Praise for Casanova

"Davey Davis is a master of moods, beauty ripping like—as in one of Davis's own metaphors—a firework display reflected on dark and shifting water."

—**TORREY PETERS**, author of *Detransition, Baby*

"*Casanova* 20 is another stunner from one of the great writers of haunting fiction for our violent, sick, sometimes beautiful world. Davis has written a melancholy, lonely, fully embodied novel about art and desire and the self and how people get through. I was spellbound by every page of this uneasy and utterly surprising book."

—**LYDIA KIESLING**, author of *Mobility*

"Enrapturing, entrancing dual narrative about bodily betrayals both real and imagined, fixation, neurosis, beauty, charisma, hotness, youth, death, impermanence, needs, wants, desire, regret, being proactive, being a vector, asking and not asking for what you actually want, and being and not being gay—sometimes at the same time!" —**HARRON WALKER**, author of *Aggregated Discontent*

"What if you were unbearably hot for your entire life and one day, without warning, it stopped? One half of Davey Davis's third novel, *Casanova* 20, explores one straight man's grief over this conundrum, while the other side plays the story of an older gay painter watching his mother, sister, and then himself succumb to an unexplained but fatal illness . . . Davis is, as always, sharp and unexpected, even as they dig into themes around sex and illness . . . As with everything else in the novel, the answers are both straightforward and mysterious. It turns out twink death can happen to straights, too." —**MORGAN M. PAGE**, cowriter of *Framing Agnes* and *Boys Don't Cry*

Praise for *X*

"*X* is lyrical and nonlinear, with sentences that feel like carved obsidian: dark, sharp and shiny . . . The overall effect is masterly, a perfect mating of style and subject . . . [It] will leave you, in the same way it leaves its narrator, wondering: What are you ignoring? What can't you admit to yourself? And is it already too late, or have you just given up?" **—HUGH RYAN**, *The New York Times Book Review*

"Davis is a remarkably self-assured author, and *X* is a dizzying, beautiful novel, and a fascinating look at a subculture that mainstream American art has frequently shied away from."
—MICHAEL SCHAUB, NPR

"Davey Davis's *X* is the real deal, lacerating the reader with its swagger, prose, and heat. It's delicious; it's so gay; it locates and names the state as easily as it locates and names desire."
—SARAH THANKAM MATHEWS, *The Cut*

"Whether in their debut novel *the earthquake room* or in their consistently fascinating substack DAVID, Davey Davis is one of the sharpest chroniclers of contemporary queer culture. Their writing goes beyond discourse, excavating the complexities of topics our communities love to simplify. Their new book, *X*, is a noir based in a present much like our own. It's as sticky, thought-provoking, and, simply, entertaining, as we've come to expect from Davey."
—DREW GREGORY, *Autostraddle*

"A sadist longs for true crimes: physically sexual, violently emotional in a world where other people are being deported. Filled with clever and thoughtful turns of phrase, and drawing on traditions of noir, camp, memoir, and erotic thrillers. Davis depicts the

trans/nonbinary/queer subculture of Brooklyn as an all-consuming underground network of friends, playmates, lovers, and clients, with occasional forays into office jobs, self-absorbed on the edges of a larger society of official cruelty. They unflinchingly draw taut the tightrope between ego aggression and political passivity that so many live on." **—SARAH SCHULMAN**, author of
Let the Record Show

"Hard-boiled style meets dyke drama in the clubs and play parties of queer Brooklyn. In an atmosphere of creeping fascism, Davey Davis gives us a fascinating protagonist . . . X is both a delight to read and a penetrating study on the intimacy of violence and the violence of intimacy." **—MCKENZIE WARK**, author of
Reverse Cowgirl

Casanova 20

Or,

Hot World

A HETEROSEXUAL NOVEL

BY DAVEY DAVIS

Catapult  New York

CASANOVA 20: OR, HOT WORLD

This is a work of fiction. All of the characters, organizations, and events portrayed in this novel are either products of the author's imagination or are used fictitiously.

First Catapult edition: 2025

ISBN: 978-1-64622-283-4

Library of Congress Control Number: 2025937415

Cover design by Victoria Maxfield
Cover image © Touchstones Rochdale Art Gallery / Bridgeman Images
Book design by tracy danes

Catapult
New York, NY
books.catapult.co

Printed in the United States of America

1 3 5 7 9 10 8 6 4 2

For Marcello

Casanova 20

Before

What happened to him? asked Adrian.

At the sound of his voice, the man with one arm turned around. When he saw the little boy he started, as if something hot had touched his bare skin. Mom seized Adrian by the arm the man hadn't, but it was too late. He came for him, his shadow devouring Adrian's like droplets converging on glass.

What did I tell you—? The rest disappeared in the crackle of Mom's shopping bag. She dragged Adrian into the salon and lifted him onto a chair. In the window behind him, the man with one arm was waiting, fingering the dusted edge of his frayed rayon lapel as he paced the sidewalk like a jaguar in a cage.

Look at me. Mom squeezed Adrian's chin, forcing his face forward. He looked at her. Her lips were always flat, even when she was speaking. He strained against her, trying to turn around again, but she held him fast . . . *And that's why I said to never, ever . . .* It was as if she hadn't even heard his question, although he knew she had. Adrian wanted to know what it looked like beneath the flap of the man's empty sleeve, which was neatly pinned against his rib cage, but Mom wouldn't tell him.

He's gone, called Miss Linda. She was at the door, her right cheek almost flush with the glass as she peered up the street. *I think it's fine now*. She already knew about Adrian.

Released from his mother's grip, Adrian turned around to find that the window was empty. *Mom—*

No more talking, Mom said. From her knees, she pushed her shopping bag under his chair and reached for his shoelaces. *Now you stay right here until I'm done*. She firmly cinched the bow. *And be a good boy*. She stood and backed away, her mouth still in its line, but when she turned to face Miss Linda's mirror, all her teeth were showing.

Adrian began tearing coupons out of a magazine, careful not to rip anywhere but the perforated paper. After what felt like forever, he turned around again. The man with one arm was back. He ran his fingers through his hair like a movie star, smiling as he would still be smiling when, forty-two minutes hence, he would take hold of Adrian, so very gently, while Mom screamed, her hair incandescent with Miss Linda's chemicals.

———————————◇———————————

Padding through the earliest rooms of his consciousness, gauzy chambers of fork-mashed fruit and curvaceous arthropods unearthed to gleam, Adrian began his life believing that the world saw something that his family—Mom, Dad, Grandma, and Auntie

Rachel—did not. At home, after all, no one stared at him. No one begged to lay a finger on his shirtsleeve. No one wept over his reciprocal touch.

A few weeks after Adrian's sixth birthday, the five of them were at the public swimming pool when a wild-eyed woman began to follow him to and from the diving board, surreptitiously reaching for his hand each time he prepared to ascend the grainy steps of the short, slippery ladder. When Mom complained, the lifeguard banished her from the premises, only to insist that the perfectly conscious child needed a bout of CPR. Still dripping, Adrian's family went home, never to return.

That night, Mom put Adrian to bed early and joined the other adults in the living room for a summit of sorts. They had always ignored the attention the boy drew, for which he was never given an explanation. Addressing it seemed pointless, even somewhat obscene, but they could no longer deny that it was only worsening as he grew. Something would have to be done to keep the family safe. Pepper spray? Karate lessons? A face covering for public outings? This was Auntie Rachel's idea. *Like one of those hyper kids they put on a leash*, she said.

Although there was a shared sense of relief in speaking freely about something that until then had been only alluded to, even between Mom and Dad, little else was accomplished that night. While every point of order spawned lively, and at times even heated, debate, each was eventually abandoned. When it came to the problems Adrian's body created, his family would eventually discover that it was better to wait and see, leaping to action only when there was no alternative. They preferred to view Adrian as a troublemaker rather than a puzzle, a fantasy that allowed them the comfortable thrill of resenting a person who couldn't yet see over the kitchen counter.

———————————◇———————————

The Payless was redolent with back-to-school smells: leather, plastic, glue. Grandma was leading Adrian down the aisle, her soft hand warm around his, when a man in a charcoal suit emerged from behind a shoe rack to slip a finger beneath the strap of his overalls.

Grandma turned red as an apple. *Pervert!* she cried, pulling Adrian back into her bouquet of baby powder and Earl Grey. His body collided with hers, his head striking the brass detailing on her purse and the underwire of her bra. He thought they would both fall over, but Grandma planted her feet and held firm, covering his eyes until the man was gone.

In the car, the soothing drone of Christian talk radio washed over Adrian as he reflected on the incident. He knew that when Grandma shouted it—*Pervert!*—she had been talking about the man in the suit. But in a way the word was for him, too. Had the man been different from the other adults who came to talk to Adrian, sometimes kneeling to beg for his name or to take pictures with their cameras, plaintive hands extended in grotesque mimicry of ceremonies he was decades too young to participate in? He didn't think so. Did this mean that *pervert* was a word that Grandma thought of more than she said? Adrian wasn't sure.

Whatever *it* was that made Adrian this way, his family accepted full responsibility. He belonged to them, after all. There was an undeniable resemblance, including the jawline that, diluted to perfection in the little boy, had once expressed itself with an almost comical squareness in the paternal great-grandfather, Grandma's dad. (Near the end of his long and laconic life, he was affectionately known as Grandpa Popeye, Pops for short.) Mom maintained a nearly unspoken regret for the tiara-crowned prize-winner her pretty son might have been; Dad spent not a little time wondering what all this would mean for a red-blooded American boy. But swapped bassinets, infidelity, or other mischief were never considered. Whether his family liked it or not, Adrian was one of them, of this they had no doubt.

But his parents looked like everyone else, as did their parents and siblings. Adrian, a shocking anomaly with a smile like a lazy angel, did not. This made him a problem without a solution, and if that was the case, his family concluded, then what good was there in dwelling on it?

Not everyone fits in, Dad remarked one evening after his son was in bed. He was thinking about an epileptic girl he had gone to grade school with—specialist visits in the big city, wooden spoons in the teacher's drawer. *Some people are just different,* he said, feeling open-minded.

The women exhaled in concert, their sighs of agreement emerging from beneath almost-identical silver necklaces. They were all learning to not just resign themselves to Adrian but to indulge in their resignation. Sensible as only the unimaginative can be, his family felt that they had merely been unlucky, as everyone who has ever lived sometimes is, in the event of Adrian's birth.

And so Adrian was neither praised nor punished for *it*, or for the attention *it* drew. If an outsider commented on *it*, they were

curtly dismissed; if something more was needed, his family became skilled at figuring out what that might be, from ducking
out the back to bribing doormen to calling the police. Once they
were safely home again, Adrian would be sent to his room, while
his family gathered around the coffee table to nurse their tension
headaches with bottles of wine and pills from wan childproofed
bottles.

Happened again . . . Too much . . . We can't just . . .

Their voices shot down the hallway, striking Adrian's bedroom
door like plated rings on an angry fist. The spall and shrapnel of
the same frustrations pierced his dreams: Dad baritone, Mom sarcastic, Grandma shrill, Auntie Rachel drunk.

But over the years, their venting became background noise, like
the morning din of Dad's dust-grouted clock radio. Adrian knew
his family wanted to keep him safe. His family knew that there
was only so much that could be done without locking him away
in a closet, a measure they avoided less for its cruelty than for its
melodrama; what they hated, above all else, was to make a scene.
Perhaps this is why more drastic solutions, like plastic surgery,
never occurred to them.

You know, Dad said, tapping his wristwatch against the belly of his
wineglass, *in a way I feel better when something happens. Otherwise you're just standing around and waiting.*

Makes my skin crawl, said Auntie Rachel. Never married, despite
her best efforts, she was bewildered by her nephew's women and
infuriated by his men.

It gets so tense, said Mom. Though she would never admit it, even to her husband, she didn't care to be alone with Adrian in public. In her memory, the man with one arm—who at her scream had released her son with a subtle push, as if lifting a homing pigeon to the sky—had already been replaced by even stranger strangers and worse violations.

You're doing the best you can, said Grandma. She had returned from the kitchen with a new bottle, which Dad set to uncorking like a starving man with a can opener.

―――――――――◇―――――――――

By the time Adrian was big enough to push the shopping cart by himself, his family was more comfortable with the crises seen to their conclusions than the ones they managed to avoid. It was only then, when they could summon the manager, or gesticulate with their coffin-like cellular phones, or selflessly plant their bodies between the boy and his aggressors, that Adrian's carefully managed life was justified.

A few times, Dad—less lantern-jawed than Pops but with an imposing build thickened from weeknights on the weight bench in the garage—had hit another man. When blood beaded the gnarled stems of half-off melons, the Albertsons produce section joined the list of locations that Adrian would forever associate with raised voices and filial anger, along with the coffee drive-thru on the Esplanade; the concessions stand at the stadium where the town's amateur baseball team played home games; and Josué Auto Body, where a broken dartboard gamely dangled behind the counter. But these were the only times that Adrian's family acknowledged *it* in his presence. Like death, his beauty was dreadful, inevitable, and never to be spoken of in front of the boy unless it couldn't be avoided.

Adrian's more distant relatives, the ones who saw him only at holidays and the odd wedding, were certain he would grow out of *it*.

Testosterone will do the trick, promised an in-law, reaching a manicured hand for the boy in her lap. The eight-year-old, his face pinched with sleepiness like a sun-stunned bunny's crushed velveteen, had stayed up late playing on the computer with his cousins. Stroking the hair that Grandma trimmed over the kitchen sink, the in-law experienced the brief but overwhelming impulse to bring her lips down to the down fuzzing Adrian's neck like lichen. Through an archway, Auntie Rachel carved pale slabs of meat for another child, her homely braids hanging down her back.

The in-law was wrong. Adrian only became more beautiful as he got older, and by then he was too big to be held in laps, too wise to have his fate spelled out over his head. For reasons unknown even to Auntie Rachel, a professional gossip, the in-law became an outlaw before Easter, and so her resolve against *it* was never again put to the test.

As if keeping pace with his growing ability to defend himself, *it* seemed to intensify as Adrian aged. When he attracted followers on his walk home from school, Auntie Rachel was enlisted as his chauffeur. After a blitz of late-night heavy breathers, the family number was removed from the phone book, but there was nothing to be done once their street address had been discovered. From the third grade onward, the mailman arrived at least once per week with amorous postcards, billets-doux, poems, and death threats, sometimes with cash enclosed, and regularly beginning with the question: *What is your name?* Though they read every missive, Adrian's family refused to acknowledge these correspondents' intent, whether implied or spelled out in pastose flourishes of juicy blue ballpoint. Instead, they took swift, silent action: a primitive digital home-surveillance system was purchased, the landline was usually disconnected, and every bit of fan mail was ripped to shreds over the garbage can in the front yard, in case anyone was watching from an unmarked car.

Over the course of his childhood, Adrian was nearly kidnapped twice. Privately, Dad was surprised it was only the two times, and he suspected other attempts had been unknowingly evaded. He shuddered to think of what would have happened if the family hadn't been comfortable enough to afford certain security measures: cameras, alarms, his handgun, a German shepherd honorably discharged from the local K-9 unit presented to Adrian on his tenth birthday.

Race: Caucasian, Hair: BRN, Eyes: BRN. After Adrian was nearly taken the second time, the form at the police station demanded demographics, but there was no prompt for the beatific cast of his lips, nor for the white-hot follicles limning his fauny hairline, nor for the way his small body moved, like candlelight on cave walls. It was the beginning of the school year, and Adrian's summer burnish still shone from beneath his crisp white T-shirt; a medievalist would have been reminded of a sorcerer's bowl of alkahest, with its backwash of liquid gold. Where would any of that fit on a clipboard?

Since Mom and Dad wanted the issue resolved as quickly and dis-creetly as possible, no charges were pressed. On the way home, they took Adrian for an ice cream cone with an unprecedented second scoop. He never again saw the woman who tried to collect him from school in a hot-pink Honda speckled with lime-green paint, and nor, as was the custom, did anyone in his family speak of her.

She was, however, remembered. The following year, Adrian was enrolled in a private school on the east side of town, which Mom grudgingly budgeted for. Tuition was a stretch, but Grandma was happy to help. Pops had died rich, having made smart investments in judiciously redlined real estate back in the forties. *Worth every penny*, said Grandma when she showed Adrian the school brochure, its glossy pages filled with laughing children and proud parents. Although Adrian had never met her father, she liked to remind her grandson of his enduring providence.

In Adrian's favorite movies, the cops always got the bad guys, but not before several exciting games of cat and mouse, the dramatic tension stretched by explosive car chases and unseen leers through wintry panes of glass. From his place on the carpet in front of the TV, Adrian was excited to find out what the villain had come for, to see precisely what was at risk if the cops didn't get their man in time. He admired logical plotlines driven by characters with clear motivations; although the people who followed him, and chased him, and waited for him in minivans did so with complete focus, Adrian sometimes got the sense that they had no idea what exactly they wanted to do with him. His sex education, derived primar-ily from their words and letters (one he remembered particularly well had arrived on his lunch tray, a folded three-by-five-inch card propped against the greasy milk carton), was more advanced than that of most children his age, and yet, for all their prurience, his admirers seemed to want more than even that. What that was, however, remained a mystery.

His family referred to them as his *friends*, a little snidely, as if the people who wanted Adrian were rude neighbor children, or lice. *One of your* friends, Auntie Rachel would mutter when the handsome young waiter, check in hand, asked if he could touch her nephew's hair.

On the way home from dinner, Adrian studied his family's heads from the back seat: the right side of Dad's crew cut, Mom's flat-ironed tresses, Auntie Rachel's braids, Grandma's fluffy white bob. He touched his own hair, pretending for a moment that he was a good dog receiving pets. He didn't like his *friends*, who often frightened him. They gave him a distinctly unpleasant feeling. Grimy, like the windows of the family Suburban when Dad hadn't washed it in a few weeks.

Quietly wriggling out of his seat belt, Adrian clambered as far back as he could go and pressed his finger against the window. Behind its halo of steam, a truck tailgated the Suburban with surgical control. On its front bumper, a cartoon smiley face grinned opposite an American-flag decal. From the driver's side, an arm ended in a waving palm, elongated an extra inch by black stiletto acrylics.

Peering from the window, Adrian attempted to match the smiley face with his own high, humorless grin. The driver kept waving, inexorably friendly as a Walmart greeter. Adrian's smile dropped with his finger. He didn't want them to think he was waving back, having learned that appeasement only made his *friends* more insistent.

You'd better be in your seat back there! In the rearview, Mom's mouth had flattened until it almost disappeared.

———————————◇———————————

The first woman found Adrian in a bookstore, a national chain whose employees were forbidden to read on the job. Cuddled into his oversized chair, he bore witness to brave Maurizio, who clung to the mizzenmast of the dauntless *Beatrice* as a squall threatened to drag her to the bottom of the Mediterranean. Like Grandma, he occasionally licked his finger before turning a page. He didn't hear the woman, smoothly sotto voce, until her gloved hand landed on his shoulder and brought him, blinking, back to the real world.

The woman had something special for Adrian. *A present,* she promised. Her hair and eyes were brown, like his. *Come with me. Just for a few minutes.* For all anyone knew, she was his mother, whispering that it was time to go home.

The woman offered her other hand, this one ungloved. She had clean fingernails and an engagement ring, dull as an old penny. Knuckle stuck between pages 62 and 63, Adrian considered her proposition. He liked presents, but it seemed to him that putting his hand in hers would mean something that he did not yet understand, and ought not to. He looked down at his novel, which was of the Choose Your Own Adventure variety, as advertised by the swooping sticker that burned across brave Maurizio's broad and brawny chest. His reading had taught him that forking paths have limitless tines, each leading to its own endless garden. He knew he shouldn't leave the bookstore with the woman, but she wasn't asking him to leave. He didn't put his hand in hers, but he did follow her to the family bathroom, where they stayed for almost twenty minutes.

A month later, it was the first man's turn. He taught at Adrian's school, in a beveled building with crows on the roof. Adrian's friend, a girl named Estela, was in the man's class. Although she was one year older, Estela was small and shy like Adrian, and like Adrian went mostly unnoticed by the other children (until he was deep into high school, no one his age cared about *it*). Adrian liked Estela because she liked to read, too, and, for reasons he didn't understand, because she wore the same Halloween costume every year: purple balloons taped to a black leotard, with a brown cardboard stem affixed on her headband. As Grapes, Estela was forced to move among the store-bought superheroes and pop stars, plastic belts of Adonis clinging lewdly to their torsos, with a caution that resembled majesty.

You're so beautiful, the man told Adrian. *So, so beautiful.*

Adrian would soon forget how they came to be alone together in the beveled building with crows on the roof. In his memory he was simply there, running his finger up and down the stainless steel leg of the desk while the man talked to him. Nor would he remember much of what the man said, though he knew there were many compliments. Adrian never responded to compliments in kind. For the man, he had none to give, and besides, he knew even at his age that he wouldn't have listened.

It was the reason the woman and the man found Adrian. They would not have noticed Adrian if he had been like Estela, a normal-looking child who resembled her normal-looking parents. *It* compelled them to him, though neither understood why any better than he did.

I love you, said the woman. The tilted mirror above the bathroom sink reflected the ambergris tiles on the floor, the black base of the plastic garbage can, the pearl stitching on her beige trousers. She gently squeezed Adrian's nape, soft as lapin, with her gloved hand. The other, still nude, pulled down the inky zipper and wormed inside his hoodie to warm the cold skin above his elbow. The faucet echoed in their fluorescent grotto of Lysol and stale urine, the harried crunch of the air-sterilization system marking each new unit of forty-five seconds like a private aeon.

Only once did someone try to enter the family bathroom. The door handle suddenly twisted, then cracked, locking at its limit. The woman jerked as if she'd been electrified. Adrian didn't move a muscle. Together they stared at the handle, breathless, until it whirred back into its default position. If there were any retreating footsteps, the hallway carpet—thick and long befouled by slimy bathroom traffic and cheap-heeled booksellers dreaming of a cigarette—silenced them. There was nothing. No clearing throat, no curious tap. The woman returned her attention to Adrian. Her breath was restored, but with a jagged edge.

A few minutes later, she zipped up Adrian's jacket and told him to leave. He went back to his chair, where he found Mom squinting down at page 62 of his Choose Your Own Adventure. On the way to the car, he reached for her hand. He wondered if the woman was still in the bathroom, all alone.

Adrian didn't see the woman or the man again. Later in his life, he wouldn't remember if this was by his own design, or theirs, or circumstance. He would never know, if he ever had.

Did the woman remember? She did, or thought she did. In the bookstore bathroom, she felt like a lightning bolt, bright and hot and predestined. But as she made her way past checkout and through the sliding front doors, her senses clouded. She hesitated on the curb, attempting to gather her thoughts. The parking lot seemed to sink down into the earth, its air weighted with premium unleaded and fryer grease from the Chinese buffet the next building over. She doubted she could walk in a straight line, let alone drive it, but she summoned her focus. She staggered to her car and collapsed behind the steering wheel, key buried in the ignition, purse vomiting gum and change on the seat beside her. Though she had to pull over three times to collect herself, she eventually made it home, where she went straight to bed. She slept for almost twelve hours, coming to the next morning with the worst headache of her life.

Though the headache eventually wore off, the cloudiness persisted. After her time with Adrian in the bookstore bathroom, the woman began struggling to remember things. She found herself staring down at her shoes or over her dashboard as she grasped for a name, a word, her own phone number. She had often described herself as a *positive person*, but after Adrian she was irritable and touchy, wishing only to be left alone. She stopped attending her book club or calling her friends, even Becky, who needed so much help with the baby. When her fiancé, Pantaleón, got into bed, the woman already had her back to him, her side of the mattress cold beneath her body.

Panta was aware that his fiancée masturbated (the burly personal massager was stabled like a prized stallion on the lower level of her nightstand), though not that she had stopped going to work in order to do it for hours at a time, each orgasm punctuated by a desperate bout of tears. It was *him* that she didn't want, Panta believed. He suspected his new orthodontia, which he had gotten for the wedding but which, after the eruption of a rogue wisdom tooth, would not be removed in time for the ceremony, where he watched the white shroud trudge down the aisle to meet him. A few weeks later, his new wife asked for an annulment. Panta's braces outlived his marriage, which should not have surprised him but did.

Did the man from the beveled building with crows on the roof remember? As the SUV pulled into the abandoned parking garage by the mall, the one with the stop sign assassinated by pellet guns, Adrian had abruptly requested to be taken back to school. Panic surged through the man (—*how had this happened? The police*—). A two-lane bridge that didn't see much traffic between rush hours came to him as if in a dream, followed by another apparition: one body, then two, then a whole SUV sinking into algae sheer and flocculent as the Milky Way.

Go back? the man repeated. He could see that Adrian was not afraid, and, quickly as it had come, the panic ebbed. Sitting with his hands in his lap, the boy was soberly watching himself watch himself in the mirror protruding from his side of the car, as if the man weren't there with him. (It was Adrian's private feeling that if he had to be seen, he should at least be permitted to see, too.)

All this could be salvaged, the man realized. Nothing had happened yet. It wasn't too late—he was just taking the boy on a field trip. The bridge and the bodies faded. The man pulled back out of the parking garage, his body purged of violent impulse.

But as they passed the park a few blocks away from the school, the man hit the blinker and cranked the wheel. The park's corner lot, secluded from the street by a wall of pink and white oleander (shedding blossoms, noticed Adrian, the way circus-animal cookies crumb in their snack-size plastic), was empty. It shouldn't have been, on such a beautiful spring day, but it was. Under a flowering saucer magnolia, the shining tires made a vermiculated mulch of the fallen petals, though Adrian was not aware of this, seeing only, for a little while, the man's pink pores and some white crumbly crud erupting from the armrest's metal trash receptacle.

Afterward, the man drove Adrian to a gas station a few blocks from the school. Adrian completed the trip on foot, where he didn't have to wait more than ten minutes for the family Suburban, its bulk expertly maneuvered by Auntie Rachel. He never saw the man from the beveled building with crows on the roof again.

As he had with the woman in the bookstore, Adrian kept his encounter with the man to himself. Though he would later suspect that the experience had helped solidify his preference for women, he would maintain a deep, if distant, compassion for men as a group. In the SUV, the man's fear had tightened his brow and hardened his hands, but it hadn't stopped him, and this had endeared him to Adrian, who until then had never known a grown-up to need courage: his family was indefatigable, and as for his *friends*, people with the interiority of movie zombies, frenzy was all they seemed capable of.

The man drove home through the twilight. He jumped the curb below the neighbor's oak trees, each pruned into an unnatural symmetry by predawn crews of Honduran landscapers, and didn't bother to repark. He couldn't stand to be in the car for another second—it was hot and airless, like an untested bomb shelter. Exhausted by the walk to his front door, he sank into the porch swing he never used, his heels lifting off the deck's faded yellow pine. He realized he had left his wallet in the SUV but couldn't bring himself to retrieve it.

An hour passed. He grew thirsty but no less fatigued, so he stayed there on the swing, rocking in the breeze and pulling his hair.

When his wife got home from work, he was still out there. He wouldn't say a word, and she couldn't persuade him to come inside for some bourbon, something to eat. She had her drink alone, peeking at her husband from the front window, watching his knuckles whiten rhythmically against the back of his head. At midnight, she went to bed.

The man stayed on the swing until the landscapers returned for another day's work. He wept, because his life had been changed.

<hr />

A few months later, Adrian turned twelve. Having been apprised of his *situation*, as Dad put it, his new private school, under certain misconceptions, attempted to assign him an all-female security detail. Their selection was to be based on the guards' ability to maintain normal heart rates while viewing photographs of the boy, but when none were able to do (one was so taken by his top left incisor, left boyishly chipped after a soccer game, that she withdrew her application at once), the detail was scrapped. *You just have to laugh*, said Auntie Rachel.

During school hours, Adrian was on his own. Thankfully, the school's faculty and staff were mostly professional toward him,

and the other kids, already aware of his reputation, carefully ignored him for the most part. He didn't make many friends, but
he never had enemies, either. He got decent grades and spent
his lunches in the library reading fantasy novels and playing online chess with the librarian, Mr. Jenkins, who sketched Adrian's
mouth on napkins stained by his customary breakfast of a sugar
round and burned coffee.

From his first semester at the private school, Adrian's family sensed
a change in him. Instead of hiding behind Mom, he began to greet
adults with unwavering eye contact, even a handshake sometimes.
He debuted a ginger but winning smile, the germ of a permanent
habit, to shepherd onlookers through their initial awe. Most people were taken by Adrian, but few wished to abandon themselves
to him once they'd seen their lust laid bare by social niceties. The
ferocity of some *friends*, he discovered, could be nipped in the bud
if managed confidently. Almost without realizing it, he learned to
speak quickly, forgive easily, and forget right away.

He's growing up, Dad said one Tuesday evening. They had risked
a trip to the skating rink, where his son whipped by so quickly his
face almost went unnoticed. While he waited to feel something
like pride, heartburn climbed the back of his throat.

I just hope he doesn't get the wrong idea, said Mom. She was relieved when her husband didn't ask her what she meant by this,
because she didn't quite know, either.

As Adrian's adolescence peaked, the way his *friends* found him
began to feel more like a surprise party than an ambush. Relieved

somewhat of the burden of self-defense, his curiosity about other people flowered. He felt as if he could assess his *friends* one by one, attempting to see each person as they were before deciding if he should fear them. Instead of awaiting them with the passivity that is the fate of all children, he anticipated them with the pleasureful certainty of one who knows he is beloved.

Suddenly sensitive to *it*, girls his age began to notice Adrian. He had always liked girls: Veronica Lake on Grandma's strobing television set, her slender skyward arms merging with the antennae; the way Auntie Rachel pulled her winter tights, ophidian cables twisting, over her hard, round knees; Estela's big sister, Mimi, who had a training bra in her dresser drawer and a Barbie phone perched on the nightstand by her twin bed. They began flocking to him, along with the grown women—some older than his mother, than his grandmother, even—who had sought him out since childhood.

Adrian forgot about the woman from the bookstore, though every once in a while she would return just as he was falling asleep, her eyes rearranging in the black above his head like ghosts: voluptuous, limpid, and clean. He would suddenly remember the bookstore bathroom, where she hadn't closed her mouth except to kiss him; where he had seen, between bisous, that one of the lower incisors had collapsed against its compatriot, each rooted in honest yellow. He wondered if her fragrance, a strange but delicious blend of tropical fruit and cat piss, was perfume or if she smelled that way all the time.

When Adrian would waken the next morning, the woman was gone again, even less than a dream. This is how memory works, or doesn't.

With men, especially straight ones, Adrian discovered that his beauty was almost always enough. This was not always the case with women. Sometimes they required a little work, but putting *it* to the test was more than worth it. Though Adrian had never had an aptitude for sports (recall his tooth, that athletic casualty), he was naturally disciplined when so inclined. With patience, *it* grew stronger, but also more controlled.

By the time he was eighteen, Adrian could summon *it* in order to resemble the kind of man that the women he encountered were most attracted to: for blondes he was stoic; scientists mysterious; writers witty; baristas exciting; leftists like-minded; cops uninhibited; teachers romantic; mothers gentle; mothers rough; strippers capable; bakers soulful; social workers horny; divorcées easy; HR administrators nice; bisexuals boyish; line cooks indulgent; cashiers funny; optimists charming; readers erudite; CEOs implacable; musicians clever. Women found themselves blowing kisses, some for the first time.

It's possible that *it* was a kind of intuition, not that Adrian ever thought of it in quite this way. If *it* was a sense, like sight or touch, then Adrian had been cultivating it since that day in the bookstore bathroom, the day he chose his own adventure. *It* was how he had known to speak very little to the woman, to neither smile nor to grimace, and to be firm yet cautious when he reached to stroke her hair, its bird's nest of bobby pins crowned with a single vulgar barrette.

If Adrian had entered private school at the dawn of his understanding of *it*, he graduated almost six years later with a firm grasp of its implications on his life: that he was different, even if he couldn't say exactly how, and that this difference was mostly good.

◇

Though Adrian was not close with any other beautiful people, he had always studied them, fascinated by their shared phenomenon. Was it a superficial similarity, or did it indicate a deeper connection? Although occasionally a *friend* was almost as beautiful as he, he never encountered *it* in another person.

He eventually came to the conclusion that if there was a class of beautiful people, he was not a member. Otherwise, Adrian reasoned, he would have been able to leverage his looks like a commodity, eventually finding his way to some measure of power or celebrity, like the famous actors he was so frequently compared to (none of whom looked a thing like him, in his opinion). Adrian had neither of these things, and wasn't sure he ever could. Not that he wanted for anything, except for the next woman, of course.

While Adrian was clearly different from other beautiful people, they could surely have related to the social virtuosity his beauty allowed him to develop from a young age. In his twenties, when dating apps became available, he quickly began using them like a grocery list, a trick he learned from gay men (though if he had to be with a man, he preferred other straight ones). He knew all the parks and went to all the museums. He made eye contact like a gambler. He climbed thousands of stairs to find women fainting for him, strewn over beds like winter coats, warm and heavy, sometimes wet.

Occasionally—often, even—there were husbands, men of that sort. Though he did his best to avoid them, these men had a way of causing bad things to happen. They were why Adrian had to sweet-talk a US marshal when he joined the mile-high club; why he jumped a chain-link fence and raced a one-eyed rottweiler through a used-car lot; why he almost lost his life over an aquiline sous chef who sucked his fingers as she came. He remained beautiful despite these men, even after the fistfights, the vaudevillian lapel-lifts and heave-hos, the threat of an acid attack by a spurned accountant who would have gone through with it if he had known where to get the stuff. (Adrian had believed him, not because the accountant was crazy but because Adrian had been with his wife, of whom the accountant was envious. Adrian was the first and last beauty that would ever concern themself with the pair, and his wife had been chosen, not he. Who could tolerate such a loneliness?) *Not the moneymaker!* someone else might have cried, throwing up his arms, or perhaps even fighting back. Not so for Adrian, who knew that *it* was a sturdier, sexier thing than the skin stretched over his skull.

Even when a woman wasn't directly involved, husbands and men like them still tended to find Adrian. While drinking illegally at a New Orleans dive named for a fat Chalcolithic goddess, he heard a voice behind his ear: *Pretty boy.* The words were both warning and consequence, sandwiching the hit like a slab of lunch meat. His vision pixelated by eyelashes, tears, and the neon's bleeding gridelin, he awoke on the floor with his tongue everywhere. The man on the stool next to him had misplaced his wallet, and Adrian was his first and final suspect. Before the bouncer could drag him away, the pugilist helped Adrian to his feet and, with a gruff but courtly humility, kissed his wilting hand.

While he waited in the urgent care exam room, Adrian watched a fly hurl itself against the windowsill, striking the hard plastic over and over again. Fingering his hot new face, he had an epiphany:

it wasn't the women that these men were angry about, not really. Knowing this would make him both more endangered and less. The fly was ramming the glass, the chirr of its wings permeating the silence, when the door swung open.

Baby, said the RN, reaching for his brow. She wished for latex, a cape and a tiny fitted hat, like in the old days, when everything was in black and white. She was a sensitive woman, blessed with the Sight by way of her Aunt Despie, and her Granny Sinclair before her, but that talent was not necessary to sense *it*, even with his face like that, and at this hour of her shift, too, when her ilium rode her spine like a drunken cowboy in red-hot spurs. Her boyfriend, who flashed his VIC for the 10 percent discount at Clément's Boxing Gym, would never find out about Adrian.

Our secret, said the RN, as if he didn't know. Despite the pain, Adrian found he could focus on her quite easily. He wasn't afraid for his face—*it* didn't care about swelling or scar tissue. She gave him a kiss for each suture, then joined him on the exam table. When it was time to leave, there was no bill, only extra painkillers from her personal stash.

In the parking lot, Adrian found that it was almost morning. He put a capsule in his mouth, its foul flavor reviving him for the walk back to the hotel where his *friend*, a lesbian dentist with a gambling problem, had sobered up enough to wonder if the beautiful young man had been nothing more than a dream. He checked his phone—it was only a couple of miles away. He set out as briskly as he could, tonguing his teeth in search of loose fillings.

Cypress and sweet gum dripped with gentle rainfall, pearling with chains of plastic globes that turned wrought iron fences into long, slender throats. Adrian thought fondly of his RN, whose soft body had responded with ticklish eagerness, and whom he would never see again. This fact was not incompatible with his love for her, which was a miracle that could be experienced every day of the rest of his life, if he wanted. Passing sunken trailers and stunted banana trees, he tried to picture the man in her life, relishing a connection that didn't precisely exist. If he had been there with him, walking alongside Adrian into the early gloam of Magazine Street, Adrian would have put his arm out and around him, drawing him close as a lover.

Despite the challenges that partnered women presented, Adrian loved them best. Every woman was unique, of course—no one could know this better than he—but the ones who were spoken for were alike in their desire for freedom. Many of them had low self-esteem. Adrian didn't mind. In his eyes, there were few real flaws a woman could have, though he did avoid those who didn't like to talk. He preferred to listen, and not just to flattery, although he enjoyed this more than he would ever admit. As a group, women were practiced in defending the compliments they made to other women, just as those other women were practiced in deflecting them. But Adrian absorbed admiration without question, whether or not it was genuine (it almost always was). Women found this intoxicating. Taken women, irresistible to Adrian, were unable to resist. Unlike the lesbian dentist—a practiced liar, like all good addicts—Adrian almost never lied. He didn't need to.

This was Adrian's life. There was never a need for a home or even a bed of his own. Every woman was available to him, each a soulmate after a fashion, generous with her resources and wanting nothing more than Adrian himself. Nothing more, nothing less. Swinging from his perch, a garbageman whistled for his attention as the truck rumbled past, but Adrian, already floating, thought it was the morning song of some exotic Southern bird.

———◇———

When Adrian moved to New York City a few weeks after graduating from the private school, his family let its disapproval be known without a single argument. Mom's emails dried up, Dad's phone always seemed to be off, Auntie Rachel never checked her voicemail. Even Grandma, filed away in a rubberized facility after her knee replacements, lived long enough to offer a surprisingly supple flick of the wrist when Adrian was asked after by the other crones at Yahtzee night. From her, he heard nothing at all.

One afternoon, Adrian cornered his aunt on the phone for what was to be their final call. Before he could ask why she'd been avoiding him, she beat him to the punch. *How could you just abandon us, after everything we've sacrificed for you?* she demanded. *How are you going to keep yourself safe without your family?* He didn't know what to say, so he told her he had to go. She didn't insist and he never called her back.

There was no grandiose ultimatum, no official ending. Other than a card for Christmas, and another for his birthday, each with all four signatures in Mom's handwriting, Adrian stopped hearing from them altogether. His family faded like a plume of smoke in a still room, and he let them. What else is to be done about smoke?

At any rate, he had a well-placed trust in his own ability to adapt. In no time at all, two suitcases and a couple hundred bucks bloomed into an apartment, a new pair of Jordans, and three credit cards impressed with other peoples' first and last names. Of course, Adrian did wonder. Had he been deracinated, like an ingrown hair, by a loveless family? Or did he share in that fault, if only a little, by not insisting on himself?

He would never know for sure. Two years after he moved away, one of the first infernos of California's incipient fire season swept through Yahi Valley while the morning dew still trembled on the lawn. In a matter of minutes, the cul-de-sac where he learned to ride a bike and play HORSE on the neighbor's haggard hoop was incinerated. Dad and Mom and Auntie Rachel, who had moved into Grandma's old bedroom, were burnt like so many match heads. Their funerals, held cost-effectively in aggregate (unlike Adrian, the recession never had an infancy), marked the last time that he ever set foot in the town where he was born.

Over the next few years, the rest of his family disappeared, less dramatically if no less irrevocably: Grandma to the grave, the rest to mutual apathy.

⸺⸺⸺◈⸺⸺⸺

From his first day in New York, Adrian had no schedule to maintain, no goals to meet, no master plan for his future as a citizen of the world. He kept it that way, seeing the city as a plane of as-yet unfulfilled pleasures through which he moved like fingers roaming the curves of a ripe cornucopia. Still young, he had nothing but time, though of course women were an imperative. Luckily for him, they were also practical. His *friends* of the feminine persuasion gave him everything he needed, from spending money to couture clothing to, one time, a mini yacht he quickly bored of and abandoned in a windless Hamptons harbor without a second thought.

Though *it* certainly had shape, texture, even heft, Adrian had resigned himself to its mystery long ago. *It* came when he called, racing with his heart, fluttering like his breath, advancing and receding as if yoked to his very consciousness. But obedience was not understanding. The essence of Adrian's beauty, the sum of its parts, was hidden away, and to seek it was like searching for the sun in a fogbank, or a train behind the fire of its own headlamps: he could never see what he knew to be there. Yet his certainty of *it* transcended both faith and logic. *It* was not reducible to his appearance or to his personality (appearance's false complement, even for the very beautiful). *It* was something more, in fact, something beyond his comprehension, or so Adrian came to believe, though he thought of it less and less over the years.

Not that Adrian felt he had to justify his beauty, to himself or anyone else. Women loved him for it, which was all he needed to know. Like *it*, being with them came naturally to him, like satisfying hunger, or thirst, or his cock's hot, tight counterweight deep in his groin.

———————————◇———————————

Adrian's twenties drew to a close as the new century's began. With them came the first pandemic of the epoch. Like a tsunami, its approach was mostly overlooked until it was long past too late.

At first, Adrian didn't give the virus much thought. No one did. Of course he'd heard the rumors from his phone and Mark's TV, from eavesdropping on the train and talking to the high-strung father of four who ran the corner deli. Based on the headlines coming out of Wuhan and trending in niche corners of the internet, this new disease wasn't all that interesting unless you were an epidemiologist or a politician with brand-new stock in hospital ventilators. As the winter progressed, the story became a part of the digital static, consistent but gossamer as a viral meme.

Adrian was untying his shoes in the locker room of the Bed-Stuy Y on a chilly March evening when he received the notification: due to skyrocketing positive rates of the novel coronavirus, Governor Cuomo had issued an emergency stay-at-home order for the state of New York.

Stay-at-home order? Adrian set his phone on the bench beside him, steadying himself on the smooth treated wood. His friend Mark had texted him from California the night before. He hadn't bothered to really read the message because it had included the words *inside, talk soon,* and *serious,* which were contorted by his skim into something vaguely chastising—making it easy for Adrian to ignore it altogether. He had been distracted by Belle anyway, who at the first hint of competition had plucked his phone from his hand and laughingly dangled it over the fish tank. After Adrian got home from her Ridgewood loft bed, built over a sprawl of putrefying laundry and loose catnip, he had slept all day, only just waking in time for an early dinner of mediocre banh mi with Cora. This statewide notification was as new for him as it had been for Mark twenty-four hours before.

Should he be worried? He looked around. The locker room dripped and hummed as if alive, but he was alone. There was no one else on whom he could base his feelings. He checked Twitter, scanned Google, flicked through a few logjammed Reddit posts. Panic had gripped the city and was rising around the country, but what about this new notification had made the Bed-Stuy Y any less safe than it had been five minutes ago? Something was changing, that much was obvious, but it hadn't changed completely. Not yet.

Even now, Adrian didn't respond to Mark's text. He'd get around to it later, he thought, putting his phone back in his bag. He stored his things, squeezed the locker shut, and walked to the sauna, free for the moment from his pocket Cassandra, the rough white towel horseshoed around his neck.

It was almost closing time, so he wasn't surprised to find only one other man there, relaxing on a bench against the back wall. They smiled at each other. Adrian wondered if the man had received the same notification, if he knew yet. He hoped he hadn't, didn't. Tonight, Adrian felt like being alone with his thoughts, an activity best accomplished in the company of other people.

He sat a few feet away on the same bench. The man was young and very handsome, the kind who tended to be intimidated by Adrian unless they were already horny; once they were hard, it didn't matter that he was the more beautiful. He liked the man's beard, black as the tribal patterns on his biceps. His pump was still shapely. Sweat danced over his broad forehead in the fluorescent light.

When a staff member came in to announce that it was closing time, Adrian was already heading to the showers. After he rinsed, he went back to his locker to get dressed, tonguing the coal-colored hair coiled in his teeth, where he turned off his phone without checking it again.

———————◇———————

Within a matter of days, New York City snapped shut. The country stalled around it, states going dark one after another like floors
chunking dark in a closing factory. That first pandemic spring,
the talking heads and public intellectuals compared the political situation to whichever world-ending crisis best suited their
lobbyist-funded agenda: 9/11, Pearl Harbor, the Crash of '29. The
less incendiary recalled the Spanish flu a century ago, or even further, the Black Plague, but no one wanted to hear about that, much
less learn any lessons from them. There was too much to think
about, let alone to know.

The pandemic didn't make sex more difficult for Adrian. In fact, it
had never been easier. But meeting women, then talking to them
for a little while, then finding someplace . . . The whole process,
once exhilarating or relaxing, sometimes both at once, had become
desperate. It was the same when meeting men, which was an even
bigger surprise to Adrian. Having never needed to make an effort
with them, he took them for granted. Now, for the first time in his
life, gender didn't matter. Woman or man, Adrian could smell on
them the reek of terror and grief and suspicion, as if their desire
had reached fruition in the Bed-Stuy Y sauna's antre of semen and
chlorine. The layoffs, the shutdowns, the supply chain gridlock,
the police massacres, the stashes of frozen bodies abandoned by
Cuomo's cronies—despite most of it having almost no direct effect
on his own life, it shocked Adrian. Witnessing the carnage from
his phone felt like watching a high-production limited series on
Mark's big screen, his adrenaline spiking from the depths of the
sectional couch.

Like everyone else, Adrian felt bitterly unlucky. When he wasn't
at Mark's apartment with his cat, George, he spent hours at home
in his unmade bed, curled up on the slippery sheets and homely

full-size mattress he wouldn't let Mark upgrade, forgetting to eat as he dwelled on the desiderata of a crumbling world. He had an utterly new desire: to be someone else. If he had to have been trapped in a universe in which the pandemic was inevitable, why couldn't it have come when he was quite young or else quite old? Despite the practical dangers of being a child or a grandfather at a time like this, he fervently believed it wouldn't have felt so bad. For the first time since they met, Adrian envied Mark his age, which even Mark would have admitted could be called *old*. Without any guilt, he envied Mark his dying mother, too. At least her failing life had given him a reason to be in Northern California, away from the ghost trains and nightly clamor of pots and pans.

Someone else in Adrian's position may have felt compelled to introspection, to analyze their relative safety and uncover a sense of gratitude for their exemption from immediate danger. This was an instinct that Adrian had occasionally experienced but rarely indulged in. Now that the pandemic was here, he steadfastly avoided it. He already had to think about death every time he wooed a wife, compelled an undergrad, enraptured a county judge. The danger of husbands and boyfriends lost some of its luster. Adrian did not fear death, but now his lovers did, and this put them in the future, stealing them away from their precious interval together. Though free from possessiveness in general, Adrian was jealous of his lovers' attention. An instant cannot bear even the slightest external pressure. A moment vanishes when it becomes self-aware.

The first year of the pandemic inverted Adrian's natural life. Now love was an invitation to fear rather than an escape, a monarch butterfly's brindle giving way to a tiger's rippling anterior. Though the pandemic changed very little about his day-to-day that first year—he didn't have a workplace to endanger him, roommates to argue with, a body that put him at higher risk—Adrian wished for it to end with an urgency that was, he felt, unique in all of New York City.

------------◇------------

For obvious reasons, the word *friend* had never sounded altogether nice to Adrian. But he did have friends, real ones, among the conveniently powerful lovers, the impatient aspirants waiting to prove themselves, the starstruck NPCs who could scarcely gather the courage to speak in his presence. He trusted everyone equally, save for this special handful of people, whom he trusted less, which he considered an act of almost egregious generosity. With his *friends*, he gave of himself completely, if only for a few minutes or hours. With his friends, he gave of himself carefully and conditionally, a gift made all the more precious for its extreme rarity. His friends, Adrian believed, understood this, Mark most of all.

Growing up, Adrian had never felt alone. How could he, with his family and *friends* always nearby? That first pandemic summer, his *friends* spooking like wild horses and his friends nowhere to be found, he felt in his bones the yearning for another person's company. Mark was still in Almendra, his mother's illness having taken a sharp turn for the worse just as the local hospitals were overwhelmed by plague. After hosting a couple of frantic fundraisers, the gay bar where Cora worked shuttered permanently, and by June she was too depressed to leave her bed except to take her turn in line outside the Key Foods, eyes livid with insomnia. Then there was Mary, who by coincidence had been back home in Perth when it all began, sunning her summer-stained feet for Instagram. She would ride out her forced hiatus from the Land of the Free at her parents' house, she told Adrian, and invited him for a visit whenever he could make the journey, travel restrictions permitting. Adrian said he would, and mostly meant it.

With everyone he cared about gone, literally or otherwise, Adrian found himself adrift in a city he no longer knew, feeling as if he was on the verge of losing something, if it hadn't already been lost. He felt smothered by his mask and alienated by a sadness that, as it turned out, not even women could assuage. He missed Mark and Cora and Mary. Texts, phone calls, and Zoom meetings only made them seem farther away.

In June, after a man was murdered by police in Minneapolis, New York City torched two NYPD precincts in a maelstrom of coordinated grief. Though Adrian often observed the protest marches from his window—they were everywhere that summer, at all hours of the day and night across the entire borough—he had no interest in joining them. Racism and all that was bad, sure, but he would rather get a root canal than think about politics (though of course he'd never had a root canal, and never would).

But it wasn't long before the commotion lured him out from under his sheets and down to the front door. From his stoop, he looked down on Prospect Place's merger with Washington Avenue, which was bustling with hundreds of lively, sweaty people. When they chanted, or screamed at a squad car, or called to each other, their voices were strong and clear. Adrian felt a wave of desire. He wanted to be among them, even if he was disinterested in their purpose. He descended slowly, but vaulted the last three steps, gold chain levitating under his shirt (*A reminder*, Clifford had whispered, slipping it over Adrian's head, where it caught the loose curls like filigree in a tumbleweed).

The protest enveloped him like a sultry wind. Sweating in the summer heat, the people waved flags and shook their fists at drones; they distributed water bottles and keffiyehs; they ate ice cream and rode skateboards; they carried sleepy children and improvised explosives. Adrian kept to the outside of the crowd so he could get away if he needed to, but this made him easier to spot. Before long, women were waving him down from cars. Men were belting improvised songs about heartbreak. Women came too close, carrying *New Yorker* tote bags and wearing *Freak Nasty* hoodies, to ask him the color of his eyes (*Eyes: BRN* never satisfied them, as if the DMV could be argued with). Men fought for his gaze, then stared him down when they achieved it, flexing their forearms.

Adrian's desire melted away. After marching for a few blocks, he peeled off onto an empty side street. Behind him, the crowd roared. Ahead, the plane trees shrieked with insects.

⸻ ◇ ⸻

When the weather started to cool again, Adrian's friends finally began to materialize. Mark came back from Almendra after his mother's funeral, trying to conceal his grief with his exhaustion. Cora got hired at another bar, a straight one, not far from Adrian's apartment, her depression now supplanted by a far more sociable anxiety. Mary texted daily about her plans to return as soon as the first vaccines were available, whenever that would be. Soon, the president had promised the nation. Soon, everyone told themselves.

In January, Mark went back to Almendra again, this time to care for his sister, Ruth, who was also sick. (*The last time*, he promised, reaching for George's flickering tail.) Adrian spent the rest of the winter drinking with Cora at her bar or lying around Mark's apartment. Or he was with a *friend*. The beginning of 2021 belonged to Julio, who lived to lie, and Bambi, Winsome, and Valerie, all of whom had apartments on the same city block. And then there were the many *friends* he would never see a second time, even if some of their numbers ended up in his phone.

With nothing much else to do, winter was twice as interminable in what Americans referred to as lockdown, although the curfews had ended months before. Though he scrupulously responded to Adrian's texts, Mark initiated them only when he wanted to drink (though he didn't say so, and didn't need to). Cora drank so much she forgot to text. Mary, who had taken up with a married man in the fall, now usually had her phone on *Do not disturb*, and anyway, though she and Adrian shared more waking hours than one might have expected, there never seemed to be enough time for a proper call.

But there was still the vaccine to look forward to. Once it arrived in the spring, Adrian figured he would return to the clubs and movie theaters and sporting events along with everyone else, reclaiming life as it once was.

———————————◇———————————

Before the pandemic, Adrian never got tested. Not for the less intimidating social diseases, not even for HIV. Not on purpose, anyway. Although Mark, being a gay man of a certain age, had tried to intervene once or twice, he knew there was no forcing his young friend to do anything. Adrian had always avoided the doctor, ever since his pediatrician interrupted a vaccination to lay a cold wet kiss in the heart of his palm. *Disgusting!* Grandma cried, red as an apple again. Adrian wasn't taken back to the doctor except for a health exam ahead of private school enrollment; since his teeth were perfectly straight, Mom rationalized, no dentistry was ever called for.

By the time he was on his own, Adrian's medical hesitancy had become a habit. It didn't matter. Congenitally healthy and miraculously lucky, he was an insurance provider's perfect patient. In his many years of trysts without precautions, by what miracle had he never gotten ill? He tried not to think about it. Thus far, this tactic worked better than it had for anyone in the history of anything.

Naturally, Adrian never got tested for the new virus, either. He had certainly never gotten symptoms. Moved by the popular confidence in the vaccines, he made an appointment the moment one became available. The news said that the pharmaceutical companies would open up New York again, with only a year of their lives lost to this horrible pandemic. For Adrian, nothing except sex felt better than believing that this was the truth. He couldn't wait to go back, back to when women weren't sad and everything was easy.

Adrian

Although he walks from Windsor Terrace at a leisurely pace, he still arrives at Medgar Evers a half hour before his vaccine appointment. Adrian, who is almost never bored, doesn't mind waiting. He pulls on his N95, sieving the luscious air through its plastic fibers, and dutifully queues up. When the wind blows, cherry blossoms fall. A few cling to his leather boots.

He's not last in line for long. Everyone in New York City wants their vaccine yesterday. Friends have come in groups, laughing and joking and taking photos of the cherry trees. Nearby, someone paraphrases someone else's tweet about climate change. *Yeah, 2020 was hard. But it'll still be the easiest year of the rest of our lives.* They pull their masks away from their faces when they speak.

Adrian smiles. More and more, people seem to regard hope for the future as some kind of punch line. But today, 2020 feels like a bad dream. Not even his fear of needles can affect his good mood. When a cherry blossom pins itself to his shoulder, he permits himself to feel blessed.

The line begins to move. It snakes through a series of checkpoints, where Adrian must display his QR code to four separate jack-booted intakes, into a multipurpose room full of makeshift booths. A reservist directs Adrian to the one in the corner, where another reservist is changing her gloves. Though his heart has begun to race, he takes his seat, wriggles out of his jacket, and rolls up his sleeve. He forces himself to keep his eyes open, scanning the room for *friend*ly faces.

There you go.

He hardly felt it. Didn't even get dizzy, like he usually does. Although he's not in the risky habit of smiling publicly, Adrian beams under his mask as he takes back his ID, along with a crisp new vax card. He admires the brand name of his vaccine, the in-cantation that he will now need to enter theaters, bars, and other public places, where people have already begun flocking, where women are already waiting for him as if the pandemic never hap-pened. He could kiss it. Instead, he looks up and scans the room again. What he wants, more than anything, is to feel his happiness with someone else.

But of course, here is the reservist, right in front of him. Adrian quickly assesses her. Her forehead is smooth and her fatigues are sexy and her body smells like something a teenage girl would smear on her lips. He gets to his feet and leans against the wall of the makeshift booth. *Wanna take a break?* he says, *it* surging so powerfully he can feel his cheeks burn.

But the reservist's eyes are trained on her iPad as she gestures to-ward the line behind him. *Next!* she calls, tapping the screen.

It's only when he's left the multipurpose room, following the signs down the hallway, that Adrian realizes his mouth is hanging open under his mask. He snaps it shut and lifts his fingers to touch his face. Still warm. Perhaps the reservist hadn't heard him. Or perhaps she did but was afraid of getting in trouble, though such things usually didn't concern his *friends*, not when it came to him. Or perhaps she was one of the people—so few that he can remember every one of their faces—that just didn't want Adrian.

There are more signs leading to an underground gymnasium, where another reservist directs him to a folding chair. Is he making eyes at him? It's unclear, but possibility relaxes Adrian a little. There has to be an explanation for the other one, something he simply hasn't thought of yet. Reassured, he sits impatiently, watching the reservists direct people into and out of chairs. When the window for anaphylactic shock has passed, he is ordered back upstairs, light on his feet as a hungry cat.

Outside of Medgar Evers, the diamond-cut afternoon has been replaced with a milky, allergenic dusk. He heads to Eastern Parkway up an avenue teeming with buses, bikes, and bare faces. People grin at one another, vape from cupped hands, jostle restive babies, lean in while yanking buds from ear canals to shout, *What you say?* The cars in the street and the garbage bags on the sidewalk are lubed with mist. The corner fruit stands do brisk business, the plums glowing like gemstones when they're held up to the light for inspection.

Adrian feels as if he has time-traveled back to last year, before the spring had taken hold, before the governor's stay-at-home order in the Bed-Stuy Y, back to when he had never looked further ahead

than a day or two at a time. He believes that everyone walking toward Prospect Park feels the same as he does, that they, too, have a
fresh SpongeBob Band-Aid and bloodstreams pullulating with the
antibodies that will keep them safe forever. That they're bathing
in the same relief, its potency underlaid with a sense of civic accomplishment that Adrian, who doesn't vote and uses his jury
summons to collect nail clippings, has never experienced before.
That the happiness that hibernated through the longest winter of
his life is coming awake for them, too. Adrian is enamored. Instead
of training his eyes on the ground, as he usually does when he isn't
seeking out a new *friend*, he lavishes their faces with attention, his
pace slowing to a stroll as he nears the park.

But he keeps his own mask on. Over the past year, he has discovered how much easier it is to be in public with one. Even when *it*
is going full throttle, covering his face seems to dim it, bringing him
closer to true anonymity than he's ever been. This gives him a great
and almost guilty pleasure. When he chooses to go unseen—or less
seen, anyway—he feels wise and judgmental. Was this what normal people felt like? Masked, he can watch without being watched
back, and he has been pleased to discover how much he enjoys it.

Adrian makes room for a man and a woman holding hands, their
eyes locked together, as they pass him by. His thoughts return to
the reservist, the details of her face (what he could see of it, anyway) already in the outer limits of his recollection. Perhaps his
mask had simply worked too well. He feels a little silly. Behind
him, the couple's laughter caroms off the art deco prewar building
that looms overhead. What does it matter now that Adrian is safe
from COVID, and it's a beautiful spring day, and his friend Mark
is coming back to New York, and he can be in love with anyone,
and often is?

Adrian's jacket is just warm enough for the twilight air. Not yet ready to go home, he turns left onto the great cement patio of the Brooklyn Public Library. Now that he's vaccinated, his right to be unmasked indoors will soon be restored, but he wants to stay outside for a while longer, feeling the sunset's light, if not its heat. The library steps spill out into Grand Army Plaza from beneath the golden hieroglyphs that burnish the building's cool limestone facade, severely generous as a glacier. Though the steps are as low and few as they are broad and wide, he feels as if he's overlooking a busy ant colony. He watches the people move below him, his vision microscoping when he so chooses, zooming in on a figure, a face, an expression. From here, the world happens and he watches.

Adrian enjoys New Yorkers. Their global reputation for brusqueness, even rudeness, becomes absurd if one spends a week among them, moving with their native tides of traffic and train schedule. It is their certainty that makes them so intimidating to people from the suburbs and smaller cities, a terribly alert unselfconsciousness that sets them apart from other Americans. But something has changed about them over the past year. As the masks have begun falling away, Adrian has noticed that their faces, paler and softer about the chin, hold a new awareness. A strange expression has arrived, a perma-pose that never drops, not when greeting, or catcalling, or leaping out of a motorbike's path.

Adrian realizes that he's been seeing this expression throughout the city, a look that remains even when nothing should be there, during those times when it ought to be echoing the mind's emptiness. Since the masks started coming off, even the dull liminalities of the train platform and bodega counter have become wind tunnels of consciousness. No escape, no release. It dawns on him that something—everything—has changed again. When did it happen? Why didn't he notice until just now?

Adrian snakes a hand under his jacket, then his shirt, to touch his Band-Aid. Just before nightfall Grand Army is always busy, and never more so than when the weather begins to warm. Men and women and children and animals, all the races and ethnicities he can identify on sight and plenty he can't. Some walk, some are carried or pushed, some wheel themselves. Some stand jingling change, or prop themselves in camping chairs, or wedge their bodies onto the marble steps of condemned storefronts, balefully watching Adrian back. Working their jaws and rubbing their foreheads with fingers stiff as twigs, the people around him have removed their masks after a long, brutal year to find that something is missing.

Adrian's mood begins to sink, descending like a tea bag weighted with gravel. He pulls the loops of his mask from around his ears and exposes his face to the evening. The wind touches his smooth cheek, his unwavering chin, and he follows it with his fingers. Is his face like theirs? Does it look different, as if something has gone missing? But also as if some new burden has arrived? He thinks again of the reservist, and his insouciance—*Wanna take a break?*—humiliates him. Adrian is not used to feeling humiliated. He tries to remember when he was last with a woman. To his consternation, he has to really think about it. It was not today, or yesterday. It was, in fact, Sunday. The time before that, Saturday, he was with a man. The fact that it was a man doesn't worry him, precisely, but neither does it seem right.

Anxiety thrills through him like cold water carving a dark ravine. His hand returns to the Band-Aid. Plastic crowds the rough cotton gauze, tickling his fingertip. The faces of Grand Army Plaza suddenly look ugly and mean, as if a filter has followed him off-app to contort every person in his line of sight like the twisting innards of a paint can. For some reason, he is reminded of Mark.

Adrian pulls his phone from his pocket, but his thumbs hover over the empty screen. He has never been very good at expressing himself, even when it comes to simple things: what he wants, what he needs, what he is feeling. Mark often seems to know what Adrian is thinking without him having to say a word, but he doesn't even understand himself right now. The language he's searching for is present but inaccessible, like a corpse petrified in peat. He puts his phone away. He places his mask on the step beside him, litter that will be left behind when he goes to find Cora at the bar. When he doesn't feel like talking, she is more than happy to fill the silence herself.

As Adrian walks toward St. Johns Place, a man without shoes asks him for a dollar. When Adrian gives it to him, the man shyly puts it in his pocket. *I'm in love*, he says, but as he continues on his way, Adrian realizes, with something like shock, that he is not the object of the man's emotion.

I'm in love. It could have been for anyone, perhaps even everyone, excepting him. Today, Adrian is just as anonymous with his mask on as without. He is not beautiful anymore.

Mark

Mark brings a gust of wildfire smoke into Calvary with him. As its scent fades into the attar of pine and leather, a sense of affectionate obligation flowers in his chest. He crosses the nave. The sun, low behind the stained glass, sends piebald shadows to dance over his shoulders. At the top of the stairwell, his hand finds the rail, avoiding a patch of splinters by habit.

They didn't come here when he was a kid, didn't attend church at all until Mark was nine or ten, when Mom began seeing the pastor at the Episcopalian over on Prieto. Sunday services for almost a year, until Mom broke off her engagement to Darryl and embraced her agnosticism once more. As Mark descends, the steps shift and flex, Calvary moving with him. The first time he felt its wooden planks under his shoes, he was almost forty years old.

The basement is as wide and low as the nave is narrow and high. Only a few inches above Mark's head, long, dirty windows, sliced by black legs and passing tires, frame Miwok Street. No cigarettes or vapes are allowed down here, but Pall Malls linger in the upholstery, a welcome change from the smoke outside. Since 2003, A Vision For You—held on Mondays, Wednesdays, Thursdays, and

Fridays at 7:00 p.m.—has been his meeting whenever he's back in Almendra. Has it changed at all in that time? Not that he can see. There is the cheap backup podium, papered with crumbling sheet music. There in the corner are the empty storage tubs, each the length of a wooden shipping pallet. There is the peeling card table and its tankard of coffee, boiling hot, as Mark discovers when he squeezes out the first cup of the meeting. And over there, he sees, is the chair he sat in the last time he was here.

It isn't literally the same chair, of course, only an identical one situated in the original chair's place, an end seat in the second-to-last row on the left side of the aisle. It had been the only available chair when Mark arrived that evening, late because he had to call a neighbor for a jump after Ruth had left the headlights on. As he sat down on March 19, 2020, he'd remembered to turn off his phone.

Only when the meeting was over did he sift through the deluge of rounded squares for the first MSNBC notification. It was Governor Newsom announcing the stay-at-home order: the pandemic had officially begun in the Golden State. Mark hurried upstairs, slipping through the smokers already gathering at Calvary's side door and trotting to the truck, where he read the message a second time.

He had texted Adrian, then put his phone away. The others could wait. Fuck it. Why not bum a cigarette, under the circumstances? But watching a pigtailed mother of one—Caitlin, he was pretty sure her name was—shoot a diaphanous donut into the air, he thought better of it and started the engine. He checked his phone again. Adrian hadn't responded, of course. He peeled out of the parking lot, dragging gravel over the faded white lines of the intersection.

Ruth was waiting at the front door, Grammy's quilt draped over her shoulders. She held her phone out for him. *Breaking news . . . issued a stay-at-home order . . . to slow the spread . . .*

Already saw it, said Mark, brushing past her.

You're probably next, she said, echoing the internet, where it was rumored that New York's stay-at-home order wasn't long in coming. The quilt swept the floor behind her like a wedding veil.

As they made themselves comfortable on the couch, the texts began pouring in, their phones singing like pinball machines. Unlike everyone else Mark was talking to—Lucinda, Tyree, even his agent, Derek, all responding promptly, unlike Adrian, that little idiot—Ruth didn't seem worried in the slightest. When he caught a glimpse of her screen, she was playing one of those candy games, flicking away her notifications like houseflies.

Where's Mom? Mark asked.

Asleep. His sister sighed like a weary princess.

Only a year ago, Mark thinks. He regards the chair from last time: thirty inches tall, onyx in color, capable of opening or closing in one fluid movement. He entertains himself by writing an artist's statement for it, as if it were on display in a museum. *An advent and artifact of the twentieth century, the twelve-step-meeting chair is an object affectively rich with irony, sentimentality, and ressentiment . . .* He takes a step toward it, then stops. The chair feels unlucky.

Mark glances down—the coffee, his hand, his shoes—then up at the ceiling, only a few inches above his head. He has the sudden urge to leave, although there is nowhere that he really wants to be. Not in Almendra, anyway, with the sickness and the smoke. He could go back to the house, but Ruth is there, trying to sleep. Sometimes in her own bed, but usually in Mom's, overseen by the shadow box of Grammy's vintage egg cups: Bakelite shepherds kissing Bakelite shepherdesses, garish red berries nesting in holly. The clock on the basement wall says he is twenty minutes early. He could still leave without drawing any notice.

Mark takes a deep breath to steady himself. Splitting the difference, he sits resolutely down in his third-choice chair, distant enough from his second choice that it almost feels random, and sets the coffee on the carpet. He'll stay, as he's stayed despite himself so many times before. With each new person that comes downstairs, he relaxes a little more. The sounds of his fidgeting—his keys tapping against the chair, his boots scraping the carpet's tight, hoary fibers—disappear in their voices.

I still wear mine most of the time I'm out of the house, says one unmasked woman. *Well, I'm vaccinated*, replies another.

They've almost got this one under control, says a man in weathered Wranglers, pointing up to sea level. *Like hell they do*, replies a man in cobalt track pants. *My brother's a firefighter, he says it's one of the worst he's seen.*

Mark doesn't care for coffee, but he needs it tonight. He's been having trouble sleeping, like Mom did toward the end. The nightmare came over and over, though she said she could derive no meaning from it: a clown lighting a playing card aflame, observed by a laughing monkey and a man in a red hat. That was the word she had used: *observed*. When she woke up, she would call Mark to her room and beg him to read aloud from one of her old *Time* magazines. Almost beseechingly, as if he had ever in his life said no to her.

Mark almost never dreams. His sleeplessness is a garden-variety insomnia, an excruciating self-awareness that transforms his mattress into a wooden cot and gives the wine bottles in the pantry little voices that taunt him through the walls. At 2:00 a.m. this morning, persecuted by an inexplicable dread for A Vision For You, his local meeting for almost twenty years, he had made himself a deal. If he could see the sky when he woke up, then he would go. If he didn't, he would permit himself to skip and stay home with his sister. It was a lazy compromise—the fire, though unseasonable for the spring, had been raging for six days. But nature called his bluff. A few hours after Mark finally nodded off, a cold front, long and gibbous on the meteorologist's map, blew in from the Pacific, dispersing the haze and cooling the farmlands. When a stomachache woke him well before his alarm, the AQI report confirmed what he could see through the window: the new sun made amber tea in the foothills, giving way to a sky as blue as a cereal box. Though the smoke returned that afternoon, the news reported that the fire was now 70 percent contained.

Mark hadn't wanted to come to A Vision For You on the evening of March 19, 2020, either. There he was in his hometown—sleepy Almendra, population: 11,393—to help Ruth take care of Mom, and yet there were all these meetings to attend. *Haven't you paid your dues yet?* asked Ruth. Mom supported his sobriety, of course, but had always regarded the program with suspicion. *Who knows what kind of people you'd find at a thing like that,* she said in her unknowingly knowing way. *I go almost every day when I'm at home,* Mark lied. The truth was that the monotony of the rooms, where any entertaining histrionics were canceled out by survival's brutal banality, was a welcome reprieve from the pettishness of his mother, the crankiness of his sister.

In retrospect, Mark supposes that he should have been grateful for one final in-person meeting before the world went Zoom. That night, as he and Ruth waited for more news from the living room couch, scrolling feeds and messaging friends all over the world, he had rubbed his bloated belly and worried. When it occurred to them, it was simultaneous. They turned their heads and locked eyes: What if *they* had this new virus?

They rushed to Google. Neither were coughing, but that didn't mean they didn't have it. The symptoms didn't seem all that different from the common cold, or allergies, or something else more or less normal. Even if they became very sick, they would have to get tested to know for sure. Where and how, out here in the sticks, wasn't clear.

Leaning forward, Ruth had peered down the hallway toward Mom's bedroom. *What if she gets it?* She sounded more wary than concerned.

Maybe we all already have it, Mark said. There was comfort there, in the possibility of a known quantity. But then who had been Patient Zero? Could Mark have picked it up a few weeks ago at Tyree's gallery opening in SoHo, or on the way home, with the unexpected layover in O'Hare? He could have even gotten it in Almendra, at the grocery store or the bank, and brought it back to his mother, an elderly woman already in ill health. A cold sweat broke out on his forehead.

Although Mark's inbox was flooded with sobering news—the Guggenheim, which was supposed to be exhibiting a few pieces from his collection, *The Gargoyles*, had closed; the Biennale was on indefinite hold; one of Derek's other clients, a woman seven years younger than Mark, was so ill she'd needed to be hospitalized and intubated—none of it meant anything particularly bad for him. He was where he needed to be, here with Mom and Ruth (the pair arguing whether his presence was necessary, their positions on the issue depending on the day and the other's current stance). Adrian was safe in New York, taking care of George (though knowing his young friend's proclivities, Mark wondered how safe that could possibly be). There were Zoom links for his meetings; for the next year, he would attend them remotely, listening to people in London and Minneapolis talk about their mothers, boyfriends, kids, bosses. There were masks and gloves for their runs to the grocery store and the pharmacy. As the pandemic dawned, Mark had nowhere to be and somewhere to stay, and money was no object. He had felt lucky that night, if not good. Ruth emerged from the kitchen with a bottle of Pepto-Bismol in one hand and an inch of bourbon in the other. They raised their glasses—hers liquor, his peppermint tea—and chased them with belts of pink goo, grimacing down at their screens.

Along with antacids and tea, the goo was part of Mark's system—part trial and error, part superstition—for managing the GI symptoms that had been coming and going for months now, much longer than anyone had been talking about this new virus, he reassured himself. No, all his recent time by the toilet, or on it, couldn't be COVID. It was something else, something with more staying power. A tumor. A hormonal imbalance. He should be so lucky to have developed something as minor as a gluten allergy. Wasn't everyone coming down with those now?

And then there were Ruth's symptoms—the headaches, the exhaustion, the weight loss—but there were explanations for those, too. Taking care of Mom for all these months was bound to take a toll, after all. That was why Mark had come in the first place, and his timing couldn't have been better: two weeks before the pandemic, six before the doctors threw up their hands, and four months to the day before his mother died forever. There had been no official diagnosis for her mystery illness, for which the California state government, desperate for deaths that the new disease couldn't be blamed for, was surely grateful.

People continue filing downstairs into the basement. Some wear masks, some don't (Mark doesn't). A woman takes a seat three chairs away from him. Pilly fleece, a mane of unkempt hair, and a face Mom would have archly referred to as *interesting*, like a character actor from a David Lynch movie. He doesn't think he has seen her before, though in all likelihood he has. Is she memorable? Dark curls with white at the forehead, like a spotlit cloud in the night sky. Her coloring reminds him of George. At that, a little knife inside him.

Mom's final opinion had been the same as the ones preceding it: that she was almost certainly afflicted with an unknown autoimmune illness, which had likely been unleashed from her genes by her stress, her diet, or, perhaps, her 1970s, the decade when she gave herself a 50 percent discount on the Winstons she bought on the clock at S & M Produce.

At the moment, it's impossible to say what triggered it, though we're learning a lot these days about how unhealthy the modern American lifestyle really is, said the doctor, crassly rubbing his septum. There was a rainbow pin on his lapel, the bright enamel weighing down the drooping fabric. The doctor was masked, as all of them were, but his lineless forehead and liquid joints suggested that he couldn't have been more than thirty-five. Mom was so old that her impending death didn't even obligate him to perform a professional display of sadness. He spoke confidently about Mom's *timeline* with big, casual gestures, handing Ruth brochures that she would drop in the garbage can as soon as he left the room.

Mom is dying, Mark had realized, not for the first time. He looked over at Ruth. Hunched in a corner of the sunless exam room, his sister reminded him of a mushroom, spongy and pale. She seemed far away, whereas Mom, wrapped in paper on the chilly metal table, was, despite her resemblance to a sugar-powdered sweetmeat, like an extension of his own body. When he put his arm around her, she leaned against it, as if testing the strength of his grip.

A few weeks later, on the same day, Mark and Ruth would learn from their own doctors (via socially distanced Zoom calls, like the goddamned Jetsons) that the tests Mom's doctor had recommended strongly suggested that they had the same illness as she. *It's still early days, compared to her*, said Mark's specialist. *You likely have many months, if not a year or two. But it is happening, I'm sorry to say.*

Mark and Ruth suddenly had their own timelines and care teams. *I can't talk about it*, Mom said, going to her room and closing the door behind her. Ruth, whose illness appeared to be more advanced than Mark's, was grateful to be left alone; Mark was merely nauseous. The night of their eerily coincidental death sentences, he and his sister sat in the living room until dawn with the TV turned off, listening to Almendra's silence, now strange to Mark after all his years in New York. Was he sad? Only when he thought of Adrian, and so he tried not to. That night, he and Ruth talked very little.

When the new symptoms began in 2019, Mom hadn't said anything, at first because they had resembled the normal effects of aging, and then because she was embarrassed by their increasing urgency and intensity. *No one needs to see anyone like that*, she later explained to Mark. In that way, Ruth wasn't like Mom at all. She didn't get embarrassed—she never had. Mom had been ladylike until the end. As Ruth's condition worsened, she shat with the door open and hurled with abandon, without ceremony or shame or apology. Not that there was anyone to apologize to. Though the first months of the pandemic had prevented people from visiting, Mom had received dozens of letters, phone calls, and frozen meals from neighbors and acquaintances in town; her coffee klatch had sent flowers and her community service society had fundraised for a souped-up hospital mattress. Ruth, who'd lived in Almendra since her birth, could count her local friends on one hand, which shook when she held it up for her brother to see the pinkish spots that were appearing around her swelling knuckles. *We're doomed*, she said. Mark was grateful when she laughed. It gave him permission—not to laugh himself, but to relinquish his impulse to fret. For Ruth, contempt always won out over fear.

There wasn't time to adjust, only to act. Mark called Adrian. *I guess I'm staying here until the end*, he told him. *But we don't know when that is, probably a few more months at most.* He told him that Ruth was sick, too. But he didn't say anything about himself. Adrian was quiet, even for Adrian. When Mark hung up, he had the unnerving feeling of having talked to the mirror for the past twenty minutes.

Mark spent the next four months smearing Cetaphil on Mom's papery skin and massaging her matchstick muscles. Maybe he would trade in his oils for ceramics, he joked (wouldn't Derek just love that). He made all her meals (though it was Adrian who was the chef), trying to recreate the blandly fat-conscious dishes he remembered from his childhood: tuna salad with diced red onions on white bread, cottage cheese with canned pineapple, skinless chicken with rice pilaf and parsley. When it was time to eat, he sat Mom on the couch behind a TV tray and propped the iPad against the salt and pepper shakers so she could watch old episodes of Lawrence Welk and Dick Cavett on YouTube. At first she fed herself, but soon she began asking for help; her arms were tired, she explained, and her aim was off. From the cushion beside her, he spoon-fed his mother, self-consciously scraping her sparkling chin clean between bites. It was impossible not to think about her doing the same for him when he was young, so early in his development he couldn't even remember it, but he never mentioned this; for Mom, such comparisons would only lead to embarrassment, not poignance. No matter how small her meals were, there were always leftovers, which he put in the fridge for him and Ruth to pick over later.

The weather warmed fast. The mornings Mark woke up sick—nausea, diarrhea, headaches, sometimes vertigo—were increasing in regularity, but his energy had still been fairly good back then. He downloaded TikTok to watch the videos of cute cats that Adrian sent, and soon enough the algorithm was feeding him more of people helping their elderly loved ones use the toilet, brush their teeth, tie their shoes. He did more of the feminine caretaking tasks, like washing Mom's feet and braiding her hair, than Ruth. Ignoring her own symptoms until the inevitable crash knocked her flat for a week, his restless sister was better suited for running errands and hounding phone reps when Mom's insurance refused to cover the medication she needed to stave off the suffering, real suffering, the kind that made people go looking for a gun to swallow. Mark was with Mom. Ruth was with the world, what was left of it.

While they waited for Mom to die, Mark didn't work, not one time. In the garage, which he normally used as a makeshift studio when he was in town, the linseed and turpentine gathered a coat of yellow powder, fine as yeast. He didn't even sketch. When Derek called, he didn't answer. The inevitable conversation was too much to bear. He sent a few emails and entertained a few texts, but that was all. If he couldn't even tell Adrian what was happening, how in the hell could he tell anyone else?

Mark's on sabbatical now, Ruth told Mom, raising her voice to make sure her brother would hear. *The world's just going to have to make do with one less genius around.*

Mark had never been precious about his work—perhaps preciously, he thought of himself as more of a craftsman than an artist—but he was shocked by how easy it was to just stop. Once, he came into Mom's room to find her on the bed with her eyes fixed on the ceiling, her flannel nightie pooling around her shriveled limbs. Reminded of Lucian Freud's portrait of his own mother, he was momentarily tempted. But that was it. It wasn't that his knuckles, now spotting like his sister's, had begun to trouble him, or that he felt uninspired, or that he was overwhelmed by his caretaking—if his mother wasn't sleeping, they lounged for most of the day, talking or playing cards if she was up to it. She left bed only for dinner, which he served while the sun was still high above the horizon. *Early-bird special*, he joked. With Ruth glued to her movies, in the evenings he was alone, free to do whatever he wanted until he turned in at around ten or so.

If Mark didn't have a Zoom meeting or a phone call with Adrian—
he was avoiding everyone else back in New York—he would go on
a walk. Down the driveway to Ohlone, turning right on Tehama,
keeping to the dusty path alongside the private gravel road. A break
in the barbed wire revealed a narrow trail through madrone, black
walnut, and elm trees, leading to the creek where he had come to
read comic books as a boy. The creek had no Anglo name that Mark
had ever heard, and he'd been born here in Almendra, not fifteen
miles down the road, back when hospitals still made their own for-
mula. Even these days, the creek might survive until almost mid-
summer, scattering over sunbaked circlets of algae-scabbed rock.
He threw stones, sending skippers to bounce between glancing
water and darkening horizon. (Did Adrian know how? Mark had
always struggled to imagine his young friend's childhood, which
he never talked about, as if he had come to life fully formed, an
adult from day one.) He squatted, sniffing the soil, the slime, the
scat. Birds blackened as the stars pierced the twilight's dying span-
drels. He held out his thumb and squinted—skylines and sunsets,
skylines and sunsets—but the gesture was vestigial. Painting was
Mark's life, but he was not alive anymore, not in the way he had
always been. He hoped that he would die in New York, where he
had lived his life, his real life. Was anyone there thinking of him,
right this moment? (He knew that Adrian cared about him, but
did he miss him? His doubt gave him a strange pleasure.) When he
could no longer see his shoelaces, he would begin making his way
back home again.

Feeling a tickle in his throat, Mark hastily searches his pockets for
a tissue. He brings them to all his meetings, just in case. Since last
year, he often talks about Mom, using words like *dead* and *gone*,
rather than *grief* or *empty*; he does not talk about his own failing
health, or his sister's. People listen attentively, but if they cry, it's

for themselves. (Who does Mark cry for?) He finds the tissue and vigorously blows his nose.

Sitting nearby are a few people who had known Mom during her life: there's Jake the libertarian arborist, and over there is Mom's cousin's daughter, Tina, who dropped out of herb school after she married that guy with the earthworm farm. How well had they known her? In her final months, she became almost unrecognizable to her own son. She hadn't even complained, and Mom had always complained. Her slow end had begun a lifetime ago with a mysterious fever as Mark was finishing elementary school and Ruth was entering the third grade, followed by an ever-growing list of clinically inexplicable symptoms: fainting spells, leg pains, food allergies, migraine, early menopause, arthritic hands, and chronic fatigue, not to mention her vertigo. (*My Ménière's*, she'd been saying since she was still buying Mark's underwear for him.)

And yet the transition from sick to dying had been so sudden. From the sixteen weeks between prognosis to deathbed, the illness winnowed Mom down to a stranger that Mark hadn't the time to know. Preoccupied with her own annihilation in a way that was totally in character yet utterly novel, this new Mom hadn't seemed interested in him, either. He found himself missing the woman who had often been annoying and pathetic, whose perennial sickliness, while tedious, had been her way of holding him close. His guilt for leaving her to Ruth for all these years, scabbed over with time and exasperation with his sister's victim complex, had become in its recrudescence the shameful wish that Mom would have died differently—quickly and suddenly, in her sleep or in a crash. Even a death long and agonizing and littered with endless goodbyes would have been better than the gradual fading of this calm and measured woman who no longer talked over her

daughter or preened for her only son's pity. Well, maybe not better. But it would have been something Mark recognized. But the
hypochondriac eventually had gotten what she wanted, hadn't
she? Shouldn't she have been satisfied?

Of course, Mark can't say any of this to anyone. Not to the people
at his meeting. Not to the neighbors he runs into at the post office. Not to the teller at the credit union, a heavily tattooed young
woman that Mom babysat years before her very first permanent
Tweety Bird. He thinks he could say it to Adrian, but could he do
that without admitting everything else? The longer he waits, the
more impossible this seems.

At the funeral, Mark read Mom's eulogy from a piece of lined legal
paper. He had written it at the kitchen table while Ruth rewatched
a Lubitsch, *Der something or other*, in the living room, the cellu-
loid muttering and laughing through the doorway. The service
was at the Episcopalian church over on Prieto because Calvary
had closed for electrical renovations (perhaps Mom would have
found this funny). He had never minded public speaking, but that
afternoon he had felt queasy about it. The mourners didn't appear
to notice, listening with scrupulous respect to the son of the dead
woman, the famous painter who had come back, after all these
years, to take care of her in her final days. Mark knew he ought
not to have been moved by it, but he was. Almendra wasn't far
from San Francisco, but it was still a hick town mostly untouched
by its gentrification, even if, to his enduring wonder, a sparse but
spirited Pride parade now ran the length of Main Street—four city
blocks—at the start of every June.

And though—the eulogy went, in his own narrow cursive. Mark
had stopped. For a moment, he thought he had written *Arturo*,

and he almost read his name aloud. The mourners understood his pause to be a sign of overwhelming emotion and offered him a wave of encouraging nods. He cleared his throat, collected himself, kept going. Someone—a woman in an ugly grey blouse whom Mark didn't recognize—wept audibly in one of the back rows. When he finished, he folded the legal paper and returned to his chair next to Ruth, who patted his knee with uncharacteristic affection. She would not be speaking after him, though Mom had asked her to.

Had Ruth been thinking about Arturo, too? Arturo was always there, but after the funeral he hunted instead of haunted. When the guests gave Mark their condolences through their surgical masks and N95s, assuring him that Mom would be missed, he thought about Arturo. As Mom was lowered into the soil of Sonoma County, he thought about Arturo, whose body was in New York, less than a mile from where Adrian and George were waiting patiently for him in Windsor Terrace. When he and Ruth were washing casserole dishes at dusk, the sunlight coagulating in the smoke (French Camp Fire, 4,343 acres burned, 36 percent contained), he thought about Arturo.

Perhaps the doctors were wrong and he and his sister wouldn't die just yet, Mark had speculated, drying his hands on a daisy-printed dishcloth. Perhaps Mom's death would be a bookend to his lover's: death, death. As if he and his sister and everyone their age would keep going on, forever.

Clenching the tissue in his fist, Mark leans forward again to pull his phone from his pocket. The lock screen is a photo of Adrian holding George in his arms. They're in Mark's room, sitting on the bed. Adrian's teeth hover over the cat like mistletoe; he is more beautiful than a Bernini. Mark had considered painting the photo but never ended up doing it. Something about it having been taken on an iPhone then used as digital wallpaper, becoming the background of a dirty habit he kept in his pocket, right over his ass. No. The photo, if you could even call it that, was tainted. The painting would not be what he wanted. It would go from a sensation to an image. It would be a waste of time.

The cough suddenly erupts. Mark reaches for his coffee, but it's still too hot. As he coughs he blows his nose again, tasting the dead trees in the back of his throat, worrying that it won't stop. Wouldn't that be funny, if this forced him to leave the meeting, after all that hemming and hawing? He sets the coffee down, squares his hips in the chair, and holds a shaking fist to his mouth. He must look old. *Well*, he thinks, *I guess I am.*

A young man comes down the stairs and crosses the aisle to sit a few rows ahead. Without turning his head, Mark can see the baseball cap, the sinistral leather boot, the tidy black beard. His throat fighting to contract, he suppresses the burn stripping his esophagus. The young man turns his body toward him, reaching to rub his ear, but as their eyes are about to meet, the cough bursts through Mark's defenses and he doubles over in his chair. When he comes up for air, the young man is looking away.

As the cough settles, Mark's eyes keep returning to the young man, who is clearly straight, like the guys he dreamed of when he was a boy, here in Almendra. Now Mark is the older one, the object of daddy issues, or else a sad old lech waiting in the wings. During their year at the Episcopalian church over on Prieto, there had been an olive-skinned deacon with a five o'clock shadow, much better looking than Darryl, Mom's pig-pink boyfriend giving the sermon. The deacon wore the same pair of hunter-green slacks to every service. From the pew he shared with Mom and Ruth, Mark had imagined leaning against the deacon's legs, feeling where the slender pieces of fabric held his leather belt in place. He would be rigid but passive, conforming his body to the deacon's, bending into its uprightness, his head to the grown man's heartbeat. Mark had sensed that something was meant to happen after this, but he didn't know what it was. In his fantasy, he and the deacon were under a willow tree together, alone in the center of a vast, shimmering meadow. Mark didn't know where this was supposed to be. He had never seen a willow tree outside of the movies—*Oklahoma!*, *Gone with the Wind*, etc.

The cough begins again. Mark honks from deep in his chest, choking on the hot, bitter fluids that drip from his nasal cavity, catching spit in the crook of his arm. But as his mouth kisses the inside of his elbow, he can't help but smile: he has never been younger, only a different person. A few people, the young man among them, keep their eyes fixed on the podium, as if trying to spare him some public humiliation.

———————— ◇ ————————

When Mark gets home from his meeting, Ruth is watching a movie. It's all she can do now, but then, it was all she ever did. With the exception of her college years in the Bay Area, Ruth has always watched television—the spindle-legged Chromacolor, then the cable-ready Panasonic, then the century's first flat-screen, which was followed by the fifty-inch upgrade Mark had given Mom and Ruth for Christmas a few years ago—in the living room, seated in one of a series of faded recliners that were always parked between the Dutch leather club chair and the lumpy red two-seater. When

Mom died, Ruth moved the flat-screen to the foot of Mom's bed. For some reason, this bothers him.

When Ruth was accepted at SFSU's School of Cinema, Mark had thought she might really go through with it. Shocking everyone, she would leave Mom in Almendra for good, maybe even become a professor someday, the first person in their family to not only finish college but earn an advanced degree. Instead, she dropped out in the middle of her second semester, on account of broken things: the only romantic relationship that Mark ever knew of, with a mousy, snub-nosed man named Clark; her Volkswagen Something or Other, driven by said Clark into a dead live oak on the dark and stormy night of the breakup; and Mom's leg, after she fell from a ladder while taking in the laundry minutes before that same storm, the atmospheric river of the decade, descended on Sonoma County. At twenty-two, Ruth moved back to their childhood home in Almendra, the notes for her thesis on Frances Farmer wadded up in the bottom of her vintage cardboard suitcase.

She never left home again, aside from the spring of 1995, during one of Mom's rare spells of good health, when their fights were worse than they'd ever been. After Ruth smashed Grammy's china cabinet with a cobwebbed ball-peen hammer she found in the back shed, Mark decided an intervention was in order. He invited his sister to visit him and Arturo in New York. To his disappointment, she took him up on his offer.

For the better part of three months, Ruth sat on their couch, chain-smoking and watching TCM. *Don't you want to explore the city?* Mark asked, mystified by her sloth. It was her first time away from California, other than a few road trips into Nevada and Oregon when they were children. But Ruth only left their apartment in the Village to see movies at Film Forum or the Waverly, circling ads for directors—Preminger, Lupino, Borzage, Hou—with a golf pencil. Late at night, after he and Arturo were in bed, she would slink back into the apartment with cups of black coffee ("WE ARE HAPPY TO SERVE YOU") and gardenias wrapped in wet white paper, like soggy cold cuts. The flowers helped with her homesickness, she said, though Mark couldn't guess why. They withered on the kitchen table, where Arturo was obliged to work because the TV was blaring at all hours a few feet from his desk.

Let's go outside, Mark begged. *The tulips are beautiful this time of year.* Only once did she oblige, donning a floppy denim hat that was so big its only function must have been, Mark believed, to embarrass him. *You look like the flying nun*, he groused. On the street, he tried to set the pace with a brisk stride, but she lagged behind, and no matter how much he slowed, she wouldn't keep up. *Why are you being so neurotic?* he kept asking her. When they reached the parklet on Hudson and Eighth, bristling with yellow and fuchsia bulbs, she refused to walk through it with him, skirting the black bars from the sidewalk instead, hat wiggling absurdly in the breeze.

When Ruth finally left for Almendra, where Mom, her vertigo returned, had forgiven her daughter for the cabinet, Arturo made a big show of locking the door behind her and her vintage cardboard suitcase. *You're lucky you're cute*, he told Mark.

Mark stands in the doorway, squinting. The TV's blue light washes his sister, her wasted body shrimping against the headboard. When he arrived in January, he had been shocked by how much she had deteriorated in the four months since Mom's funeral. *Why didn't you tell me?* he asked. *I would have come sooner.*

She snorted, waving him off with her gnarled hand. She knew, as he did, that he would have, as resentful as he was concerned.

On the screen, the camera crawls inch by painstaking inch over the living room of an apartment, revealing a couch, a nondescript coffee table, and the beginning of a hallway. There are three darkened windows, the walls around them draped in black velvet. In each window hangs a doll's head painted like a smiling harlequin clown. The camera continues to pan, but more and more unsteadily, as if held by someone not strong enough to lift it for very long. It turns to follow the hallway to its terminus, a black door. The door is slightly ajar, a faint light coming through from the other side. Whoever is holding the camera pushes the door open, perhaps with their foot. The lens comes to rest on a bed in the center of the room, where a nude woman is lying on her back. The origin of the light is unclear. The camera approaches the woman from above. It steadies, taking in her black hair and red lipstick and white skin. Her eyes are closed and her mouth is parted by gravity. The visual language of the camera changes from caress to examination. It approaches in short, choppy zooms, like a microscope, cutting her into brusque, dehumanizing frames. There is no breath, no movement. Mark can't tell if the woman is dead or sleeping.

But already he's lost interest. Rubbing a knuckle in his eye, he goes to the kitchen, where he can look out the window into the backyard, a much more engaging tableau than Ruth's weird movie that no one's ever heard of. Out there, the garden eats itself beneath a comforter of fermented fruit, its molding tangelos pillowed by the earth. A half cord of wood gathers cobwebs by the trough where he burns leaves. Against the fence, a stack of pallid newspapers stirs in the breeze. The last of them, since Ruth canceled the subscription a few weeks ago. Mom being gone was her excuse, but Mark knows how difficult it has become for his sister to limp to the end of the driveway every morning, where an elderly man reaches around the breastbone of a laughing Labrador to throw plastic-wrapped bundles from the window of his Tacoma. Mark leans on the countertop, tapping his fingers. It's looking a little disheveled back there. Tomorrow, his stomach permitting, he'll do some clearing and have a bonfire, stoke it red. St. Paul's robes on the road to Damascus.

From Mom's room, a scream, followed by a slap. A baritone voice shouts in a Romance language he can't put his finger on, cut through by the sound of Ruth coughing, her curdled lungs fighting for air. Mark thinks about the handsome young man from the meeting. He thinks about Arturo, who had loved handsome young men. (What would he have thought of Adrian?) Her coughing dies down enough for him to hear wordless moans from what sounds like a woman—perhaps the one on the bed, with the black hair and red lips. It occurs to him that his sister will never get laid again, although he has no idea when the last time was for her (it couldn't have been Clark, could it?). He won't ask, and so he'll never know. When she coughs again, his own throat begins to percolate. But as he takes a breath in preparation, her coughing worsens, and his throat calms. Every time he tries, she coughs. His lungs begin to ache. Her coughing prevents him from coughing.

Irritated, Mark goes back down the hall to Mom's room, where Ruth has just rewrapped Grammy's quilt around her narrow shoulders. She hacks into her palms, satin lilies of the valley and felt roses of Sharon shuddering by her ears. *This one is about intimacy*, she says, her voice thick with phlegm.

On the screen, the woman is still on the bed. She lifts an arm to point at the camera, an accusation, and her eyes flip open, filled with a white glow. No pupil, no iris, no involutions of blood vessels. The special effects are interesting, Mark has to concede.

That actress wrote the script, but she's not even credited, Ruth says. *Her husband pushed her from a moving car not long after production. Dead at thirty-six.*

Mark doesn't reply. It isn't required. When they were kids, Ruth always spoke for her older brother. *Slow,* said his second-grade teacher. *Lazy,* corrected his fifth-grade teacher. *Sensitive,* insisted Mom. As an adult, his reserve makes him seem mysterious, a quality often commented upon by the press. This aspect of his persona—what Derek calls his *brand*—seems to fascinate the so-called public that the PR people obsess over.

Ruth's eyes never leave the screen. Her chin droops grotesquely as she hacks, a crumpled fist his only safeguard from an invisible explosion of germs. Her tongue rolls, a strip of raw bacon. Mark hates the noises she makes, hates looking at her like this, but his distaste is bundled with a soft and silken relief: his hatred means that she is safe. How could his sister die when he doesn't like her? That just wouldn't be fair.

Mark's belly relaxes. He coughs. Now brother and sister cough together, his eyes on her, her eyes on the screen. Eyes closed again, the black-haired woman is now floating in a bathtub. The harlequins' heads bob in the water around her soft armpits.

On the wall behind the TV is a framed photo of Mom. From 2016 or '17, Mark guesses. She is sitting at the kitchen table, a ceramic ladle in one hand and her cane between her knees. Mark doesn't remember being there, and supposes Ruth took the photo.

Mark's phone buzzes in his pocket. *BREAKING: The number of Americans dead from COVID-19 surpasses 500,000.*

Mark deletes the text. The COVID updates depress him, but he doesn't know how to make them stop. He doesn't know anyone, personally, who died of it, a fact that makes him feel more and more strange as last year recedes into the past. When he was young, back in New York, it was different. Death was everywhere, for everyone he knew. He still doesn't know why he was spared. He thinks of his painting *Funeral* (oil on canvas, 1991), which was recently acquired by a tech millionaire. Six months later, it was disbursed to a museum of American LGBTQI art history after the millionaire's body rejected his third heart transplant. Mark hasn't been to see it since the sale. Warehoused now, is how he thinks of it.

No one had made any assumptions about Arturo, who had died long after antiretrovirals and all that. But the connection was there, with the tensile strength of a moored ship in a choppy bay: a homosexual; a long, wasting illness; Arturo's youth with ACT UP. Seven years later, the connections still eddy, and occasionally Mark feels something akin to shame, a sensation that has outlived his lover, tainting his days, his death, and the life that Mark had contributed to both. What will happen when Mark is dead, when there is no one else who had known Arturo as he'd known him? What will replace the truth of Arturo's life? Associations, movements, demographics; some words, some dates. When it's Mark's turn, will that truth be replaced? Is there a truth to be replaced? Is Arturo memorable? All that Mark retains from the first year after his death are tepid bowls of corn flakes; the lawyer's horn-rimmed glasses, lenses flecked like a dalmatian's coat; and the effort of assembling his face into the shape that would allow him to avoid any more questions than were strictly necessary. To offers of a home-cooked meal, of a ride here or there, of an embrace: *No, thank you, I'm really all right.* No matter the Samaritan, their efforts stank of intrusion, of a salacious desire to know, by way of Mark's grief, the most beautiful man that he had ever known. *But Arturo is mine,* Mark had thought, over and over. *Mine, mine, mine.* What does the truth matter when it isn't willingly given?

His coughing has abated, as has his sister's. Now the only sound comes from the TV, where the woman is floating in a bathtub. He must get some more rapid tests the next time he's in town, he thinks, if there are any in stock. When he was young, he didn't matter, and he feared a death that he could see and touch in the ravaged bodies of his friends. Now the world holds him in such esteem that the new death almost feels unreal. What a strange, impersonal way to be terrorized. When he was in New York over the winter, he told a few people that Mom died from COVID. He doesn't know why. When he confessed this lie to Ruth a few weeks ago, he had expected his sister to laugh or maybe even get angry.

It's not a big deal, she said, giving her soup a brisk stir. *Can you hand me the salt?*

Mark goes back to the kitchen and opens the fridge. Not much in there, now that there's really only him to feed. When Ruth is able to eat, he pours powders from plastic sacs into small bowls and reconstitutes them with water of varying temperatures. There are bricks of hardened goo developed to restore fat, fight atrophy, and preserve cognitive function, which he melts, mushes, or purees. Dense as this palliative nourishment is, it takes up very little space next to his cartons of milk and eggs, his moist baggie of cheddar, his slinky filets of shrink-wrapped salmon. In the freezer: ice trays, Popsicles, a mysterious block of aluminum foil. He wishes again that he had thought to preserve something that Mom had made, or the remnants of something that he had made for her. Like a slice of wedding cake—something that he could reheat to smell, then freeze again for safekeeping, a sensual memory defying physics and good taste for all eternity. He wonders if the ladle that Mom is holding in the photo is stowed in the kitchen somewhere. If he finds it, touches it, will it still be warm? He has stopped telling people that Mom died from COVID, but only because there is no one new to inform.

Mark's stomach doesn't hurt, thankfully, and he does have an appetite, but nothing in the kitchen catches his interest. He looks at the garden again. Mom planted it with Darryl. They worked it together on Saturday mornings, and late Sunday afternoons when they returned from the Episcopalian church over on Prieto. Back then, the dirt had been tidy. Now it's mussed, like thinning hair. The trees had been young and supple. Now, almost fifty years later, they have grown high and immovable, lushly mature. Though a line of irises has started to unfurl, the boxes are barren, the vines sag from their trellises, and last autumn's corn husks lie like the moribund, begging for the pyre. Mark had guessed that Ruth would abandon the garden when Mom died, and he had been right about that, too.

Adrian

The woman leans from the bed to kiss his shoulder on his way out, but she doesn't try to stop him. *It* had been dormant back in Washington Square Park, but when she flashed the hotel key card with a mischievous grin, Adrian took her up on her offer without a second thought. They had spent the afternoon in bed, laughing more than they spoke. But now that he's in the elevator again, he worries. What was it that the woman had been attracted to, if not *it*?

He decides to forget about it and get on with his evening. His apartment is closer, but he's going to Mark's. He hasn't been since yesterday morning, and George will want food and attention.

He walks down Broadway with his eyes in the sky, looking for the ram-horned demons bestriding the old red building sandwiched between two taller, sandier high-rises. There they are. He stops by a hydrant and squints. Though the beasts' shoulders are hunched, their snouts are long and delicate and their claws lie across their breasts with the patrician delicacy of a certain iteration of Dracula. Ever since Mark finished painting *The Gargoyles*, a few months before the pandemic began, Adrian has begun to notice such grotesqueries everywhere: in movies and in books and in real life, too. Here in the city, so much younger than the metropoles of Europe, they're more common than he would have thought. He discovered this pair, prettier than Mark's by a mile, last year. Now he makes a point of coming to see them whenever he's in the neighborhood.

Oh, fuck.

Adrian is spun around on his heels before he even feels the blow, dense as brick, to the left side of his body.

Sorry, says the man with the acne and muscle definition of a successful gymfluencer. *Didn't see you there.*

Adrian's disquiet freezes the air around him, dulling the sounds of revving engines, jackhammers, sidewalk chatter. He steadies himself against the hydrant, pinching the octagonal nipple on top of its dome until his fingers turn white. Feeling something like shame, he resumes his way to the train.

Before he turns the corner, Adrian looks back at the figures bronzing in the late-afternoon sun. Now the sky is so bright he can see them only briefly, like subliminal messages on 35 mm film, before the sun forces his eyes shut. Could a gargoyle even be pretty? If it were, well, then, it wasn't a gargoyle anymore, only a statue, no longer fulfilling its purpose of . . . what, exactly? He realizes he doesn't know what gargoyles are *for*. He'll have to ask Mark sometime.

When Adrian comes above ground again, the sun has set, but only just. April showers the streets of Park Slope, where over the past few years the corners have begun sprouting surveillance machinery disguised with cheery edutainment chyrons and broken charging ports. He enjoys strolling through this neighborhood at this time of year, when the pavement is leaden with rain and the iron fences, knit and purled into holy black geometries, are bedizened in honeysuckle.

But as he walks, his worry deepens. There is a nanny with a double-decker stroller and a poodle on a leash; a postman in a crimson durag digging through his canvas; a pair of elderly twins dressed identically, their long white hair in braids down their curving backs; and a girl who looks so much like his friend Mary, with her black pixie and brave bone structure (Adrian has always thought she looks like someone who could take a punch, yet squares up so sturdily that she never has to), that he almost calls her name before remembering she's on the other side of the world.

He notices them all, and yet none seem to notice him, though he isn't wearing a mask. Do they even see him? If not, why not? He can come up with excuses—the nanny is busy, the postman is preoccupied, the twins are losing their sight, and the Mary clone, well, perhaps she got some devastatingly bad news today and can't see any farther than her own footsteps. He can remind himself of the Greenwich hotel pillow that still smells like Mark's shampoo. He pulls out his phone to look at himself through the camera, and his face appears as it always has. But none of it sets him at ease.

When Mark's text drops down into the screen, Adrian is relieved to see that it comes with an errand. He puts his phone away and quickens his pace.

———————————◆———————————

After feeding George, Adrian takes the stepladder to the hall closet. On the top shelf is an unlabeled cardboard box. He pulls it open and dumps dozens of unsealed white envelopes onto the hardwood.

Getting to his knees, he spreads them across the floor. Peeking through the lower lip of each is a stack of glossy, rectangular photographs, which, according to the dates printed on the face of each envelope, are from when he was very young, or even before he was born. Opening one, he finds a profusion of four-by-six-inch Fire Islands, where he and Mark spent a week every summer until COVID. This Mark is much younger, proving that the hair Adrian thinks of as brown was once a rich, almost rosy mahogany.

Adrian takes his time admiring his friend's past. Here he is toasting the lens with a Rheingold. Here he is in a kitchen, a string of lacquered chili peppers hanging from the wood paneling, with his arm around Arturo, whom Adrian knows only from photos like these; Arturo is pointing out a watchful doe in the window. Here they are on the beach with another man that Adrian doesn't recognize. On the back of the photo, in handwriting that isn't Mark's: *A conversation piece.* It's signed *Leo.* The last photo shows the third man—perhaps he is Leo?—stretched nude on a towel, his feet buried below the sand's blond crust. Hair curls up and down his midline like a row of dampened fiddlehead ferns and his mouth is rounded in campy shock at the hand that's reaching from out of frame for the tan line left by his Speedo. Adrian recognizes the short, squared fingernails, the calloused thumbs, the gold ring that Mark still wears in Arturo's memory.

Adrian looks at this photo for much longer than the others. Its staged sensuality makes him feel weird. He realizes he never really sees Mark like this: sexually playful, coarsely immature. He's not sure he likes it. He thinks about the woman he left behind him at the hotel and, for some reason, the reservist who vaccinated him a few weeks ago. Although he's just gotten here, he wants to go back out again; he is suddenly ravenous for attention, like he was when he first moved to New York. Back then, his approach to his *friends* had been less polished than it is now. Sometimes he went only with *friends* that he felt an intense desire for, or who could give him everything that he asked for, and he had a lot to ask for, in those days. But sometimes he would stand on the corner, any corner, and think to himself, *Whoever requests me next will have me,* and they would. If he goes to that corner now, what will happen?

Adrian puts the Fire Island photos back in their envelope and continues his search. It doesn't take long to find the one Mark wants. Leaving the box on the ground, he goes to the kitchen with it between his thumb and middle finger, careful not to smudge it. He places it on the countertop and opens the camera app, moving his phone around so his picture doesn't have a glare.

Found it, he texts Mark. *She looks so pretty :)*

It's Ruth from a long time ago, here in New York. He can tell because he recognizes the park behind her, one of the little ones in the West Village, not far from the Jane, the hotel where he was just this afternoon. Golden-brown hair, pale but freckled, skinny and unsmiling, she doesn't look all that different from now. She's wearing a blue hat that's so big it could be an umbrella.

Adrian thinks about texting her, too, but he doesn't. He's never known someone who was dying before and doesn't know what to say.

Mark

Mark.

Last spring, Mark bought a baby monitor in case Mom needed him at night. This spring, it's in a drawer somewhere. Ruth prefers to yell. *Use it or lose it,* as she likes to say.

Mark.

There is a path through Mom's house. Though imaginary, it's almost as old as Mark is. He follows it from his room, through the kitchen, to the hallway that leads to Mom's room, where it ends at a varnished knot in the hardwood that pricks his toes. Is Mom's room memorable?

Mark.

I'm here.

It's 3:36 a.m. He consoles himself with the knowledge that he would have awoken soon, anyway, with his own problems. Vomit or diarrhea, spin the wheel. Maybe some joint pain for variety.

Sick again, Ruth says.

Mark helps her out of bed and guides her to the bathroom. Shifting her weight from his shoulder, his sister sighs as she eases down onto the edge of the bathtub. He lifts the lid and the seat. He goes under the sink for a new roll and slides it onto the plastic spear that Mom bought at the Costco in Novato.

You need help?

Get out.

Mark doesn't say what he's thinking. He closes the door behind him and sits on the bed. On the TV, *Losing Ground* is on pause. He recognizes the still, even without any characters in it, because she's been watching this one a lot lately. Ruth has always loved movies about artists making art.

To pass the time, he misses George, who he calls his baby (that makes him the daddy and Adrian the mommy). Mom had been a baby at the end, blinking sleepily, crying weakly. Ruth is like an angry toddler. Mark pretends his thigh is George's flank and strokes it through his sweatpants. Will he be like this when it's his turn? Mean to Adrian in the middle of the night and distant during the day, but needful always, demanding things his young friend hasn't in his power to give?

He hears his sister lower herself to the tile, all alone behind the wall. Mark attempts to interpret her sounds: Coughs or retches? Preparatory or productive? Being clinical helps him rise above his feelings. He fears that one night they will overwhelm him and he'll lose control. That his large and hairy hands will tear into the sinking flesh around Ruth's biceps, pinched from almost a year of slow starvation. He thinks of a song he wrote a long time ago; of a painting he won't survive to paint.

After a long silence, Ruth begins to splatter and crack into the water. Mark wrinkles his nose, seizing the bridge as if to hold his head together. He didn't feel resentful when it was Mom. He's not sure why he feels this way now. Because he's finally worn out from watching his family die? Or is it Ruth specifically? She is often cruel, now, even for her. Mom couldn't have been called gracious, but she did thank him, on occasion. Or else she was in too much pain to pay attention to him in any way that didn't involve getting her needs met. That was okay. With Ruth, it's something else.

Mark.

The noises have stopped. Mark goes to the door, takes hold of the handle.

Mark!

Yeah?

Can you fucking—

He rolls his eyes. Her sputum lands in the commode like something heavier, like wet clay. More noise. He pulls out his phone and checks the time. It's too early for this shit. He and Arturo used to bring a small backgammon board to entertain themselves in cafés and airports when they traveled. He's glad Arturo isn't here. He would be embarrassed to put him through this.

Mark . . .

When he opens the door, Mark jumps. Ruth is already on her feet, leaning against the frame. Anticipating her fingers on his shoulder, he makes the decision to not flinch.

All done? he asks.

Yeah.

Sighing, he wraps his arm around her waist and accepts her weight again. When they were kids, they watched Boy Scouts escort old ladies across the street on TV. Now his sister is the old lady. Skinnier than she's ever been, which is convenient, because Mark is weaker; he's not as strong as he was even last summer. They stagger back down the hallway and into the bedroom together. She clings to him until she can feel the mattress beneath her, then pushes him away. Ruth is not the kind of woman who could take any joy in becoming smaller. For this, Mark pities her.

She attempts to get comfortable. When Mark tries to help, she holds up the flat of her hand, her mouth squeezed into an ugly bud. Her hair is loose, a white-threaded arras browned by lightlessness. The strands make an insectile sound when they spread across the pillow. *Turn it on,* she says, pointing at the TV, but then she digs the remote out from somewhere and does it herself.

A period piece. A handsome young man, pale and chestnut-haired and peclessly slender, paints with oils on a canvas. He wears black trousers, white hose, a fitted cream waistcoat. He looks like the kind of guy who would wear a wig to a ball. An interstitial with lacy trim interrupts the young man's hand, mid-stroke, to announce, in a loopy font, *Mastery happens when rules feel like freedom.* Offscreen, violins quaver and shriek. When the interstitial disappears, the handsome young painter is back, but now the camera has pulled away, bringing into view the painter's subject, another handsome young man, equally slender, but with light brown skin and a mustache like a piratical Gene Kelly. The subject is lying nude on a chaise longue, his legs slightly parted. The painter peers into the shadows there, scowling in concentration.

He looks like your friend, Ruth says.

She means Adrian, though Mark isn't sure which of the two actors she's comparing him to. Maybe she doesn't, either. She hasn't seen Adrian since before the pandemic, when he passed through on his way back from Taiwan, where he'd exchanged New York's wet heat for a more tropical kind with one of his *friends*, a lawyer named Karen. Mark had gone to collect him at the end of the driveway, where Adrian was waiting beneath a walnut tree in a shaft of sunlight as soft as a cloud of perfume.

Didn't bring much, did you? Mark said, lifting the suitcase. Like the backpack Adrian was wearing, it was small and expensive, with a hard plastic shell.

You know me.

How much was the car? He wanted to touch his friend, but it didn't feel right. It rarely did, especially here.

Adrian shrugged. The Uber from SFO had been sponsored by a third-generation Dole Corp exec with three gold-capped molars to prove there were no hard feelings after Adrian declined a first-class ticket to Honolulu. *Wrong direction*, Adrian had explained.

While Adrian went to say hello to Mom, Mark took his bags to his bedroom. When he came back down the hallway to the kitchen, Ruth was waiting, hipping her fists. *Not the office?* she said, lifting an eyebrow.

His sister was no prude, but the thought of explaining to her, yet again, that he and Adrian weren't lovers made him want to pull her hair, like when they were kids. She wasn't looking for an explanation, anyway. Congratulating himself for not taking the bait, Mark peeled back the foil from the glittering pork chops. When he turned around again, she was in the doorway, embracing Adrian like a long-lost son.

Mark was shocked. Over the years, he had noticed that some people took a strong dislike to Adrian once their pulses had the chance to slow. The fantasy having run its course, his beauty became an imposition, as if his body were merely a rude bid for attention. Though Ruth, too, had gaped like a codfish when Mark introduced his friend, she had afterward been aggrieved by him for years, forcing her smiles and refusing small talk, unless there was an opportunity to ask pointed questions about how he and Adrian had met, or where his young friend disappeared to at night.

Adrian! cried Ruth, vigorously patting his back.

Hi, Ruth, said Adrian, smiling over her shoulder.

At a loss, Mark began serving the pork chops. Ruth led his friend to the table, fondling the fabric of his shirtsleeve between her fingers. Adrian reported that Mom's vertigo, which was always at its worst in the summertime, was acting up, so she was going to stay in bed.

More for the rest of us! said Ruth, rubbing her palms together. *I hope you're hungry.* She seized Adrian's plate and started scooping salad.

Mark was suspicious. Ruth peppered Adrian with questions—had he enjoyed Taipei? What was it like?—but every time their guest attempted to answer, she interrupted with yet another question, each more effusive than the last. His sister's behavior reminded him of their friend Cora, who often didn't seem to actually like Adrian, although Mark knew that she did, very much; Cora's was a conflicted interest, dressed up in a little camp. Was it a lesbian thing? He had always wondered about his sister. She had more chemistry with her pork chop than she ever had with Clark, that man she dated. If she were gay like her older brother, it would be hard on Mom, but would that even matter at this point? Ruth had long been what Grammy would have called an old maid. Handing his sister the wine bottle, Mark examined Adrian's polite attentiveness for something real, signs of feeling that resembled his own skepticism or resentment, but as usual he was only the most beautiful mirror in the world. If his friend had noticed that anything with Ruth was different, he didn't betray it.

Let me, babe, said Ruth, reaching for Adrian's glass, still half full of trembling liquid. Built without central AC, the house was sprouting with ceiling and floor fans to offset the heat—the temperature was still hovering above 90 degrees as the light faded—whose whir and hum muted the flatware's tang on the plates and the squeal of Mark's chair on the linoleum.

Thank you, said Adrian. In Taipei, he went on, Karen had taken him shopping, and to see an old temple in a historic neighborhood, which was decorated with statuary of peacock-plumed dragons and chimeras leering with joyous fury. He set down his wineglass to touch Mark's wrist. *Like* The Gargoyles, he said. *I took pictures.*

For me? thought Mark. He was moved. Adrian was loyal but forgetful. To be remembered while he was traveling with one of his *friends* was better than a dozen roses.

And is Karen your girlfriend? prompted Ruth, wine drooling down the stem of her glass.

No, Mark interjected, surprising himself. His sister knew very well that Adrian didn't have girlfriends, didn't date at all. His male *friends* aside, Adrian was straight and romantically solitary. A bachelor, though the anachronism didn't suit him at all. (*Doesn't it seem a little soon?* Ruth had asked after meeting Adrian for the first time, less than a year after Arturo died. *He's not even gay!* Mark had hissed.) Perhaps these subtleties were lost on those who didn't spend much time in the company of gay men, who understood that behavior and identity were very different things. He could feel another headache, the third this week, pressing its big belly against his eye sockets.

Adrian righted the ship. *She's just a friend*, he said. Karen, who practiced international law, lived between Taipei, Munich, and New York. They had met at a tapas bar in Williamsburg, where he was getting a nightcap with Cora, and before he knew it he was in her luxury apartment with the sea view, watching chemtrails tailgate freighters, their whitecaps streaming like bolides in the twilit sky. There was a new ring on his middle finger: silver inlaid with watery stones.

Karen wouldn't last, of course. None of them did. In a week or two, the ring would be misplaced, or sold, or traded for another bauble, or even given away on the street as an act of generosity or distraction. Years ago, Mark had set up a safe-deposit box as a loss-prevention measure and given Adrian the key. As far as he knew, the box was still there in DUMBO, empty as the wineglass Ruth was refilling.

Adrian kept going, although it was uncharacteristic for him to speak at length, or for Ruth to allow someone else to do so. Was any of it natural, Mark wondered, or was it all just to ease the tension, a skill at which Adrian was especially adept? He had come to trust his friend with his life, but trusting was different than knowing.

By the time Mark returned from the pantry with the balsamic vinegar, Ruth had regained control of the conversation. She was telling Adrian about the rich weirdo who left all those VHS tapes to SFSU when he died. *Hundreds of them. Literally,* she said. A few weeks ago, an old friend from grad school who specialized in moving-image archiving had asked her to help him start processing them. *Working with him is an amazing opportunity,* Ruth said. *Twentieth-century American experimental cinema is sort of his thing.*

Mark reached for his water, wondering what part of this free labor amounted to an *amazing opportunity.*

That's what you went to school for, right? Adrian asked. *Film?*

Well, I didn't finish, Ruth said. She seemed to suppress a smirk, as if this failure had actually been an accomplishment. *Mom needed me here. Mark was off in New York.*

Mark let his fork fall to the table. His pork chop was simply too dry. He had warned her about overcooking them.

What's fascinating about these tapes, Ruth said, ignoring the clatter, *is that the movies on them—the ones we've seen, anyway—are of quite high production value. Like, really high. But here's the crazy thing: no one knows who made them.*

Mark had already heard all this, about the intrigue of it all. Though most of the actors in the movies appeared to speak American English as their first language, none of them could be identified. *And these aren't De Sica's nonactors. Amateurs that were cast to critique notions of authenticity*, Ruth said. *Many appear to be trained professionals. It's just that no one has ever laid eyes on them before.* Outside of context clues from within the films and the ages of the tapes on which they were preserved, the movies couldn't be dated with any certainty. It was as if a ghost studio had risen from the Mojave Desert (though one couldn't assume even that location, of course) sometime between the Great War's beginning and the Cold War's end to churn out a string of more or less feature-length films—some seemingly avant-garde; some conventional enough for, say, Oscar consideration, if Ruth could flatter herself as a judge of such things—then converted the films to tapes before disappearing into the ether.

Wow, said Adrian. Was he being sarcastic? Mark wondered. He could never tell. Unlike him and Ruth, his friend perspired evenly, as if he'd come to the table through a thin veil of water. Even in this heat he was immune to flushing, though Mark had observed him affect discoloration when there was the need to appear delicate or indisposed. His own face, of a similar complexion as Adrian's, but longer and cut with deep wrinkles, at once harder and softer with age, was more sensitive to the elements, reddening with exertion, sun exposure, anger. In theory, he and Adrian looked alike—*Race: Caucasian, Hair: BRN, Eyes: BRN*. The difference was that Mark looked like any other man, whereas Adrian—colting, honeyed, undeniable—did not. And yet straight people often guessed that Adrian was his son, though other gay men tended to land a little closer to the mark. The inflection of the glances they shared often told the story that Ruth seemed hell-bent on imposing, and that even Mark sometimes wished were true: that Adrian, a complacent little philistine with daddy issues, wasn't his platonic companion but his boyfriend, a half-wit gold digger who had latched onto a wealthy painter of some fame, rather than a Saudi Arabian prince or ailing Muscovian oligarch.

It's a real mystery, agreed Ruth, swilling more wine onto the walnut. Her eyes were shining.

Mark wanted to be generous. *Ken's been keeping you busy, Ruth*, he contributed. He disliked Ken, whom he had met only once at a barbecue that Ruth had taken him to. Ken, who was married to a woman, spoke to Ruth as if they were sleeping together and to Mark as if they were peers.

There's just so much to do, said Ruth. Her eyes were back on Adrian, who also seemed to have given up on his pork chop. *Not only do they have no idea where these films come from, but many of them contain explicitly queer content, much of it non-pornographic. As if the Production Code—do you know what that was?—just never happened. The whole thing is fascinating on its own, but from a queer studies perspective, especially, this collection is just super valuable. It's just incredible. If the sister of the dead guy hadn't found it, it all would have just disappeared.*

Wow, said Adrian again, playing with his fork.

There's salad left, Mark said, lifting the bowl to show him.

It's just so important, you know? Ruth said, putting her hand on Adrian's forearm. *Preserving queer culture. Especially these days.*

Yeah, said Adrian.

Ruth hesitated, as if she expected him to expand on this. When he didn't, she turned to her brother, frowning. *Mark, open another bottle, would you?* She addressed herself to Adrian again, stroking his shoulder like a cat. *Do I remember Mark saying something about you leaving Brooklyn for good?*

From the other side of the counter, Mark grimaced. He had said no such thing. What he had said, when Ruth had dragged him to Duffy's on Third Street a few nights ago, was that Adrian sometimes talked about moving away. He had traveled extensively with his *friends* since he came to New York, but he had never lived anywhere else as an adult. Mark didn't want him to leave the city, not now, when he felt more responsible for him than ever. *Of course you don't*, Ruth had said, patting his arm, boozy as fruitcake.

The label on the bottle promised the wine would be malic. Mark's mouth watered. Inhaling deeply, he pushed the metal into the cork as the scents of sweat, garlic, pepper, vinegar, jasmine, nasturtium, rotting camellia buds, and, with a pop, tannins entered his body. Above the sink, mosquitos batted against the yellow window, attended by hawks whose legs dangled like the prongs and probes of deep-sea creatures. He returned to the table with the opened bottle. Ruth took it from him, her eyes glowing like coins in the failing light.

Well, said Adrian, *I might go back to Taipei.* The room he had stayed in would be there for him if he wanted to visit again, perhaps for the winter, as Karen had suggested. Ruth poured more wine, her hand beige and bulbous behind the glass, like ginger raw from the earth.

From the hallway came the creak of a bird-light step. Mom was up. Mark craned his neck, but he couldn't see her through the doorway. He didn't want to leave Ruth and Adrian alone, but then he heard a gasp, followed by a thump, as if something heavy had fallen. He leapt to his feet.

In the living room, Mom leaned against the two-seater, panting slightly. She wore her flannel nightie in the heat. Her face was pale. *Couldn't find my glasses*, she said. A potted Christmas cactus was overturned on the carpet, soil strewn around her bare feet. In the kitchen, Ruth was laughing.

Mark fished Mom's glasses from the floor and handed them to her. The cactus had fallen from its place on the side table, next to a framed photo that had appeared, as if by magic, after Arturo died: Mom and Arturo in the backyard. Someone's hand (Ruth's?) holding a sparkler. A puff of whipped cream on Mom's nose, Arturo's mouth in an O. Mom's teeth crooked, Arturo's hair thin. Though toward the end their relationship had softened, Mom had never loved Arturo. What had his death meant to her? Was Arturo memorable?

Oh, you stop it! cried Ruth in the kitchen. Adrian was laughing, too.

Here. Mark took Mom by the elbows. He wanted to get her back to her room. He'd clean up the dirt later.

My glasses, said Mom. She held them in her hand.

They passed by the doorway to the kitchen. Back hall, sunset window, art on the wall—*Aunt Charlie's* (Conté crayon, 1993), *Untitled 1* (oil on canvas, 1999), *Untitled 2* (oil on canvas, 1999), all by Mark—dining table, three chairs, Ruth's foot, Adrian's silver ring.

Ah—!

Mark's sense of himself in space realigned with a crunch: he had bashed Mom's little arm against the doorframe. Now her glasses were on the floor again.

Mark!

Sorry, sorry.

My arm—

I'm sorry!

Even from Mom's bedroom, Mark could hear every word that Ruth said. *And that's what I was telling him about that director,* she screamed. *A closeted Fordian. And Freudian.*

Adrian didn't know a thing about movies. Although most people assumed he was a bimbo, that didn't stop them from subjecting him to their culture, which had always struck Mark as unfair. Adrian wasn't stupid, though it was true that he was mostly ignorant of cinema, current affairs, wine, books. Art, too. Nor did Adrian care much for Mark's work, a fact that he had never concealed. Supportive, yes. Appreciative, not at all. From the beginning of their friendship, Mark had pretended to be miffed by this, even hurt. Secretly, however, Adrian's distaste made him feel cool. Like he was so secure that he could keep someone around who was *real* with him. This seemed so transparent a fantasy that he sometimes worried other people would spot his own self-regard from across the room, as plain as the mole on his neck.

After Mom was settled into bed again, Mark went back into the kitchen, where Adrian was refilling Ruth's glass. *Thank you, babe,* she said, seizing another handful of his T-shirt. Mark rolled his eyes. *We were just talking about how complicated family can be,* she said, making a sly face at Adrian. He didn't notice because he was looking at his phone, one eye blinded by the sun from the back hall.

Talking about me? Mark hoped he sounded playful. The light in Adrian's hair had an espresso-like quality, warm and textured. Could it be recreated with oils? The thought of trying made him feel unexpectedly virile. He thought of Karen and the Dole Corp executive.

Ruth laughed, as if that were an answer. She returned her attention to Adrian. *Is your family still out here?* she asked.

No. Mark could tell by the way Adrian's fingers moved that he was messaging with someone. A woman? A married farmer? A kid his age? *They're dead.*

Oh, said Ruth.

Only then did Adrian look up. *It's fine.*

I'm so sorry, said Ruth.

It's fine, Adrian repeated. His eyes were glassy but deep. Though he hadn't visited in years, Mark's memory unearthed the Monterey Bay Aquarium, where schools of tuna swam donut-shaped tanks in unblinking perpetuity.

Honey, his sister said, reaching for Adrian again, *if you ever wanted to, you know, talk—*

Ruth, could you please shut the fuck up?

Ruth and Adrian turned toward Mark in unison, glowing like radioactive dolls in the sunlight streaming in from the window down the hall that opened onto the backyard. It was too bright to see through the glass, but Mark knew the backyard perfectly, even after four decades in New York, even after the eight years he stayed away when Mom kicked him out. Purple tea roses, rabid green kudzu. Swaying maple, unctuous magnolia. Concrete that burned through the calluses on the soles of his feet. A cool, prickling patch of lawn, spotted with stubborn yellow and clods of earthworm-bubbled dirt. The garden—zucchinis, tomatoes, countless herbs—bound with rusted chain link, circled by orange, apricot, and cherry trees, and finally overseen by the massive sycamores he and Ruth had scaled to chase rats and squirrels through

the leaves and back down again to the unfinished basement, un-
usual in a nineteenth-century house built in a countryside tor-
tured by fault lines. The rodents would disappear behind the cold
cement walls, but sometimes he and his sister stayed down there
together, pressing into the earthen floor with their bare feet, inhaling the dust and mold and moisture, resisting the glamor of pink
fiberglass and labels with skull and crossbones. The place where
they would later smoke grass, play cards, keep a record player.
Where Mark would eventually start bringing men; once, someone
who had been pulling a stump out of the neighbor's front yard, his
dirty hands never touching Mark's clean white briefs.

Ruth went to her room and slammed the door behind her. The
tabletop was dark, oily, cluttered, the empty bottles gathered like a
pack of baying wolves, eyeless snouts moonward.

Um. I'm going to take this. Adrian held his phone to his ear as he
went down the back hallway to Mark's room. The door snapped
closed behind him, cutting his voice in half. From Ruth's room—
the smallest in the house, where she had insisted on staying even
after Mark had moved out—came the perplexing plod of jazz piano. Ahmad Jamal.

Mark cleared the table and washed the dishes alone. When he was
done, he went to Mom's room with a plate of food in one hand and
a glass of iced tea in the other. He walked past the cactus on the
carpet, still face down in the soil and broken ceramic.

Mom was watching *The Golden Girls* on mute, her head propped
against the headboard. She had taken off her flannel nightie and
was now wearing only a white shift, like a paper doll without her
paper clothes, and flimsy cotton socks folded over at the ankle.

Mark could see the welt on her right arm from the doorway. Tomorrow it would be a fat, aching bruise. Holding out the plate like an offering, he tried to think of how to mention it in a way that acknowledged his guilt without making himself feel worse than he had to.

As if to spare him, Mom spoke first. *How was dinner?* She held her hands out. *Did you set out the good ones for Adrian?*

Don't worry, said Mark. *It all looked very nice. Place mats, too.*

Poking her porkchop, she made a face over her salad. *Got kind of loud in there a few times.*

Her peevishness relieved him. *Ruth's in a good mood*, Mark said, setting her tea on the nightstand. Did that sound bitchy? When he sat on the edge of the bed, she moved her leg away. *It's nice to have Adrian here.*

He must be tired from his trip. With her fingers, she scraped a piece of carrot off her fork.

You wouldn't know it.

That's good. Must be nice to be young.

How is it?

Mom always ate slowly, chewing without looking up. Had she heard him? As Mark was about to repeat himself, Mom used her fork to point at the wall between them and the kitchen.

So he was out there visiting a friend? A girlfriend? She stabbed at her pork chop. *Not that it matters, I guess.*

The first time Mom had died, Mark was seventeen. She was resurrected eight years later when she broke her leg and Ruth returned from school to care for her, which coincided with the first intensification of her many illnesses; when the Ménière's, her old flame, became the least of her worries. Barely in her forties, there had been the arthritis, the seizures, the extreme weight loss. Mark remembered Ruth's voice over the pay phone on Essex and Broome, higher and quieter than he'd ever heard it. His fearless sister was afraid. That was why he went back to Almendra, after all that time, after all those years of silence. Mom couldn't be any more dead than he'd already made her, he reasoned. With his help, her health improved; he started coming home for Christmas again. Now that another death was approaching, did Mark feel as if he could mention her first? No, he realized. He did not.

Adrian was seeing a lady friend, he compromised. Mom had never asked about the nature of his relationship with Adrian; like everyone of her generation, she politely presumed heterosexuality of everyone. He had forgotten to bring her a napkin, but he decided to wait and see if she would ask for one.

A friend's a friend, said Mom mysteriously. *Seems like you're a good friend to him.*

It didn't seem like the right word for Adrian, *friend*. The old euphemism that Mom had used for Arturo, almost to the end, until they had gotten married and she had no choice. But what was Adrian if not Mark's friend? Not his lover, not his colleague, not his companion, not his roommate, though they spent many of their nights together in Mark's bed, chaste as could be. Mentee, protégé? Adrian had never painted in his life and had no wish to. If Adrian moved away from New York, leaving Mark behind, perhaps then he would become something else. It would be a demotion, somehow.

Thank you, said Mark. *I try to be.*

Setting her plate on the nightstand, Mom asked if he would bring her the pillbox from the bathroom. *The big one.*

Of course, Mark said. As he leaned to kiss her hair, she ran her fingers over the bruise on her arm.

<hr />

When Mark returned to New York after Mom's funeral, the fall weather was the same as it had been all summer in California: burning bright unless sunless, when smoke brought down the mercury with a mantle of iron that stretched across the sky. JFK was almost as hot as Almendra, but the air was clear and sweet with gasoline, and there, leaning against the hood, was Adrian, grinning around the friendly bulk of a giddy traffic attendant. After so long without seeing him—the longest since they'd met, Mark realized— he took his breath away.

I have a surprise, Adrian said when Mark got into the car. He leaned into the back seat and unzipped something.

George nosed past Mark's hand and clambered into his lap, planting his dainty feet on his thighs with his tail high in the air. Mark smiled hard, his eyes watering. Adrian honked at the attendant, who was trying to record him with his phone, and jerked away from the curb, their bodies jiggling with the suspension. George settled in his lap as if they were on the couch at home. *I missed you*, Mark said, holding his hindquarters in the palm of his hand. He knew how to apply just the right amount of pressure to his sturdy little forehead. Even in the depths of rush-hour traffic, the cat never stopped purring.

For a few minutes there was a blissful nothing. Then Adrian reached to adjust the rearview, bending his fingers into the same shape that Mom used to hold her baby-blue hairbrush. It all came back. Was Mom memorable? For the whole flight, Mark's stomach, big and bloated, had ached too much for him to sleep. He had watched his uneasy reflection in the porthole, and now he watched it again in the windshield. He still looked like his mother, even more like his sister: the brown hair, the long nose, the small mouth that opened into a wide, rare smile.

Adrian

Adrian can never remember if his apartment is on the third or fourth floor. If a guest is coming over (which almost never happens), he gets around this by telling them he lives at the top of the stairs. He often intends to count the landings and settle it once and for all, but by the time he gets to his door, he's already forgotten. He's always been like that. Mark sends him to the grocery store with a handwritten shopping list, including checkboxes, lined up like houses in a prefab neighborhood.

Not only is the front door unlocked, but when Adrian peers down the barrel of the shotgun he can see that the light in his bedroom is still on. He's glad Mark isn't here to scold him this morning. Mark lived here when he was Adrian's age, just as he was giving up on music. Back then, he paid $350 a month in rent. If the apartment were on the market now, it might go for six times that much. When Mark started making money as an artist, he bought it. When he moved to Windsor Terrace in 1999, he kept it, subletting to friends in town for shows, residencies, and divorces. When he met Adrian in 2015, the apartment happened to be empty. A month later, Adrian moved in.

All yours, Mark said, setting the keys on the counter by Adrian's hand. He had been to Adrian's former place, a mildewed Harlem studio paid for by a *friend* whom Adrian would describe only as *married*. Only once, but once was enough. Adrian can never remember how much the mortgage is. Not that it matters, since he's not paying. But he thinks that it would be nice if he did remember.

Adrian closes the door behind him, slips out of his shoes, and goes to the window. Outside is a view: a rusty church tower piercing clouds of cream, the blue and orange Jenga of a condo under construction, a pair of mourning doves scratching in a flowerpot. In the building directly across the way, the silhouettes of a loafing cat and a shampoo bottle frame a stretching nude. Despite their nudity, Adrian still doesn't know if his neighbor is a man or a woman, though he sees them almost every day.

He hasn't had coffee yet, having come directly from the Midtown hotel room of a real estate agent he picked up in the Union Square Whole Foods. He puts the kettle on. While he waits, he peers down into the yard. The only person with a key, aside from the landlord, is the man who comes to take care of the roses. One day he looked up from his work and saw Adrian in the window. Their eyes met, or so Adrian thought. After that, the man began coming two, three, even four times per week. The yard went from well-kept to brutally manicured, every rose beautiful enough to deserve a bell jar. Adrian began keeping the drapes closed.

But today there is no rose man, so Adrian leaves them open. (He feels both relief and anxiety. If the rose man saw him today, would he *see* him?) He locates the clean French press and grinds the beans. As he's pouring the boiling water, his phone rattles on the counter. He puts it between his ear and his shoulder and places the plunger over the cylinder.

I'm here, says Mark. *At JFK.*

Now? Adrian checks the calendar, squinting at Mark's small, precise print. A few inches above it floats one of Mark's studies, *Grant's St. Tropez* (charcoal, 2005), tastefully framed. There are a few of them in the apartment. Mark once referred to them as Adrian's retirement plan. According to the calendar, Mark's return flight from SFO isn't until next week.

Plans changed, says Mark. *I'll tell you all about it later.* Behind his voice, a woman robot drones pleasantly over the intercom.

JetBlue still? But Mark has already hung up. Adrian uses one hand to steady the cylinder, the other to depress the plunger. Mark hates cabs.

When his coffee is ready, Adrian gets the keys from a Madonna Inn ashtray, dons a pair of Prada sunglasses—given to him by a woman who starred in her own reality show about being a satellite member of the Croatian royalty, or something like that—and puts his shoes back on. He makes sure to lock up this time.

The girl from 1L is smoking at the top of the stoop. She's twenty-two or so, a little young for Adrian; he has no scruples about age differences between adults but has found that younger women are more likely to respond to his presence with stricken silence. Though she always seems to be sitting there, wide-eyed as a pastured cow, she's never said anything to him before, never offered a cigarette or a kiss, which is for the best, Adrian feels; she already knows where he lives. Today, as usual, he doesn't acknowledge her. As he walks down the stairs, he feels her watching him, but when he turns to look she's facing the other direction, fiddling with an earbud.

Mark's car smells like summer, plastic and sweat and peppermint from the mentholated chews he keeps in the console that are supposed to settle his stomach. Adrian sets the hot coffee in the cupholder. Traffic's not so terrible, his phone informs him. He scrolls while waiting for the Bluetooth to connect before choosing Sade, whose bodyguard said he'd take Adrian backstage, then didn't. When he reaches for his coffee, he realizes he can't get the squat mug out of the cupholder again without spilling, and so, after all that, he must go without.

At Arrivals, Adrian's texts and calls to Mark go unanswered. He idles a while in front of the revolving doors, but whenever someone in a yellow vest approaches to shoo him away, he hits the gas. He does a lap every few minutes. It's inconvenient, but it's easier than risking being seen.

He's in park checking his messages when the passenger door pops open behind him. A woman in head-to-toe Lululemon leans into the car, red mouth hanging from her teeth. *It* stiffens. Adrian is reminded of Grandma kneeling to squeeze the snapdragon's chin, her fingers applying pressure to his: when you pull the petals down, a mouth appears to say whatever you want.

For Sabrina? asks the woman.

Not a Lyft. Adrian shakes his head apologetically. He smiles, feeling generous.

Oops. Sorry! Sabrina closes the door behind her. With her hand on the back of her head, as if protecting a hat from a strong wind, she reenters the terminal crowd, a rolling suitcase bungling over the curb in her wake.

Adrian's panic is like water moments before it begins to simmer: invisible, unbearable. He pulls back onto the road and speeds to the parking garage, where he knows of a quiet, shadowy corner on an uppermost level that's often empty. He gets out to sit on the trunk, reeking of *it*, and waits until an elegant middle-aged woman in a service uniform passes by. Back in the car again, he learns that her hair is soft on his inner palm; she gags theatrically, ruining the aura of pudeur cast by the grandchild on the back of her phone case. When she leaves, Adrian resumes his position on the trunk. Now that he's relaxed somewhat, *it* has lost its rigidity while gaining an electrical spine. He sees the man in the dun cowboy hat and soon he's in the car again, his buzzing phone growling the plastic. *Fuck yeah*, the man says. Outside somewhere, doors slam, horns groan, jet engines shriek. The noise tips Adrian into a strange irritability. He resists the furious urge to shove the man away. Instead, he glares over his meaty shoulder, memorizing the wall outside the windshield, its paint and its print, its cracks and its corners.

It has vanished again by the time Adrian returns to Arrivals, where Mark is now waiting, two black suitcases and a duffel bag like awkward children beside him. He honks and pulls up to the curb, but his friend doesn't notice. He waves. Mark glances in his direction but remains leaning against the wall. Adrian has to get out of the car and shout Mark's name for his friend's eyes to tighten with recognition.

Mark begins loading his bags into the back seat. *Sorry I'm late*, calls Adrian. Mark waves his apology away. In January, when

Adrian brought him to Departures, the first timid flakes of snow-
fall had powdered their hair. Enclosed by winter, it had felt as if it
was just the two of them in the terminal, saying goodbye for they
didn't know how long. Now it's the beginning of Pride month, and
JFK is as busy as it was before the pandemic, hemorrhaging people
and luggage and cars and buses. The underarms of Mark's T-shirt
are already dark with sweat when he drops into the passenger seat.

Hey. Adrian reaches out his hand, then settles it behind Mark's
headrest, rubbing his thumb on the fabric. *Is everything okay?.*
What happened?

Let's go. Mark buckles in grudgingly, as if he simply hasn't the energy to risk death. Adrian might as well be the rideshare Sabrina
thought he was, here to collect a stranger. His friend, always lean,
is now skinny, his underarms flabby and his leather belt gored for
a new hole.

Okay. Adrian thinks that Mark looks bad and sad. Silently tapping
his fingers on the steering wheel, he waits to merge, surreptitiously
sniffing the cologne the cowboy left behind. Does Mark notice it?
He doesn't seem to. All the way back to Windsor Terrace, Mark
keeps his eyes trained on the road. He doesn't even look at his
phone.

Back at Adrian's apartment, the calendar on his wall says that
Ruth's funeral is tomorrow at 2:00 p.m. PST.

Mark

Mark balances his bodyweight between the mattress and the hardwood. His calf brushing against linen and metal, he extends his foot until it meets one of the suitcases, still half full of balled socks and T-shirts. His other foot remains on the mattress under the sheet. He waits. It doesn't pass. He waits. He doesn't have to pick up his phone to know what time it is.

When he sits up, the pain travels downward, slowly filling his chest and groin. Mark has begun imagining his body like one of those plastic bears that are pumped with honey and sealed with a red cap. When the bear is turned, the honey moves, pushing past swollen stalactites of air until it gradually comes to rest again. The honey is the pain.

With a sigh, Mark heaves and stands. His torso twists to the right, bringing the honey to his spine. More honey slithers toward his knees, bursting at each joint before finally landing in his ankles. Last month, after the pain had been everywhere inside her for a year—growing, crushing, eventually disabling—Ruth said that it had suddenly stopped.

I'm just tired now, she said. The bedsheet looked heavy on her body. Rain ticked behind the window. *Was it like that for Mom?*

Today, the pain is the same as it was a week ago, on Mark's final morning in the now-empty house on Ohlone. Here in Windsor Terrace, the morning begins at the same time, expands and contracts with the same pain. It isn't just his stomach anymore, the nausea in the mornings and sometimes after dinner. When he arrived in Almendra for the last time in January, the honey had gotten worse again. By then it was coursing through his hands and forearms and hips, sometimes his elbows, sometimes his knees. He could still lift his sister, who was heavier than his mother had been, but it grew more and more difficult. Over the winter, he wrapped his joints in the hot lavender compresses that Mom used to make for Christmas and birthday gifts, and he slept on rigid ice packs that lost their spines overnight. He abandoned grass, a lifelong affinity, for the more straightforward weed gummy, which he ate by the handful to little effect other than a brief, dispiriting body high that made him feel like a balloon at the end of an unlikeable child's birthday party.

Mark feels for Ruth's pills on the nightstand. He just likes to know they're there. There's more in his suitcase, all he'll need. He decides he'll resist his first of the day for a little while longer. If he doesn't eat before the pills, he'll regret it. Not that they can stop the pain that saturates his every waking moment. As he sleeps, it concentrates in his skull, where it becomes the headache that awakens him hours before his alarm, then lingers on until lunchtime at least.

He rotates his head to see what hurts when. When they got back from the airport last week, Adrian had dropped the duffel bag in the corner of Mark's bedroom, where it lies unzipped, revealing dozens of multicolored VHS tapes, like a black-husked cob of heirloom corn. In Almendra, he had searched online for one of those old TVs with a built-in VCR until he remembered a Manhattan gallerist who happened to own one, a friendly but ambitious guy who wanted Mark to owe him a favor. A few years ago, one of his artists had brought the VCR/TV for an installation but had killed himself before the end of his residency. Though his agent had come for his leftovers—there wasn't much, the artist being a minimalist—she had left the VCR/TV behind. The gallerist kept it in his office, where it multitasked as a display shelf for a potted plant and a risqué water clock. The artist had been at the beginning of his career, but the gallerist believed he would have become quite successful had he not tipped into oblivion from the thirty-ninth floor of an Upper West Side high-rise. The scandal added a frisson of adventure, an edge, to the otherwise-sleek decor of the place where he held his meetings. Mark didn't like the gallerist personally, but he called him from Mom's kitchen. In the backyard, the green leaves were oiled by rain.

Delighted to grant Mark his favor, the gallerist had the VCR/TV delivered to Windsor Terrace without delay, where Adrian was waiting for it. Only a year ago, Mark could have brought it upstairs himself. Now it would have been impossible. When he imagines attempting it with his current body, sweat pricks his skin and his anus makes itself known as the terminus of something long and unbearably sensitive. He pictures a misstep, a fall, his cracked skull, the VCR/TV landing on its eye with a great pop beside him. The honey boils in sympathy.

But the VCR/TV is now safe in his bedroom. The gallerist had assured him that it was functional, and when Mark depresses the big, square Power button, the screen jumps to life. Small white numbers and letters appear and disappear in the top right corner of the screen, whose color alternates between coal and royal blue. So far, so good. Mark reaches into the duffel bag and grabs a tape without looking. No cover, no sheath, no nothing. He slides it into the slot. He pushes Play.

The black screen flares with red sans-serif: *Hot World*. No other text announcing the director, the screenwriter, the players, the production company, *In Glorious Technicolor!* There is nothing else to be seen. A rhythm made of machines and bass begins, creating a depth that deepens the darkness with each passing second.

But the honey is moving again. Mark's fingers curl to his suddenly cramping belly. As he rushes to the bathroom, the rhythm increases in volume and frequency, buzzing the speakers embedded behind the thirteen-inch screen.

Mark is alone, so he doesn't bother closing the door behind him. Adrian comes and goes like an outdoor cat, but last night Mark asked him to stay over. *Sorry*, Adrian said, his eyes trained on his tacos. *Busy*. He sits on the edge of the tub and listens to *Hot World* throb from his bedroom. With his elbows on his thighs, he breathes as slowly as he can, feeling his heart syncopate with the music. It's probably better to be alone in this state. He'll be here for a while, as he is almost every morning these days.

In flirts George, who's lately been partial to overnights on the living room easy chair. Flicking his tail, he follows his snout to the cabinet, then to a screw on the base of the toilet. Air whistles through his nostrils in a way that Mark suspects is performative. He knows George will try to lure him back to the bedroom for his first leg of the day's sleep cycle. When the music from the VCR/ TV rises to a crescendo, the cat lifts his head and flattens his ears. When it abates, he relaxes. When he kisses Mark's naked shin, the weightless metal plate on his collar, useless on an animal that will never go outside again, leaves a cold line on his patella. The music evaporates; the nudge becomes a bite. When Mark jerks, George flees, back to the living room, perhaps. His mouth begins to water.

When the nausea first began, Mark would bring a book or his phone to the bathroom to pass the time. Back home in Almendra, there were the *National Geographics* that Mom kept in a basket next to the toilet. Ruth had an almost-unused book of word puzzles. But everything was eventually tossed to the counter or left on the floor, glossy ads and boxes of ballpoint squiggles flapping at his bare feet. The early hour, the small print, the executive thinking were always too much, and he soon gave up trying to distract himself. Like everyone else in the nineties, Mark had gone through a phase with transcendental meditation. Maybe his morning purge could be like that, he thinks. But when a new wave of pain ripples through his body, his cheekiness vanishes. He is afraid.

On the wall across from the mirror is an old show flier, one of the first things he put up when he and Arturo moved to Windsor Terrace in 1999. Mark had held the thick paper up to the overhead light, his fingers ghostly on the other side. The flier was for his band's first performance at Danceteria, back when it was still on Twenty-First: a Xerox of a mommy beauty queen and Mark's own drawing of a sexy toilet with long acrylic fingernails. No better place for it than the shitter, Mark had thought. The Buenos Aires Affair fancied themselves experimental, but their musical talents had never matched their pretensions. Even in the scene, they were never much more than acknowledged, although Mark himself was liked everywhere he went. He's still Facebook friends with the bandmates who survived the eighties. They both became high school music teachers, one in the Bronx, one in Queens.

Not long after the move, an acquaintance sent Mark a framed photograph of the two of them with John Lurie in an Italian restaurant. From 1983, maybe? '85? It had everything: the wizened old-country proprietor, the red-and-white checkered tablecloths, the ink-drawn caricatures of Sinatra and Martin on the wall behind Lurie's big beautiful nose. The accompanying letter, typed but hand-signed in a thick, altruistic curl, was intimate in a way that made Mark feel crazy. Reading it, one would think that he and the acquaintance had been much closer than they were, close enough for Christmas dinners and cross-country road trips. (What the hell, maybe Lurie was a close friend, too, all three of them the best of buddies, posing in front of giant balls of yarn and shooting up behind back-road Tastee-Freezes. Why not?) The acquaintance had implied that by sending Mark this photograph, which he had found on eBay and claimed to have paid $750 for (an exorbitant sum, Mark had to admit, considering the public's appetite for him, not to mention Lurie), he wasn't just doing Mark a favor but saving a piece of art history that would have otherwise been lost.

Arturo thought the whole thing was hilarious. *You should frame both of them, the photo and the letter!* he said. *Right here in the bathroom!* Mark didn't find it funny at all. He had smoked a whole joint by himself and was feeling paranoid. What if he put the photo up, only for the acquaintance to never come for a visit? What if he *didn't* put it up and the acquaintance *did* come visit and was offended because Mark had put it up in his *bathroom*, where people came to shit? Though Arturo begged him not to, he crumpled the letter and threw it in the wastebasket. The photo was hung next to the show flier.

Gradually, the bathroom in the Windsor Terrace apartment began taking on a theme: Mark's misspent youth as a musician, before his art took off, when he was so deep underground not even Rimbaud could find him. He realized he liked seeing his past this way, structured yet senseless, like bookshelves organized by color. Growing up in Almendra, Mark and Ruth had a crazy old neighbor whose parlor was decorated entirely with milk glass. *Mother's favorite,* Mrs. Belami said, though her mother had been dead since before the war. When the sun was setting, her parlor bristled with thousands of white rounded hobnails and miles of ruffled trim, brittle as polished bone, suffused with the Pacific's dying aura.

Mark can hear George scratching his litter in the hall closet. Now he's in here five times as often as he was before he got sick, providing him with the daily opportunity to revisit his youth at his long and gruesome leisure. Maybe the way he's decorated the bathroom betrays some kind of sublimated instinct, a desire put aside for the majority of his life. Mark doesn't reject somatics—all the rage these days—out of hand, but he loathes the idea of his body knowing things before he does. Derek represents another New York artist whose whole thing is painting unknowingly: in his sleep, on GHB, with AI. The art happens *to* him, is the conceit. Though played out, the idea never fails to intrigue stupid people and sell tickets. Even now, Mark rolls his eyes. When the honey sours somewhere under his lungs, unleashing a jet of magma that makes him tear up, his philosophical disapproval feels all the more virtuous.

When a shriek comes down the hall, Mark startles before remembering the VCR/TV. As if in response to the harrowing sounds, the honey's simmer grows in frequency. He's missing *Hot World*, though he had promised himself that he would watch all the movies, before. Mark places his palms on his thighs, gripping each like the banister of a stairwell. His belly feels like it's cooking. He turns his head. There's the photo of him with Sylvester, from before he got sober. He looks fucked-up; Sylvester, in gold beads, looks distracted. His hand had felt weightless in Mark's, like an embalmed bird.

Mark opens the toilet as he kneels. It takes only a minute for his back to begin aching. He breathes slowly and heavily. Nothing. He eases his right forearm down onto the bone of the bathtub and waits.

Over his shoulder and across from the mirror is a frameless photo of him at an almost dazzlingly youthful twenty-three. *Another Green World, Chasms Accord, Ceremonial*. Shoulder-length hair and a nail in his right ear. He's brushing shoulders with Jimmy Somerville, the pair of them finding the camera together. Mark lifts the toilet seat without looking away. Back then, everything was new except for the fear. In 1986 he made his own coffee, listening to Donna Summer on the radio or La Monte Young on vinyl. There was only one serving-bowl-size window in that Hell's Kitchen apartment, in the corner that was politely referred to as the bathroom. Now he has, to his name, a bathroom with no windows at all, two spacious bedrooms, a kitchen with a range and an island and a rocket ship of a fridge, a dining table and chairs purchased new and as part of a set, and a big comfortable couch where George likes to nest and Adrian to drape himself, inflating its already considerable value through skin contact alone. Throughout the apartment are seven generous windows, two of them overlooking Eleventh Avenue, high up off the ground. Little traffic, big trees.

Mark feels it coming. He kneels, ready. Proper. Only his eyes move, lighting and relighting on the faces faded by time: Lou Reed, Laurie Anderson, Roland Gift. The frames shine. His shoulders hunch, Basquiat's chin eclipsed by the curve of porcelain. Suddenly, his head tips forward. Out it comes. (*Do I have a meeting today?*) It seems strange that the interior of his body is hot when he feels himself to be quite cold, even wishing he had put on his wool socks before coming in here. When will food no longer be worth this, four or five or even six days a week? (*Damn. Drinks at seven.* Derek has been desperate to pin him down since he came back from Almendra. No problem, Mark will just cancel at the last minute.) At some point very soon Adrian's cooking, which Mark has been refining for almost six years, will no longer justify this excruciation. Nor will all the meals that can be purchased in restaurants or ordered for delivery: the nasi campur, the turkey sandwiches with Dijon and pesto, the scoops of chocolate-cardamom gelato, each nibble imperiled by needle-thin shards of pistachio.

His candid of Scott Walker pouts from a shelf above the toilet. Mark treasures his photograph of that beautiful man, but it's here in the bathroom all the same. He coughs. It occurs to him that this is the only room in the apartment that he didn't reorganize when Arturo died. Almost all of their photos together, the paintings (*Arturo*, oil on canvas, 1997; *Arturo*, oil on canvas, 2014), the Levi's 501s, a certain wrinkled apron, the gold ring with its engraving—they've all been put in storage. But the bathroom is the same now as it was before Arturo left him. Mark vomits again.

Mark had been living in Windsor Terrace for almost sixteen years when he installed the shelf above the toilet. Adrian, who can't be called handy but excels at following directions, had helped. That morning he was wearing a faded T-shirt that said . . . *For the Whole*

World to See, handed down by Mark because it had begun riding up over his belly over the past few years. It fit Adrian imperfectly, but to great effect, hanging over his waist and clinging to his shoulders, smooth and round as a pair of glass insulators. The T-shirt moved when Adrian did, its pale fibers revealing the skin above his briefs when he reached for the drill or ran his fingers through his curls.

Scott was in the center of the shelf, surrounded by smaller photos. There were snapshots, Polaroids, a $300 tintype made by a weird old straight man in Oakland (when Mark had arrived at his studio, the man answered the door with a piping-hot slice of pizza layered with a grotesque amount of pineapple and offered it to him with a butler's cool obsequiousness). The shelf, like the rest of the memorabilia in the bathroom, is like Mark's early years in New York: cheap, punk, aimless. The photos from everything that happened later, meticulously preserved by Arturo—the gallery openings, the award ceremonies, the magazine covers—have mostly been put in boxes, though there is still one up in the living room from the MacArthur ceremony: him with his arms around Mom and Ruth, three face cards from the same suit. The week before, Ruth went shopping at the outlets in Sacramento and brought back a pair of heels that were too high for a woman who only wore clogs. The ankle strap of one broke as she stepped out of the car, forcing her to spend the rest of the evening balanced like a flamingo on her brother's shoulder. Ruth had been so imperious, pretending not to recognize world-famous public intellectuals, that Mark's nerves melted away. You could never call his sister a coward. Unlike Mark, she'd always had a sense of humor about herself.

He flushes the toilet. His back hurts, but he's afraid to move, worried it will make him sick again. He imagines the honey has eaten away at the gristle inside his body, turning his insides into a hot entropic chaos of blood and viscera liable to overflow at the slightest disturbance. He slowly leans to open the cabinet, delicately rummages for the wet wipes. From his bedroom comes the outrage of an old-timey choo choo train. *Hot World* is still going. What could it be about? He'll rewind it, he'll find out. He coughs into a wet wipe, smoothing it over his lips. He feels, more than hears, that George is back in the bathroom with him. He is steadying himself, one hand touching the bathtub, when the cat's featherweight body collides with his.

Mark sits on the edge of the tub and tries to catch his breath. The pain has resettled in his extremities, but his stomach does feel a little better. He reaches to stroke George's spine. George has always purred easily, but so quietly you wouldn't know unless you got very close, as if holding a shell to your ear to hear the ocean. He has always wondered if the cat misses Arturo; if he understood his sudden disappearance for what it was. It occurs to him that it may not have seemed so sudden for someone who mostly knows the world through his nose.

Don't be sad, Mark tells George. His first words of the day don't echo, but they do weigh him down. Here in the bathroom is a life in which Arturo never happened. Sometimes this is a relief. Here is not a real life, one that has kept pace with the one he lives outside, in the apartment. Here is something else, a false world where a strange young man who didn't own a telephone is flanked by dead lovers and friends, hairline low and forehead tight. A young man who hadn't even met Arturo yet.

George watches him with big, luminous eyes. When Mark reaches for him, he leans into his hand before, for no discernable reason,

suddenly deciding to evade it. Mark watches him go. Tub in his
armpit, its cool against his back, he attempts to imagine death
again. He looks at the photo of himself tuning his Telecaster, an
instrument he hasn't played since before Arturo died. Sonic Youth
T-shirt, tongue pressing through his lips. He had a dimple, at one
point. He's not sure he does anymore, now that it's overtaken by
the glacial flux of age.

It's as if, Mark thinks, he has survived his own death. Now his
back aches against the tub. What if death is a cold bathroom floor
where one's body is in a discomfort only too recently descended
from pain? Could be worse. He blinks his eyes open. George's tail
flickers in the doorway, then vanishes at the sound of another horn
from the VCR/TV. From down the hall, somewhere near his bedroom door, he meows.

Okay, okay, says Mark, getting to his feet. He braces himself on
the counter and looks in the mirror. All the beauties he once was
form a cruel mise en abîme over his shoulder and above his head.
Shouldn't have turned on the light, he thinks. Flexing his lungs, he
presses himself to a certain kind of limit. When nothing happens,
he risks turning on the faucet and rinsing his mouth. He takes a
timid swallow.

But there the honey is again. He's back down on his knees, retch-
ing and sweating. Defeated, to no end: there isn't any more food
to come up. Last night's fettuccine al burro with wilted arugula,
preceded by an oily fingerbowl of Castelvetrano olives, is already
in the sewers beneath Prospect Park. This new excretion is mostly
water, with blobs of smooth yellow, minced sunshine. Where did
it all come from? If bird innards can predict the future, what might

those of an old man reveal? In the hallway, George's cries deepen and stretch, becoming howls.

But now he's done. He can tell by the way he feels hollowed out, his body hunkering without his consent. He knows that he should shower. Instead, he finds the package of wet wipes, purchased by Adrian, and takes them with him back to his bedroom.

George races ahead of him and leaps onto the bed. Now that he's gotten what he wants, he quacks with pleasure, his claws cozily pricking the coverlet. Mark reaches to stroke him; his last lover. On the VCR/TV, *Hot World* is still playing, but he depresses the button with the square printed on it, without looking at the screen, and then gets back into bed.

Adrian

Adrian lingers over the dishes. When the pots are scoured and hung, he goes back into the bedroom, where his friend eats most of his meals these days. Mark is still watching one of Ruth's movies, his fork and spoon crossed like a coat of arms on his nightstand. The bowl of scampi next to them is only half empty.

This one kinda reminds me of Buñuel, Mark says. *Surreal, yet controlled.*

Uh-huh, says Adrian, picking up the bowl and silverware. Half, he thinks, is better than none. *I'm almost done with the kitchen. Need anything else?*

Mark blinks, as if he had already forgotten Adrian was there. *Oh, no,* he says. His eyes return to the screen. *No, I'm just fine.*

If Mark were going to ask him to stay, he would have by now. *Well, good night, then,* Adrian says, a little relieved.

After Adrian finishes the dishes, he dries his hands and tucks the scampi recipe, a piece of notebook paper, back into the cookbook he found it in; he can now read Arturo's handwriting well enough that he doesn't have to ask Mark for help. Mark has come to love Adrian's cooking, and Adrian loves Mark's kitchen: the wine rack, the Mauviel and Le Creuset, the garlic vise with teeth like an antique instrument of torture. A part of him wonders if the cure to Mark's stomach problems isn't simply the right recipe made the right way. Well, the scampi wasn't it. He'll keep trying.

He sits down in the doorway to put on his shoes. The bowl of George's wet food congeals beside him, mostly untouched. The cat is nowhere to be found.

Good night, Adrian calls, locking the dead bolt behind him.

Prospect Park is nearly empty. On the edges of his vision, fireflies round as the golf balls at the driving range his *friend* Patton once took him to blip in and out of other dimensions. He attempts to keep his eye on just one, and can't. Every so often, a delivery-man shooms down the hill toward the toe of the park. Two young women on Citi Bikes pass, both wearing bonnets, one wearing cut-offs. A sad song warbles from her phone. The music roves hill and dale, copse and Porta Potty, with almost no one to hear it. No one that Adrian can see, anyway.

Adrian's route home goes through the heart of the park toward Grand Army Plaza, with its triumphal arch and horse statues. But tonight he finds himself veering off the road into the grass, toward the lake. He trips on a tree root and catches himself against the trunk. He doesn't worry. If anything bad ever happens, Mark will take care of it. He'll bring Adrian to urgent care, schedule the X-rays, foot the bill for veneers, feed him organic smoothies until he can chew again.

He picks his way down to the water. In the winter, the cottage
on the shore of the Peninsula, two hundred years old if a day,
looks like the nucleus of a Christmas snow globe. In the summer,
it almost disappears into the trees and bushes that surround it.
As always, Adrian wonders how difficult it would be to break in.
When Mark took him to Iceland, they drove a few hours outside
of Reykjavík to see a pitch-black church built at the beginning of
the last millennia. The church had been sealed against tourists,
but they could tunnel against the morning light with their hands
to see through the windows. Everything inside was as pristine and
posed as a dollhouse, the dustless pews hunched like penitents
around a caged altar. Is the furniture in the Prospect cottage like
that, Adrian wonders, deliberate and shiny and 25 percent smaller
than it is today because hormones in the chicken and American
maximalism?

He walks along the shore. Dark and motionless, the lake is its
own matte core, the silent heart of the borough. Sarsenet, like
those biking girls' bonnets, without sharing their pearlescent pink
and white. He sees more fireflies. He sees raccoons and a cat. He
wishes on a star for a cryptid, but none appears.

Adrian comes upon a trail into the trees. He takes it, remembering
the old mansion tucked away somewhere back here along a chan-
nel. He always looks for it when he comes this way through the
park, but he doesn't always find it. It comes and goes, like Narnia.
Tonight, he finds it. It's much more impressive than the cottage.
Three stories high, its white walls are surrounded by moats furred
with floating plants, gruesome sculptures—uncanny figures that remind Adrian of Mark's gargoyles—and yellow-globed streetlamps.
How hard would it be to break into this one? The doors are bolted
and nailed shut, but the thin windows are halved by slender

wooden mullions. He considers nearby cameras, as everyone must these days, but doesn't think they've been installed in the park just yet. The men getting out of the van must have thought the same.

Adrian freezes. The van idles under the light of another streetlamp with its rear doors open, where two of the men are wrestling a long, person-shaped bag from inside. Two more watch, hands outstretched, waiting to share the weight. The pair inside are facing Adrian but don't appear to see him from only a few yards away. Why not? A prodigious focus? A trick of the light?

Slowly and silently as he can, Adrian begins walking backward. Without turning away from the men and their van, he finds his footing and lowers himself into the shallow ravine behind him, slowly inching down until his eyes are level with the road. Insects trill around him. Dust collects on his teeth. Now they couldn't see him if they tried.

Speaking quietly to each other, the men bring the bag to the bridge and heft it upright, though the top deflates, as if whatever is inside is collapsing in on itself. It is clearly very heavy. Will it sink in the water? All four look over their shoulders, toward the mansion where Adrian was headed a few minutes before.

What should he do? There are cops in the park all night long. They drive laps on the road, or idle at gates and turnoffs, talking to each other through toothpicks and glaring at their computer screens. But there aren't any cops around, not that he can see, and calling 911 is always pointless. He thinks of texting Mark, but what could Mark do? He's probably asleep, anyway. Cora? She'll be at work and she won't care. If anything, she would be furious that Adrian would attempt to involve her in something so plainly sketchy. There is no one else, unless he wants to call one of his *friends*, and he isn't interested in creating a situation where he owes one of them a favor. At any rate, if he speaks or if his phone lights up, the men may notice him.

The men heave the bag over the side of the bridge. Cold, deep water—that's how you lose a body for a while. When water is warm and shallow, however, objects tend to reemerge, sometimes in a matter of hours. Adrian crouches lower, sweat pearling and plummeting inside his armpit. His thighs are beginning to burn. Tomorrow, Brooklyn will probably be in the nineties, if not higher. What will happen to the bag then?

The men walk back to the van. Their faces are all like shovels. Two are white, two Latino, Adrian surmises. Between five foot nine and six foot one in height, from late twenties to late thirties; the vital-stats sections of hookup apps have taught him how to gauge height and age with some accuracy. Now that he's seen what they look like, Adrian is worried on their behalf. He wishes that they would scatter, and fast, before one of the cop cars comes by.

But the men take their time. One stands by the front driver's side, looking at his phone. One kneels to check something in the wheel well on the back right side. They all wear black, long-sleeved shirts and pants, except for one, who wears long shorts instead, which strikes Adrian as silly, given the circumstances. Will he laugh? Would they hear?

When the engine ignites, Adrian lowers himself to his knees, the gravel scraping his skin. Instead of fading to black, the firefly just above his head disappears for the heartbeat of time that the headlights whip by. The van pulls back onto the road and guns for Flushing.

Mark

Adrian pulls the lint roller from Mark's closet and swipes it across his chest and shoulders. Down the hall, Georges Sebastian conducts the Orchestre de l'Opéra national de Paris through the living room speakers. It's the afternoon of Independence Day, and the fireworks have already begun.

Hot date? says Mark. He's in bed, a book splayed open beside him. The VCR/TV is frozen. On the screen is a monster that looks like Loch Ness and Bigfoot had a baby. This movie, a dimwitted D horror with lots of Wilhelm screams, has been hard for him to get through. Every twenty minutes or so, he hits Pause and reads his book for a while.

Maybe. Adrian primly tugs at the hem of his shirt. He looks younger than he is.

Mark thinks that the irony of his friendship with Adrian is that, after Arturo, he has never wanted another romantic partner. He feels too old for that kind of thing. Too widowed. *It's just how I was raised*, he said the first time Tyree tried to set him up on a blind date. He didn't know exactly what he meant by that, but Tyree laughed, confirming that it was some kind of joke.

Since Arturo, Mark has been surprised by his lack of interest not just in romance, but sex as well. Even with Adrian. *He fucks enough for the both of us*, he once told Lucinda, pointing at his young friend like an accusation. Adrian was in a corner with Cora, the two of them eyeing an athletic woman with a brusque haircut and black Doc Martens. For Mark, there have been a few men over the past seven years, but nothing that would qualify as an affair, let alone a relationship. They were just hookups, as Adrian calls them. These hookups were about as satisfying as masturbation, but since they required a lot more work, Mark hasn't been in a hurry to replicate them. When had the last one even been? Two years ago? Three? He remembers coming home afterward to find Adrian and George on the couch, fascinating each other with a blue feather hot-glued to a long, supple piece of wire. Whatever happened before that is gone. Not worth remembering, obviously.

Adrian puts the lint roller back in the closet. *Be back later*. He floats down the hall, leaving the door open behind him. Mark gets out of bed and pauses the movie. He feels like he could spend an hour or so on a rolling chair; like he could get a little work done.

Bye, yells Adrian. The front door closes, the easel vibrating in its wake.

Mark stretches, experiencing the confident lightheadedness of THC that's finally metabolizing. For the first time in weeks, he wasn't sick this morning, though the honey hasn't abated entirely. The insistence of it, the constant pressure. Sometimes the pain is so evenly dispersed throughout his body that it's almost numbing.

He goes to his office and sits down at his desk. There are hundreds of emails in his inbox. He lost control of it when the pandemic began, and it only got worse from there. Only once freed from normal life's sense of urgency did he realize just how many of them he received, how quickly the bolded subject lines stacked up. Rent, invoices, invitations, medical bills, investments notifications, donation requests, tax documents, spam, spam, spam. From friends, colleagues, institutions. Some of the emails have already been clicked—Adrian knows his password. Near the top is one from a distant cousin he's met only once or twice asking after a quilt rack made by Grammy's first husband. It was in Mom's possession when she died and the cousin wants his turn. Of course, he's not aware that Ruth, too, is now gone. Mark reads through the email twice, then deletes it.

Mark does this to each one: examines it carefully, as if its contents are precious or important, then tosses it into the digital dustbin. He thinks of the emails to come, the ones he won't be alive to see, and feels sadness on their behalf. Who will look after them? The ones awaiting destruction are lined up like damned ducklings. He hates that dying is harder than grieving. That grieving like this, via administration, is preferential to physical suffering. Would he accept this tedium in exchange for another year of Mom's life? For another of Ruth's? If he's honest, he doesn't know, and his selfishness immiserates him in a way that he cannot share with anyone, even Adrian, who returns from his outings, no matter how late, in time for Mark's early morning shift in front of the toilet, if only to witness, from the other room, the disintegration of his one and only body.

Mark glances over at the canvas, mottled with color. It was something he'd been working on before Mom died, something to follow

The Gargoyles. He can see, in the brushstrokes, two boys sitting next to each other on the edge of a bed. He knows a book will be shared across their laps. Mark leans closer. What will the book be? White cut leaves. The cover will not be visible, but it must still have a name. A real book, it must be. One boy bends his shoulder, a little give below the other's. Their eyes are open. Where will they look? There will be a kiss. When it will happen—before, or after, or never—is still unknown to him.

Mark slowly gets to his feet and selects a fountain pen from a jar on his desk. A gift, one meant for display, not daily use. He presses its point to the canvas. Act 1 of Bellini's *Norma* seeks its highest note as he slices through, like a razor through flesh. The aperture gapes in time with an explosion somewhere off toward the park, and a third sound—hot, furious, synthetic—collides with them. Mark jumps. The third sound, the score of dreams, is coming from his bedroom.

He finds that the screen of the VCR/TV is alive again. A new, betentacled creature, eyes rolling like Frankenstein's monster, chases a sexy young woman out of a lake. How did the tape unpause?

Mark turns it off and collapses on the mattress, panting slightly. He'll finish the movie later, maybe after he's had something to eat. He looks at the duffel bag, still bulky with unwatched tapes. He has the sense of time closing in around him. La Callas is endless.

Adrian

Adrian met Cora at a party.

With its vintage gaslights and creeping ivy, the mud-hued Cobble Hill brownstone projected an aura of old-fashioned warmth, but its interior, as Adrian and Mark discovered, was a cruel inversion of the facade. The molding had been painted over, the woodwork hidden with laminate, the fireplace deceitfully sealed. Pebbling the walls and counterspace were intimidatingly modern gadgets, controllable by the soft pad of one's thumb or a sharpened tone of voice; the laquearia in the main room was capable of doubling, sensibly and yet somehow outrageously, as solar paneling; the modern light fixtures looked like weapons. Everything, from the temperature to the nondescript music coming from discreet Bluetooth speakers, was surreptitiously monitored by exquisitely uniformed Jamaican waitstaff, each one of whom had devised a way to look both expressionless and welcoming at once.

Fancy, said Adrian, who, having found himself with *friends* in places like 10 Downing Street and Colombo's Republic Building, was just being polite. He and Mark had met only three months prior, and he still felt compelled to be on what Grandma would have called his *best behavior* around his new friend. Adrian very much wanted Mark to like him, which was why, when he became aware that his presence was distracting the two men that had approached Mark to talk about NFTs, he melted away in search of something sweet and alcoholic.

The party was at capacity with the illustrious, the wealthy, the well-connected, none of whom Adrian had ever seen before. He hadn't seen Cora before, either, and wondered if she was famous, like Mark, or a nobody, like him. They were among the youngest people in attendance, and both had come with much older dates of their own genders. Cora was deep in conversation with hers, but Adrian didn't have to wait long. As soon as her escort turned to another woman, he sidled up to ask if she had a cigarette.

Yeah, Cora said, tapping the heart-shaped leather purse slung over her shoulder. She didn't look at him twice, but he knew he had her attention. *Come on.*

They went to one of the upstairs bathrooms. It had surprisingly chintzy seashell decorations and quadruple-ply toilet paper. Afterward, while she was sorting out her panties, Cora admitted that she didn't actually have that cigarette.

Hope that's okay, she said, examining her undereyes in the mirror. She didn't appear to actually care if it was okay. *I just wanted you to come up here with me.*

Thanks. Adrian knew this was meant as a gift, and he received it as such.

So is that your boyfriend? She allowed him a moment of mirrored eye contact, then returned her focus to herself.

No, said Adrian. Even without the cigarette, he felt lightheaded. He had rarely been with anyone so sexually passive as Cora. During, she had hardly moved at all. She wouldn't look at him, either, instead gazing into the shower curtain, as if trying to decipher a message from its pink and seafoam mandalas of biologically impossible florets.

Your SD? Cora pressed on.

No. Adrian leaned forward from the wall and seized the zipper of her dress. *My friend.* He pinched the fabric beneath and pulled the piece of metal all the way to the top.

Cora tugged at her hemline. *My friend*, she echoed, *the woman I came with, knows who he is. I saw him at MoMA.*

Oh yeah, said Adrian. He hadn't known about Mark when they met, and he wonders if it would have made a difference if he had. When people found out they knew each other, they often wanted to talk about Mark's art. Adrian did his best to avoid this. They always had so many questions, which made him feel as if he were being asked to account for Mark's creativity. Adrian felt it was unjust that this was expected of him.

Are you an artist, too? asked Cora.

Adrian was surprised by her question. The answer seemed obvious to him. *No.*

Then what are you?

Adrian looked at his cuticles. When the situation called for it, he told people he was a student. One of his rare lies, which he justified because it was easier than explaining his real methods of getting by; a falsehood, he believed, only counted as a lie if he was telling it for his own pleasure, or to get something out of someone. It was a point of pride for Adrian that he didn't need prevarication to take care of himself. And at twenty-four, being a student certainly made sense, not that there tended to be follow-up questions. But he felt that he could be honest with Cora, or almost.

Something else, he said. *What are you?*

Cora laughed. *Gay, for starters.*

Adrian smiled. He loved lesbians.

You're kind of weird, said Cora, pulling lipstick out of her heart-shaped purse.

They returned to their dates, Cora a little sheepishly, Adrian with his normal equanimity. They didn't make eye contact for the rest of the evening. It was not until they met at another party a few weeks later that their friendship crystallized.

They both had ended up at the same afters at a bar in Crown Heights. Adrian was deep in conversation with a milky, milfy woman whose body bulged against her straps and laces, running over and seeping out, when he noticed a familiar plumage: a raven's wing flung open across bare shoulders. It was the lesbian from that brownstone bathroom.

Cora had noticed Adrian's *friend* before she noticed Adrian; the milf was a type for her, if not *the* type. But Adrian had gotten there first, and anyway, lovely as Cora was, she stood no chance against him. Before he left with the milf, Adrian got Cora's number. *Let's go for a walk sometime,* he said, hoping it was clear that he didn't want to be with her again (the idea of it still excited him, but only when he was alone).

Her new friendship with Adrian initiated a short, fervid spell of promiscuity for Cora. The only other time she had been with a man was during the Bush administration, though she had been a lesbian then, too. The man, a friend of a friend, had sneaked out behind the bar to smoke a cigarette, as if expecting to be scolded if he were found. Cora, a little drunk and very bored, decided to take him home when she asked him for a light and he looked embarrassed to admit that he had one. Something about this reaction was intensely attractive to her.

Cora had eyed the man, imagining the two of them in her kitchen together. Her roommates would be gone or fast asleep, so there would be no need for them to rush. She would make a drink, hand it to him, then immediately take it back again, setting it on the counter without removing her eyes from his face. Lean close, hook his shirt in her fingers. *Don't worry,* she would say, *I'll take care of everything.*

Something like that. The man, an early adopter of the Anthropocene's promise of doom, was filling the silence with a nervous homily about climate change. She pretended to listen, hot paper in her mouth, masculine hair gel on her fingers. She smelled menthol and oud, sharp flavors even bluer than the December darkness.

As she soon discovered, Cora had been wrong about the man's submissiveness, though this wasn't to say that he was dominant, either. What he had was neither innocence nor experience, and she didn't realize she craved the extremity of one or the other until it was too late. In her bed, he positioned himself on top of her and settled there, as if holding someone's place in line. Cora idled below while he moved regularly but mechanically, like a metronome. She almost made noise, then remembered that she was a lesbian and wasn't obligated to be polite. She watched him posture and struggle, taking note of his shortcomings to tell her friends about later. *Men.*

But it wasn't all bad. The man kissed decently well and had a gym-defined chest, which appealed to Cora's vanity; she was a pretty girl, after all, who deserved the attentions of attractive men. Eventually, she helped him give her an orgasm. When she was done, she told him to leave, and he did so without complaint, carrying his shoes out into the hallway rather than donning them in her living room. When she got back into bed, her sheets smelled like cigarettes and cologne, which she enjoyed with some embarrassment. She fell asleep under the leaves of *In the Shadow of Young Girls in Flower.*

After that, no more men for Cora until she met Adrian, who lived just a few blocks from her. Adrian told Mark about Cora (two new friends in such a short period of time!); Cora told no one that she was on a girl bender, one that seemed to be inflamed anew every time she met with Adrian for drinks or a walk in Prospect Park. When he and Mark went on their first trip together—County Wicklow in the springtime—Adrian had a key made so she could water his plants. Once she brought someone home from the bar and fucked her on Adrian's bed. Though she considered washing the sheets afterward, she ultimately decided not to. She didn't tell Adrian, though she had a feeling he wouldn't have cared if he knew. This pissed her off.

If Mark recognized Cora when they officially met, he didn't say so. When Adrian told Mary about his new friend, Cora, he said they had met at the bar where she worked, and that they had gotten to know each other over a game of pool. The bar and the pool had happened, it was true, but later on, the third or fourth time Adrian and Cora saw each other. Later, much later, when she and Mary compared notes, Cora wasn't surprised to learn that Adrian had lied for no reason that either of them could figure out.

⸺⸺⸺⸺◇⸺⸺⸺⸺

Cora: long black hair and never a bra. She abstains from jewelry except for the band on her wedding finger, which she wears only at the bar, to keep men away. She swears that it even works sometimes. It's ugly, which is what gives it its authenticity. It came from a pawnshop that is now a dispensary with commissioned graffiti on the windows.

The bar is empty. The heat is punishing. A July variant surges on a Tuesday afternoon. If there's nowhere they have to be, people are at home wanting to die, where they'll stay until the evening brings them back to life. Adrian has come to keep Cora company. When she's on duty, he drinks for free, but then again, he always does.

When it's dead like this, Cora reads books by people with names like Chip and Glück and Dodie while Adrian draws on an old notepad. Cora is unimpressed by everything he does, especially the things he does well, which includes his doodles of items in the bar: the jukebox, a jar of maraschino cherries. If you were to ask her what she likes about Adrian, she would be honest: his reserve, his taste in books (refreshingly bad, unstrivingly self-serving), and his uncomplicated love of animals, something that feels positively anachronistic in a world where everything is politicized, or so it seems to Cora. Today, in a departure from his portraits and still lifes, Adrian is drawing a person-shaped blob.

Cora leans over for a better look. *Nice turd*, she says.

Adrian sighs. *I saw it in the park*, he says as the bell jingles over the door. After Cora serves the customer, she places another vodka soda at her friend's elbow.

As the evening digs in its claws, the bar begins to pick up. Cora dashes around yanking levers and poring over fine print. Sometimes Adrian helps before the barback clocks in, but tonight he doesn't offer. Notepad pushed to the side, he slumps over his drink, picking at his nails.

Something is wrong, Cora thinks. She takes advantage of a lull to prep mixers. *Did I ever tell you about my Great-Grandpa Floyd?* she asks.

Great-Grandpa Floyd flew planes back in the Wright brothers' time. After serving as a combat pilot in the war, which he'd only been able to do because he'd stowed away with the merchant marines on a ship to France at eleven years old, he returned to the States to become a high-flying daredevil who thrilled audiences by walking out onto the wing of his box of bolts, *Angelica*, named for his first wife. *Angelica* didn't even break 150 miles per hour, cruising slow and low enough to keep Great-Grandpa Floyd alive until he got back in the cockpit.

That's cool, Adrian says. Over and over, he places the pencil at the top of the bar and waits for it to roll into his lap.

But it was hard to find daredevil work in America, Cora goes on, so Great-Grandpa Floyd went back to France, where Negro pilots were admired and relatively well-paid to take the risks that they did. But not long before the stock market crash, an injury grounded him permanently. It hadn't happened in the air, but rather down on Earth—in Alsace, to be precise—when a horse kicked him while he was taking a piss behind a barn.

This seems to get Adrian's attention. *Kicked him where?*

I'm not sure, says Cora. *But it was bad. After that, he couldn't fly anymore. He couldn't even run again.*

Grounded at twenty-five, Great-Grandpa Floyd made his final return to the States, where he began a new trade in New York City.

And that is why I'm a fourth-generation bartender. And probably why I was born at all. Most of those daredevil guys died young. She laughs, but Adrian doesn't join her.

If he wants to be boring, let him, she thinks. *Once the bar is really busy, he'll feel better.* It's always the same: drunk women who would have otherwise been paralyzed with fear will boldly accuse Adrian of being in the movies. Straight men in baseball caps will glower in corner barstools for hours, only approaching to order another cheap beer, never taking their eyes off him, never closing their mouths. A handful of people will be brave enough to ask if they can buy him a drink, and each will be rewarded with a refusal so polite that it's rude. Adrian's voice will be soft enough to draw in his *friends* before their admonishment hits. Occasionally, they will get angry. If necessary, the bouncer, Charles, rolling his eyes and sighing, will escort them outside. Cora enjoys watching Adrian's admirers be denied what they want.

But it doesn't take her long to observe that the crowd is weird tonight. Even when the bar reaches capacity, few people seem to notice Adrian, and fewer still attempt to talk to him, other than one of the barflies, an elder queen in terry cloth and denim, with whom Adrian already has a rapport. Even the way Reno speaks to Adrian feels off, more friendly than amorous. He's asking him about Mark. *Has he been working on anything since* The Gargoyles?

There is something different with Adrian, she's sure of it. Does he know? Cora keeps an eye on her friend, credit cards flying through her fingers. She watches his mouth slide down his face, his shoulders hunch lower and lower. He looks like a garden statue in the winter: there's no one to observe him.

Late in her shift, Cora finally feels something change. In the rainbow lights of the mirrored wall, she sees the eidolon move, hears the scrape of the stool. When she turns around, Adrian is waving goodbye from halfway down the bar. She's relieved to see him go.

———————————◇———————————

Adrian wonders if Cora is relieved to see him go. He and Charles exchange nods as another bouncer holds the door for him. Has Charles noticed the difference tonight? Is he, too, relieved to see the last of him?

Underground, Adrian trots to catch the last car on the train. It's empty except for an older man sitting in the far corner by the gangway connection. Heeding an instinct, he walks the car like a runway, sits down in the seat across from the man, and waits. Not so long ago, he wouldn't have been able to dim *it* if he tried. Now he can only hope *it* will indulge him when the time comes. He has begun to wish that *it* was a thing he could tug start, like a lawn mower, bringing it to life at his whim.

Tonight, he is lucky. Adrian feels *it* quicken just as the man notices him. He has sleepy eyes and a big chest; both begin fluttering for Adrian. A hard brake throws them against the same wall. The man watches him. Adrian stands up and sits on the other side of the car. The man doesn't move to make room.

The train hurtles on, pulling them first one way, then another. They touch each other—clothing, naked arms and wrists. The man's torso is longer than Adrian's, and his shoulders broader, but their feet appear to be about the same size. The man takes his bare knee with his cool hand and pulls his body across the bench. The man speaks to him in a language he doesn't understand, but Adrian feels, with conviction, that it is better not to know.

Adrian misses his stop. Three stops after that, the man gets off the train. Adrian fixes his shirt as the doors close behind him. There's no reason not to get off here, but he waits for a while, ignoring the conductor's babble, enjoying the feeling of *it* in his body.

He's deep into Queens when he finally debarks on an empty platform. At the top of the stairs, he sees a man waiting at the bus stop. A street sweeper blows hot air through trash, stirring the brown-papered 40 in the man's hand and cooling the sweat on Adrian's skin. It's still as hot as it was when the sun was setting. He's opening up the Uber app when a taxi pulls to a stop a few feet away.

Red plastic beads hang from the rearview. The satellite radio plays the liturgy in Mandarin. The driver is tall but stooped, crunched into his seat on the other side of the transparent divider. He smiles, warm as soup. His sweatpants are so thin they're almost diaphanous.

By the time Cora has closed the bar and gone home to bed, Adrian has left the taxi driver and burned through three more men on his long way home to Prospect Heights. The last is a rush job in the trees lining Plaza Street West, only a few blocks from his apartment. The man—fair-skinned, middle-aged, unfashionably balding when a Mr. Clean look would have flattered him nicely—trembles the entire time. Afterward, the man wipes his wet face and hurries away, descending into the station like a terrified rabbit to his warren.

Adrian inspects the bench for trash before sitting down. He rarely does this, layercaking sex, one person after another, especially with men. Though his desires are usually inarticulate, they're rarely inscrutable, and never insatiable. Not like this—not anymore. Normally he can be satisfied until next time, something he's come to pride himself on. Now he's alarmed by the awareness that he could go yet again, feeling himself already scanning the early morning streets for signs of life.

Forget what he wants—what does he need? Under Adrian's feet, a train sends steam up through the grating to dry on his hair. He imagines a sandwich, a cup of tea, a massage for his back and legs. A book? A good night's sleep? Something else? Nothing makes a dent. It takes a cigarette butt squeezed in a sidewalk crack to stimulate a real desire.

The deli by Adrian's apartment is manned by a person best described as a boy. Pensive over his phone, a spot of strawberry-kiwi Pedialyte staining the white collar of his football jersey. The boy's eyes are brown, his freckles are brown, his fingernails are normal, except for three on his left hand, which are painted black, chipped and ugly in the carefree manner of the young and slutty heterosexual male.

Admiring him, Adrian takes off his mask and waits. The boy looks up. His freckles match the flaws in his eyes. The goatee, though slender, organizes his face into masculine little blocks.

Loosie? says Adrian. *It* dances on hot coals.

The boy reaches under the counter. *Here you go.* His voice is unexpectedly deep. On the wall behind him hangs the OTC medications, condoms, phone chargers, swishers, packets of gum, and a red, black, white, and green flag.

Thank you, says Adrian, still waiting.

But the boy sticks out his chin, biting his lip. In a moment, his assessment is over. His eyes return to the screen in his hand.

Have a good one, boss, he says, already gone.

Rubbing his eyes, Adrian reaches for his phone on the nightstand. It's noon. There are new texts from Cora, Mary, Dominique in Cape Town (. . . *with me of course. he' gonna be gone for a month and . . .*), Dom in Queens (. . . *about you baby boy you think youll be up here anytime . . .*). Nothing from Mark, whom he texted last night, first from the bar, then again from the train station, then a third time from just outside the deli, a half block from home, while he smoked his bitter loosie.

Adrian knows that Mark has been awake for hours now, likely since before the sun came up. He always used to text back promptly. Even during COVID, when his mom was dying and there was that wildfire where they almost had to evacuate her place in Almendra, he always texted back, usually right away. That changed when Ruth died. Since Mark came back, it's like he's been avoiding him, even though they see each other every day.

Adrian gets out of bed, slips into his slippers, taps to the kitchen. On the fire escape: the mustard and mayo of pigeon shit, the optical illusion of a cloud balanced on a flaking bar of iron. It's hot and getting hotter, now that the sky is thickening. His phone says it's supposed to rain. He sets it on the counter and gets the beans from the freezer. While he makes his coffee, he glances back to the screen, as if now that he's finally awake Mark is more likely to respond.

Is Mark angry with him? Or is it something else? Adrian knows that his friend has been getting sicker. That he's losing even more weight, that his eyes are yellowing, that his breath smells yeasty and rank, even after he's brushed his teeth. Is it because he's depressed? The long COVID he's been hearing about? Did he get another disease, perhaps from Ruth—the same one that killed her? But then, Adrian remembers, Mark was sick before he went to Almendra. Something else must be going on.

The mill shrieks. He pulls out the drawer and shakes it to level the grounds. He glances at his phone. The screen is still dark. He hasn't asked Mark about Ruth, about any of that. Adrian has gotten the sense that questions are unwelcome, and yet in the three weeks since Mark came back from Almendra, his symptoms force him to ask questions that he knows his friend would rather not answer: *Did you get enough sleep last night? Can you eat today? Shouldn't you go to the doctor?*

Adrian stands by the window while he waits for the French press. The rose bushes down below make a magic circle around the backyard, a sanctuary that none may enter except the rose man himself. From Monday through Friday, the clamor of nearby construction pierces the walls, the backhoes rattling the foundation. The construction workers watch Adrian come and go, smiles on their faces, gentle words on their lips. But it's Saturday morning, which means Adrian can sit by the window and enjoy his coffee in citied silence: the birds, the church bells, distant traffic, reggaeton, and the ceaseless peals of the ice cream truck. Instead of reading, as he usually does, he looks through the Contacts list in his phone.

Adrian doesn't have the contact information, let alone the names, of even a fraction of his many *friends*. Even so, in his cloud are

thousands of phone numbers, some with names, some with sur-
names, some with email or home addresses. In the Notes section
of each contact are the dates when they met, and where, and how.
Sometimes he's jotted down a single detail—*Big teeth* or *Weird
laugh*—sometimes a few sentences, on occasion a paragraph.
*Asked me to go to Paris. Private jet. The food was pretty good. I slept
a lot. She actually lived outside the city, so got bored and left early.*
Adrian recalls the jet and the house and even one of the meals
he was served (a pissaladière choked with vibrant Ligurian olives),
but he doesn't remember the face of the *friend* who ate it with him.
There are too many *friends* to remember them all, even with his
notes, but that is not the point. The notes' primary function is not
nostalgia but proof. (Of what? For whom? He doesn't know.)

His thumb flicks. He's looking for someone in particular and can't
remember where he might be. He searches first under the *P*'s, then
through the *Dr.*'s. Ah, here it is, with the honorific spelled out in
full, for some reason: *Doctor Pollari*. No first name. The note says:
Mark's cardiologist. 2017. He hasn't seen Dr. Pollari in four years,
and for good reason.

A receptionist answers on the second ring. He's a friend of Dr.
Pollari's, he tells her, and would like to come see him as soon as
possible. He gives her his name and number. She says she'll call
him back. He turns on his notifications.

Adrian pours his coffee, scoops his sugar, stirs. He's considering
his first meal of the day. Maybe he'll make pasta salad, enough for
leftovers. Then he'll have an excuse to go to Mark's apartment and
coax some food into him. He doesn't decide not to tell Mark about
his decision to see Dr. Pollari—it doesn't even occur to him, and so
neither does deception.

His phone dings with a text from Cora. He pictures her at work, forearms tense, dodging a man's grasping fingers. He doesn't open it. He doesn't feel like explaining everything that's going on. She already knows Mark isn't feeling well, which is about as much as he knows himself. What else is there to say?

Mark

The tunnel that opens onto Prospect Park's Long Meadow—named *Meadowport Arch* according to Google Maps—has recently been redone. Inside, what once looked and smelled like an ancient cistern now resembles the champagne-slick hull of a virgin schooner. In the space of a few steps, the momentary cool recedes behind Mark as he emerges into the first great pasture, where Brooklyn crowds the sunshine.

He moves slowly, his feet pointed toward Windsor Terrace, where George will soon be whining for his supper. He thinks he can still make it home on his own, but it won't be easy. When he left the studio, the box weighed fifteen pounds. By the time he reached the park, it weighed fifty. At the first empty bench, he sits down to rest, panting.

And sign here, the broker had said. Mark signed. Adrian stood a few feet behind him, his old habit of attempting to avoid notice, though it was rarely successful. People always recognize him, even if they've never seen him before. Being with Adrian in public, as he was this morning, means that Mark gets to be more anonymous than he's ever been, even in his twenties, back when nobody except his friends knew his name.

And I think that's everything, said the broker, offering his hand to Mark. Adrian circumvented farewells by heading for the door, which he propped open with his foot. In his arms was the cardboard box, the odds and ends of Mark's decade in this studio. Searching for his sunglasses, which were hanging from his collar, Mark hurried to catch up.

Mark had assumed that Adrian would come home with him, but out on the sidewalk his friend handed over the box. Mark peered through the glass back into the office, sizing up the broker out of habit—why, he didn't know, since he knew anyone could be Adrian's type. But the broker, bespectacled and spare like an astigmatic jockey, was looking down at his phone. He'd already moved on with his day.

Where are you headed off to then? Mark pretended to scold. He hoped that Adrian hadn't noticed his assumption.

Adrian smiled. *I'll see you later*, he said, hands in his pockets, moving away with a schoolboy's fluid stride. Mark noticed his hair was a little long in the back; he was overdue for the barber.

Mark sets the box on the bench beside him and leans back with a sigh. Around Litchfield Villa, balls tumble, Frisbees sing, dogs gag on their leashes. Yellowed petals fade on the grass, soft and short and green. Babies arch, children run. Men, some of them beautiful, jog in tight shorts. Mark can think of no reason he might take this walk again after today. He's going to miss it.

He looks down through the lid of the cardboard. Nothing in the box is all that important, nothing irreplaceable. He thinks he could make it the rest of the way home on foot without it. But the idea of giving up and retreating to Prospect Park West to call a car makes him indignant. He *is* strong today! This morning he was sick, but when he had his egg, he kept it down. Then there was the espresso, which Adrian made in the kitchen-size La Marzocco, along with the pentazocine and a pair of 5 mg gummies. Fortified by protein, caffeine, painkiller, and THC, Mark ate some unbuttered toast with a little spinach, sauteed in avocado oil, on top.

He's exhausted, his joints burning and his guts seething. But he'll get the box home, he decides, even if he has to crawl, pushing it on the path ahead of him. The image—so dramatic!—makes him smile. When he gets back to Windsor Terrace, god willing, he'll have an appetite. He'll nap and, god even more willing, he'll awaken to eat again before watching at least two VHS tapes tonight, if not three, before turning in. *There*, Mark thinks. *It's decided.*

A giggling flock of Hasidic boys passes by. A middle-aged woman in high-waisted leggings chats with the hardware in her ear. A gap-toothed old man observes as his puppy, no bigger than a teddy bear, sniffs a garbage can. Knowing Adrian won't be at the apartment puts Mark at ease. He is awaiting, with some anxiety, his friend's demand for an explanation. He had actually believed that it was coming this morning when Adrian tripped over the duffel bag, still almost full. Next to it, pushed against the wall, was the short stack of tapes he had already watched, minus *Hot World*, which he pressed into a far corner of the duffel. On the narrow side of each watched tape, Mark had placed a strip of white painter's adhesive with their titles: *The Lady Panics*; *Grief 2*; *Rose*. There was even one called *The Gargoyles*, funnily enough. It was about a group of homeless children—the young actors had the manic double-jointedness of studio-system serfs—living on the streets of Depression-era Chicago who turn to religious grifting to survive.

Adrian regained his balance like a crane rising from a field. *Do you want me to move this?* he asked, pointing at the duffel. His voice was sweet. He was not irritated or embarrassed at almost having fallen in front of his friend.

No. Though his back ached, Mark sat up a little straighter. *It's fine there.*

He waited for Adrian to ask about the tapes, which would lead to the other questions, and then it would all come out: Mom's death, Ruth's death, the missed funeral, the sickness the three of them shared, his own death already so close. He would come clean. A preliminary relief dulled the pain, allowing him to sit up even more.

Okay, said Adrian. He went into the hall. George followed, tail at an expectant 45 degrees.

Mark fell back into the pillows. Not today then. Maybe not ever. He opened the nightstand to check for Ruth's pill bottles. All accounted for. From the kitchen, the creak of a drawer opening and, in response, George's sidereal meow: high and tiny and sharp.

On Mom's TV, the DVD menu of Brass's *Così fan tutte* had been revolving in silence for the past half hour. Mark knew because he had timed it, listening to the silence from the other side of the door. Finally, he could stand it no longer. After a peremptory knock, he barged into Mom's room.

Want me to put something else on? he demanded.

No, said Ruth. Her mouth hung open when she finished the word. She hadn't eaten since yesterday.

Mark wheeled around and rushed back down the hall. He got a can of Coke from the fridge. He pulled open the junk drawer and got the cigarettes and the white mini lighter, both left by Adrian the last time he visited Almendra. He raced down the other hall and out the back door. He climbed up on the picnic table and sat down facing the house. He lit a cigarette and popped open the can. The sun set sharp on his back, the air stringent with cut grass.

He was lighting a second cigarette when Angela came outside to say she was going home. Someone else—Brionna, she believed—would be relieving Mark the next morning.

Thanks, said Mark. Hospice had returned, this time for his sister. The RNs who came to the house weren't the ones who had cared for Mom, but the protocol was more or less the same.

Angela jiggled her thumb. *I just checked on her,* she said. *She took her meds. Should be asleep soon.*

Mark nodded, wishing that he could ignore Angela, in her red athleisure and matching orthopedic shoes. That he could snap, *That's none of my business,* every time she mentioned Ruth's failing body.

Thinking about his sister dying made him want to die. And yet he wanted to be alive so very much. He hated Angela.

Have a good night, Mark said. He waved with his free hand, steadying the cherry of his smoke against his knee.

Angela left. He kept smoking. He thought about his sister's funeral. All the same people who were at Mom's almost a year before would be invited, minus the one who had sat next to him and patted his knee, who had endured the same barrage of well-meaning but unwelcome embraces. Would anyone come? If he could find Mom's eulogy, he could recycle it, just swap out their names and a few details. A similar thought had occurred to him almost thirty years before, when they lost Leo the same hideous summer as Tenny and Junior. Mark had been the one to call Leo's parents, who, though civil, seemed as afraid of him as they had been of their son. As Leo's mother wept, Mark had thought evilly of bulk rates, and mass graves, and Hallmark cards just for fags. SORRY YOU DIED OF AIDS. But he had been steady. He didn't say the things he wanted to say, not even to Leo's father, who, he knew from Leo's deathbed, had called his own son a mistake.

Before Arturo died, he told Mark he didn't want anything, not a service, not a party, not even a private ceremony between Mark and the urn. Just nothing. Ashes to ashes, his remnants abandoned at the place where they cooked him down. Arturo's last campfire.

Mark felt as if he'd been slapped. *What about me?* he demanded.

Arturo leaned close. *My life is not your catharsis.*

This is why I hate writers, Mark snapped, submitting to his kiss.

But Mark had honored everything. He watched the incineration. He thanked someone, shook their hand, ensured his wallet and phone were still in his pockets. He took the train as if it were the most normal thing in the world, as if he had just spent the morning at Home Depot or Yankee Stadium. If he had the power to go back in time, he would not commit the heresy of resurrecting Arturo but the minor sin of meeting Adrian a little sooner, so that he wouldn't have had to spend that first week alone. So that there would have been someone to say, *Get up and I will cook for you. Go to bed and you will sleep.* He hadn't let Tyree or Lucinda come stay at his apartment, but he would have let Adrian. Adrian would have been there despite him, insinuating himself, almost without his notice, doing and cleaning and feeding George, talking very little.

Did Mark want Adrian here with him now? He tapped the bottom of the pack, as if burping a shrink-wrapped baby. With Ruth withering away in Mom's room? With the humidifier, the constipation, the smell of cheap generic body lotion? No. Adrian didn't need to see this. Nobody did.

Mark considered a third cigarette. But no, his throat was already going to hurt later. He could never get enough Coke, though. It agreed with him these days, if nothing else did. He drained the can and squeezed it in his fist. Tantrum over. Now he could go check on his sister. He stubbed his smoke, its entrails turned to powder on the picnic table.

On the other side of the doorway, Ruth was asleep under Grammy's quilt. She didn't get out of bed anymore except to use the bathroom. There was a fracture pan on a nearby shelf and a wheelchair in the hall closet. Her voice now too weak to yell, the baby monitor had reappeared, but she almost never called for him at night. He still came to check on her in the dark. Sometimes he sat outside the door, as he had a little bit ago, listening to her nothing.

Mark went back inside and through the kitchen to Ruth's bedroom, where she hadn't slept in weeks. A music box on the bureau sprouted a pirouetting dancer. On the bookshelf, he recognized a few of the books he had given her over the years, crisply unread: the prints of Bob Thompson, a short biography of Bernice Bing. Why was he so bad at knowing what she wanted? There were other books, purchased by her, all healthily dog-eared: a textbook on Japanese cinema, a biography of Oscar Micheaux, something about Agnès Varda. Pinned to the wall was a postcard of Abbas Kiarostami posing in cool sunglasses. On the dresser were dishes filled with earrings and scrunchies, satin weighted with brittle strands of brown hair.

All was as it had always been, with everything in more or less the same place as when she came back from school over thirty years ago. The long, narrow room was neat, but if he wanted, he could trace his name in the dust on the bureau, the windowsill. A dirty person's room would have felt lived in. His sister was not dirty. The stagnation was rote, not choice.

Mark put his hands on his hips. He'd been wanting to clean in here but kept putting it off. Yesterday he'd retrieved the plastic caddy and stocked it with 409, wood polish, some rags and the tube of paper towels. But after standing in the doorway for a few minutes, he put everything back. To clean Ruth's room, knowing that everything would soon need to be boxed up anyway, would be ghoulish. Bad enough that he was already going to have to do it alone.

He opened the closet. Earth tones and ragged linens, draped but not ironed. Above his head, shoeboxes brimming with tissue paper and unfocused photographs of the garden. A bike pump, its hose uncoiled. On the floor was a black duffel bag, crammed tight and zipped shut.

Mark unzipped it. Freed from their compression, the VHS tapes crackled against each other. No dust jackets, no labels. He tugged one out from the bottom of the bag, just to be sure. Anonymous. Naked.

So this was Ken's big project. He had called Ruth about it a few weeks ago when Mark was clipping her toenails on Mom's bed. Wrapped in Grammy's quilt, she listened on speakerphone, barely responding. There were some passwords and signatures he suddenly needed from her, for reasons he didn't mention. Ruth promised to forward him everything. She had to ask twice how his wife was doing. *Oh, she's just fine,* Ken said. He didn't acknowledge her sickness, didn't even ask how she was feeling. She hadn't heard from him since.

With only a little effort, Mark could lift the duffel bag. It was lighter than it looked.

———————————◇———————————

When George is finished eating, he returns to the bedroom, as he always does. With an athlete's ease, he leaps onto the bed and in a moment Mark feels his whiskers on his ribcage. Their ritual. They settle in together. Mark leans to kiss his tiny skull, assembled by god from the leftovers of small, sweet, beautiful things: marzipan and frangipani and Tinker Bell. George's fur is so smooth it's like skin. Mark imagines that he is kissing Arturo's chest, back, cheek. George purrs. In the kitchen, Adrian whistles.

Mark has just begun another movie. The day he returned from Almendra, he counted: there were fifty-two in the duffel bag. A year's worth if he watched one per week. But he didn't have that long. If the tapes were all roughly two hours in length (an unsafe assumption, but the best he could do), it wasn't even five full days of screen time.

George is licking Mark's throat when his face suddenly twists into a Munch-jawed yawn, followed by a self-satisfied snap of his teeth. His breath is fishy and familiar. He begins grooming again. Mark thinks of ancient pharaohs entombed with their cats. He resists the urge to squeeze George against his body, which he knows would only drive him away.

He will watch all fifty-two movies, before. After, there will be nothing. No service, no party. Like Arturo. He will write something down somewhere so they know that these are his wishes. He decides he won't tell Adrian anything, even if he does ask. It will be his gift to him.

As Mark strokes George's shoulders, the cat lunges to gnaw between his toes. After a minute, he drops his foot, returning his attention to Mark's caresses. Mark smiles. It feels good to be devoted to someone.

Adrian

The zodiac splays across the ceiling of Grand Central Station, each figure an omen of the human psyche: Geminis lie, Cancers cry, etc. Other than these golden asterisms, the mural is the same grey-green as a healthy upstate pond. Standing at the center of the main concourse, Adrian searches the convexity for his sun sign until the crowd forces him against the base of a great square pillar, where he resists the urge to press his forehead against the cool stone. Modern chandeliers sparkle overhead, creamy like Apple products, delicate as verglas. *It* revs.

When he sees her, Adrian takes off his mask and steps directly in front of her. Sometimes he does that, just plants himself and waits for contact. (He got Frankie like that, on Coney Island, not to mention that famous recluse with the vermillion hair, an ex-soap star who lived in the Village and shopped in Milan.) She smiles at his smile. She is deep in her second trimester. Her fingernails are bare, her bracelets audacious.

They can't go to her apartment because it's Saturday and her husband is home. She uses her phone to rent them an hour at a place in Hell's Kitchen.

While she checks them in, Adrian stares at his phone. He has learned over the years that it's more effective to not just appear distracted but to *be* distracted.

Surprisingly, the room smells like almost nothing, maybe a single Parliament filtered through postnasal drip. As she takes off her cotton knit, then her comfortable but responsibly sourced leggings, then her broad and filmy panties, a powdery fragrance permeates the air, pressing against the mirrored walls. Under Adrian's long T-shirt there's sweat, still fresh, from their brisk morning walk. He doesn't have a condom and she doesn't ask for one. Her belly is smaller and her breasts larger than he had imagined. She is somewhat violent, especially as she nears orgasm. She bursts like a blowup doll, panting into his shoulder.

She's gone when Adrian opens the bathroom door. This happens sometimes. He examines his face in the wall, then in the ceiling. One of the mirrored panels beside the hard, scentless bed is cracked. His naked body cobwebs in the glass. She left him with twenty-five minutes remaining in the room. He feels cheated. *It* won't take no for an answer. He recalls that though the clerk's shoulders were littered with dandruff, he had perfect eyebrows. Adrian dresses and goes downstairs.

The front desk is empty. There is no button or bell, so he waits, mugging for the surveillance camera. When the clerk emerges from the back room, Adrian relaxes his shoulders and leans forward, opening his mouth to speak.

The vending machine's down that hall, says the clerk. His right arm points, but his perfect eyebrows are still directed toward his screen.

As if his nose has been flicked by a giant finger, Adrian recedes from the desk. Suddenly he's on the sidewalk again, where the morning has officially transitioned from warm to hot. His appointment with Dr. Pollari in the Upper East Side is hours away, but it will take most of that time to walk. If he's moving, he's less likely to think.

Mark

Mark slides the tape into the VCR/TV, pushes Play, and gets back in bed. It's hot, despite the AC. When the notion of an ice-cold beer arises, he doesn't look past it. Instead, he takes hold of it, considers it. He immediately feels his stomach begin to cramp.

So much for that fantasy. It was one he'd been nurturing for years, ever since he got sober. It had always begun with a diagnosis. An aggressive kind of cancer, with just a few weeks left, freeing him to finally do what he'd always wanted. Not skydiving, not a trip to Antarctica. No, with death too near for consequences, Mark would go on the world's biggest, most beautiful bender. As a definite, known expiration neared, dying would become an opportunity for a thousand new firsts. The first gin and tonic served to him in a bar in decades. The first old-fashioned—bittersweet, with its scab of orange. The first IPA, thick as jet fuel, why not?

Death wasn't something that Mark had ever looked forward to, but within this fantasy it created possibilities that his life could not hold. He knew it was just an illusion of freedom, which made him feel young when he was supposed to be feeling mortal. *Well, what's wrong with that?* he used to think.

But now that he doesn't expect to see 2022, the fantasy has lost its appeal. Every morning he wakens in a haze of pain and anticipates that desire, but it doesn't come. The old cravings have gone. The idea of wine, beer, or spirits nauseates him. Even kombucha evokes the phantom tang of rubbing alcohol, sharp in the back of his throat. Perhaps what he wants isn't booze but something that won't exit his body the way it entered. He looks at the glass of water on the nightstand. *See you soon,* Mark thinks. Odds are it will reemerge as a foaming chyle in tomorrow's toilet.

He hopes Ruth's tape will distract him. The title card reads *Erômenos*, but like *Hot World*, there are no other credits. The plot is simple enough: two rich white boys fall in love at Princeton a century ago. There isn't a sex scene, per se, but they kiss each other, full-throated, more than once. Perhaps even more transgressively (though this of course depends upon when and where *Erômenos* was made), they lie down together in a soft clearing—ties loosened, one boy's eyeglasses stowed in the breast pocket of the other. Over their whispers rises the hollow bob of rowboats, just a few yards away. The lead, a serious young man with a sardonic brow, reminds Mark of a young Jean-Louis Trintignant, but of course he has never seen him before.

Hand in hand, Jean-Louis and his lover cross a carpet of vivid green into a black wall of silence, and then *Erômenos* ends. As with the other tapes, there are no closing credits.

❖

Mark spends his nights waiting for morning. He'd rather be up until dawn than awakened by pain. He knows he should sleep more, but when he does, it's fitful and nightmarish. When Mom was dying, she hadn't slept well, either. How could she have, with this awful knowing? Mark's mind is never tired, only his body.

The movies keep him company. He doesn't care if they're good. Some are, in Mark's opinion, and some aren't. (*What would Ruth think of this one?* he wonders against his will.) He liked *Erômenos*, but he was so depressed afterward that sleep was impossible. After an hour, he turned on the lamp and pushed in another tape, which he learned, after a sleepy brass band crept over an eerie umber vista, was a Daves-style Western called *He Rides By Night*.

Not that it matters when he sleeps. Mark's old life, with all the normal obligations and schedules, ended in 2020. He feels hunted by Derek's emails (. . . *new project? Monica reached out to me today* . . .), which he deletes before he even opens them. When Derek texts, Mark takes his time formulating brief, noncommittal responses. When Derek calls, he lets it go to voicemail. Mark imagines, with an almost sadistic pleasure, Derek's shock when he finds out. He feels like Bugs Bunny dangling a baby grand over Elmer Fudd's head.

Though most of his mornings are lost to pain, Mark's afternoons and evenings belong to Ruth's tapes, whether or not Adrian is with him. He discovers that while many hover around two hours, as he expected, a handful are quite short, while still others are much longer. One—about a simpleminded peddler whose quixotic adventures, some quite funny, some transpiring in moments of beauty, ultimately end in tragedy—is almost six (how all this fits on a single tape, he has no idea). Occasionally he's up through the night, until the first signs of his morning purge steal him away to the bathroom.

Have Ruth's movies made his mornings worse? They've begun to feel like the hangovers he stopped getting in 1992. Mark awakens early, to the AC unit's howl and the sheets kicked to his ankles, with a pit in his stomach and tightness in his back, with his head aching and his brain sloshing and his joints burning. Old friends. New is an aversion to the mirror, perhaps because he was young and beautiful back when he stopped drinking. Now he is old and looking even older as his fat melts away from everywhere except his belly, which resembles and feels like a hot bowling ball. He's feverish all the time and the weather is more unbearable than he can ever remember, yet it's only June. The city's most grueling month of the year still looms ahead.

The fifteenth movie Mark watches, *Stationery*, is only mildly entertaining: a teenager runs away from her foster home and hitchhikes from Los Angeles to Vancouver to meet a girl she's been exchanging letters with. He thinks that if *Stationery* were a normal release, instead of whatever this weird secret project is (a government psyop? A millionaire's fancy?), it would have been marketed as a family movie, with a PG rating because of an angry mama bear that the girl must evade on her trek through Tahoe. Or would it? Something about the girls' relationship feels vaguely homoerotic. But that would be a part of its afterlife: attaining lesbian cult status twenty years after its heyday.

Stationery ends with the two girls setting out together for the Yukon, where a kindly cousin is sure to take them in. A strangely ambiguous ending, Mark thinks, for such teenybopper script. No credits.

He wants to start another tape, but he doesn't want to wake Adrian, whose heavy head rests against his forearm. And then there's George, who's curled where Adrian's feet, too, curl. Two-toned twists fading in the single light from his lamp: Adrian tan and gold, George black and white. Eyes closed, Adrian pouts, his arms crossed on his chest. Mark has noticed that he looks more defensive in sleep than in life.

So he should sleep, too. He definitely needs it. Better to rest than cram in another movie. But as he attempts to relax, he's suddenly drowned in a craving for a vodka tonic. He can feel the glass, cold and wet, in his hand. Sweat rises to the surface of his upper lip. His heart moves fast inside him.

Adrian rolls over toward the wall, twitching but still breathing deeply. He has never known Mark to drink. What would he do if Mark began tonight, right now? Would he join him? What would they talk about if they became drunk together? What would they do?

The vodka lust retreats like a slapped hand. It's not the notion of drinking, but this uncertainty, that has finally made Mark's stomach churn. It doesn't help that Adrian made chicken-stock meatloaf draped in brown sugar–glazed bacon for dinner. Even under normal circumstances, the meatloaf would have been too rich. But for some perverse reason he had requested it, and his friend, as always, had obliged him.

Adrian took the plates—his empty, Mark's almost completely full—into the kitchen, where he used his fork to herd Mark's meatloaf into the trash. Mark wondered if he was annoyed. The possibility made him feel resentful, not that any of this was Adrian's fault. He can never decide if his friend's refusal to interrogate him is frustrating or freeing. Watching him consume his brick of beef and egg and bread, Mark had been seized by the impulse to tell him about the jellied red streaks in his hard-earned morning shit. But he hadn't done that, of course.

Adrian stirs again. Now George. Now the honey. Mark checks the time on his phone, wondering how long it will be before he's forced into the bathroom again. How many more mornings like this? He hasn't gone to the doctor since before Mom died, so he doesn't even have a clinician's best guess. Adrian will be provided for, regardless. The paperwork is ironclad, the cause of death unimportant. Whether this illness is hereditary, environmental, or both doesn't matter—it's come for his entire family, and for some reason he's the last one standing. Why it's decided to take them all within the first two years of a global pandemic is a question he's stopped asking. He doesn't care. He doesn't want to know anything anymore. He feels frantic at the idea of another dawn, at the stupefying boredom of promised pain.

The only hint of reprieve is in the idea of telling Adrian everything, though he promised himself he wouldn't. But as Mark considers what he would say, the honey comes to a simmer. The sweat on his lip blends into a general clamminess that spreads across every centimeter of skin. George's whiskers shudder and twitch.

No, Adrian can't know. It doesn't fit. Mark is reassured by the fact that everyone who might tell Adrian about his illness is now dead. He's confident he can continue to avoid telling him anything of substance, flaking on meetings and screening calls until the bitter end. Tyree and Lucinda and Derek, maybe a few others, know that he hasn't been feeling well, but who has been, this past year? Other than Adrian, no one has any idea just how sick Mark is. And not even Adrian knows the extent of it, or what comes next.

It occurs to Mark that he also hasn't told anyone, other than Adrian and Derek, that he's back from Almendra. Or even that his sister has died. Not even Tyree or Lucinda. None of them know. They've sent texts. They've called. Once, someone came by the apartment, but he didn't buzz them up, so he doesn't know who it was (though he suspects that it was sweet Lucinda; what befell the bundle of eucalyptus she surely brought with her?).

No one will find out. A feeling of peace descends upon Mark every time he reminds himself of this. Not until Adrian invites them to the funeral, anyway. Will his friends have stopped wondering about him before that happens? Is Mark memorable? To his relief, the mystery is his forever.

As well as he's planned for the future, Mark does worry about Adrian and George. Money is no object, but the world cannot be bought. He can't keep them safe when he's gone.

I'm dying. Mark says it aloud, admitting the truth to his sleeping boys. *I'm dying, too.*

The words leave the air like popped balloons. All Mark can hear is his breath, and Adrian's. Though he can't hear George's purr, he feels it at the foot of the bed, with his own foot. They'll have each other after. Will that be enough?

------------◇------------

It was with some dubiousness that Mark watched the girl follow his young new friend upstairs. She had long, dark hair and a leather purse on her shoulder. Adrian's approach to the world, or what Mark had seen of it by that point in their relationship, was as shocking as it was simple. But it was something, wasn't it? A puzzle, a distraction, a diversion. Sometimes it struck Mark as a little sad, this gay approach to a straight life; beauty was always isolating, but homosexuals had an appreciation for it that the others, he suspected, did not. At any rate, Adrian seemed happy. In the beginning, as in the end, this was all that mattered to Mark.

Halfway to the second-floor landing, Adrian reached behind him, without looking, to give the girl his hand. Like a relay racer ready for the baton, she took it. Adrian was dressed like a waiter in an '80s movie; the girl was clad in structured black, her legs bare above platform shoes. They went onward together, limbs moving in tandem, ascending to heaven on off-white stair runners. Mark glanced around to see who else had noticed them, the silty tang of watermelon and feta on his tongue.

Um, so how did that happen? Tyree was nodding toward the staircase. He meant Adrian. Mark had already discovered that ribbing was a common response from those who laid eyes on his new friend. It was a softer, more polite manner of acknowledging what they thought of as his trophy.

Mark smiled. *Just lucky, I guess.* He didn't correct the assumptions unless he had to. After Arturo, people had begun looking at him with an atomizing pity. All they saw was the negative image of his lover floating in his place, like a hologram. But when he met Adrian, this changed. He became the object of more comfortable affects: bewilderment and envy, or at least a new kind of pity, one reserved for a silly old man being used for everything except his body. Mark would have given anything to resent their condescension, as he surely would have before Arturo died. He would have to settle for the misdirection of his friend's astounding beauty.

The party tittered on. Tyree and Tamara were whispering about an up-and-coming model cum dancer who had been booked to pose nude in an alcove for the duration of the evening. The brownstone was at capacity with the illustrious, the famous, and the well-connected, none of whom Adrian would have recognized. Yet Mark had suspected that this proximity would help maintain his new friend's consideration, which was why he had invited him. It was clear that, as oblivious to social climbing as Adrian appeared to be, he was quite comfortable in such rarified company. Mark was impressed by this.

Because it was a talent, the way Adrian could remain at his side or loiter nearby, sipping something while Mark made small talk, as if his network, as Derek called it—colleagues and acquaintances and hangers-on and influencers—weren't nervously eyeing his paper straw, its suction suggestive and flattering, bringing his cheekbones to punctuated advantage. It was a talent, too, that Adrian knew precisely when to cut the cord, as happened when, after a particularly forceful slurp, a cloud of bubbles went down too fast and his eyes took on a heartbreakingly lachrymose radiance. Someone gasped; Mark saw Tyree's hand fly to his throat, the old queen. As if on cue, Adrian handed Mark his emptied glass, leaned as if to whisper in his ear, said nothing, and disappeared.

Adrian

The medical assistant closes the door behind her. Adrian is wearing a mask, which is why, he tells himself, she looked directly at him only once between reception and this big, oval room.

Dr. Pollari's office hasn't changed since he was here four years ago, when Mark brought him along for an appointment. The fist-size paperweight, a bloody prism, is still there on the desk. The window's expensive view of Central Park, bounding in the wind, continues to stretch the length of the room. The certifications framed on the wall behind the mid-century desk—summa cum laude at Harvard and honors from Columbia—are as impressive as ever.

It wasn't two weeks after that appointment that Mark had helped Adrian file a police report with Dr. Pollari's name on it. It was a perfect autumn day, crisp and spiced and cloudy, but Mark was brusque, his temper short and his shoulders hard. It was a side of him that Adrian had never seen before, though he had known it would come, sooner or later: situations like the one with Dr. Pollari were rites of passage for Adrian's friends. Few came far enough to witness the ugliness that Adrian could provoke in his more insistent *friends*. Even fewer were able to withstand it in return for Adrian's companionship.

Thankfully, that police report had been the end of things with Dr. Pollari. With the damage amounting to little more than a broken car window and some arson threats, he hadn't really been all that bad. Though he and Mark never talked about it afterward, Adrian believed the whole affair had brought them closer together.

Adrian leans forward to pick up a framed photo from the desk. Dr. Pollari, wide-mouthed and beachy, wrapped one arm around a skinny woman whose best adjective was a tie between *stoic* and *resigned*. The other arm ensnared two snub-nosed children, of inconsequential genders, under the age of ten. Scraped knees and forced smiles, like a commercial for laundry detergent. Adrian tapped the glass with a fingernail, rotating it in the light to catch sight of his gauzy fringe, his right ear. Those eight eyes had witnessed hundreds of appointments, where some patients were congratulated with good test results and others learned that their end was nigh. They had been there when Adrian walked into Dr. Pollari's office the first time, watching as the doctor forgot to finish his sentence.

Mark had moved fast. With Adrian, he knew it was best to rush through introductions. *This is Adrian*, he said, offering up his friend. *Adrian, Dr. Pollari.*

Dr. Pollari had extended his hand with aching slowness. Another person in Adrian's position may have extended their own hand farther than was comfortable rather than wait for Dr. Pollari to close the gap between them, but Adrian waited patiently. *Very nice*, said Dr. Pollari. Adrian didn't say anything.

Adrian sets down the photo and touches the gold chain beneath his collar, warm against his skin. Over the years, he has learned how to ignore his racing pulse and stomachache. Not ignore—accept. Everything happens to Adrian's body, not to Adrian. If there's one thing he knows about his *friends*, it's that holding grudges against them is not only painful but useless. Expectations only lead to disappointment, and he is far too practical, and far too experienced, to allow himself to be disappointed. He is able to grant each *friend* a clean slate with every new encounter because there's no other way to do it. Which isn't to say that he's regularly seeking new encounters with old *friends*, especially the ones like Dr. Pollari. But this is a special circumstance. Adrian has much bigger problems than the potential for a little vandalism.

As the door behind him opens, Adrian can feel himself rejoining his body. His vital signs slow, slow, slow while *it* rises to its highest frequency with contrapuntal velocity. He's here now. In contrast with his heart's torpor, he senses Dr. Pollari's begin to race; against his steady respiration, he hears Dr. Pollari's quickening, his breath so high in his throat that it echoes against the rounded walls.

Adrian turns to find Dr. Pollari still standing in the doorway, left hand on the doorknob, a Gucci timepiece on his wrist and corrective lenses over the bridge of his nose. The fly of his khakis bulges powerfully. Adrian doesn't need glasses to see each of the doctor's follicles, pores, and freckles. The part in his hair gleams like the skyline, wet with sun.

All Dr. Pollari sees is Adrian. *Well,* he says.

Hi, says Adrian.

From beneath Dr. Pollari's mask, the little sound of pursing lips precedes an abrupt silence. The first time they met, Dr. Pollari had demanded informality. *Please, call me Alex.* Mark had obeyed. Adrian had not.

Back then, four years ago, no one was wearing a mask. Today both of them are. Adrian wonders if Dr. Pollari would have recognized him if he had arrived unannounced. But that's what he's here to find out, isn't he?

Correct me if I'm wrong, says Dr. Pollari, taking a step toward him, *but doesn't this violate the terms of our agreement? Am I going to get in trouble?* The creases of a smile rise above his N95.

Adrian doesn't know. *I need your help.* He doesn't care, either.

My help?

The day Adrian met Dr. Pollari, Mark was there to receive results from a presymptomatic genetic test that he'd undergone as part of a panel extended to the clinic's more affluent clients. The Kokoschka 3000 indicated that Mark might have been predisposed to a few rare, but serious, multifactorial illnesses, Dr. Pollari explained. The possibility of developing these illnesses became more likely with age, but the doctor seemed confident that this would not happen to Mark.

I wouldn't worry too much, Dr. Pollari said, smiling encouragingly. *It's my job to keep an eye on these things. But you're very healthy, and you take good care of yourself.*

Adrian could feel Mark relaxing, as he did when George got in bed with them in the morning. He could also feel the weight of

Dr. Pollari's attention, as if George was curling up on his own chest.

When it was time to leave, Dr. Pollari came around the desk. His hand was firmer and even more insistent than before. In the elevator, Adrian received a message from an unknown sender. *I'd love to get to know you*, it said, the conditional tense undermined by the suitor's confidence.

Adrian never figured out how Dr. Pollari got his number, but it didn't matter. No pretext was needed for their second meeting, though Adrian was surprised to be invited back to the office later that evening instead of to a four-star hotel room or Midtown bachelor pad. Not that it mattered to him. He accompanied Mark home, then returned to his own apartment, where he showered and shaved in the hottest water he could tolerate before returning to the city.

If Cora or Mary had asked him about his time with Dr. Pollari, Adrian would have said, *It was fine.* This was true, although he didn't enjoy any of it, or hardly any of it. Of course, trysts with *friends* almost always had their moments. Like when Dr. Pollari put his nose, long and thin-skinned, to Adrian's throat for a deep and fervent huff. *Like flowers to me*, he whispered. Adrian suppressed a giggle but matched his smile, ignoring the cold of the mid-century desk on his bare skin, which screamed but didn't budge against their weight. Over Dr. Pollari's shoulder, the ultraviolet city, overtaken by night and wanting, was coming to its senses after the afternoon's rose-gold repose. He suddenly, desperately, wanted to be back in the depths of Manhattan, his body oxidizing with its iron and steel. But he stayed in Dr. Pollari's office for a while longer, for the contrast, and to be agreeable, and because he wanted to see if there was something on the other side of the doctor's smile. By moonrise, he had given up on finding it.

At midnight, Adrian received another text. *I want more. Come back?* But he had already forgotten his hour with Dr. Pollari. He was killing time on the ferry before a techno thing with Mary in Bushwick. Bored but luxuriating in the lunate humidity, he peered through the spray-painted windows as Manhattan passed by on its treadmill, the streets of Midtown hashmarked by avenues bright as open doors in a dark hall. He put his phone away without replying. He wouldn't have answered even if he had enjoyed their time together. For Adrian, that's how it was with men.

The next morning, he received a long, rambling email from Dr. Pollari's work account. Easy enough to ignore. The morning after that, there was a longer email, unsigned and from a private address, though its author was obvious. The red flag began its ascent. More emails. On the fourth day, a phone call. On the fifth, a series of additional calls, each with an ominous voicemail trailing behind. The flag rose apace. A week after his appointment with Dr. Pollari, Mark began receiving menacing texts and emails, too, all from different addresses consisting of numbers and special characters, their threats growing more specific and violent as the night got later.

Some of his *friends* needed encouragement to move on when it was their time. Adrian didn't like the harsher measures—disappearing, blocking, pressure applied by *friends* in good standing—but he did not hesitate to take them when necessary. In the case of Dr. Pollari, the offender was discarded so successfully that by the following week Adrian could take the ferry again without losing another thought to the unlucky doctor.

Dr. Pollari is watching him, a puff of condensation fogging the Gucci lenses.

I do need your help, Adrian says. He reminds himself that it wasn't just Mark who was there for him when Dr. Pollari's *friendship* began to sour. There was Kathleen, a former prosecutor, and Sol, who ran a company that contracted bodyguards to celebrities and politicians. Both were *friends* from Adrian's early days in New York. Remembering his friends and *friends* keeps Adrian's heart as slow as it needs to be.

And what could someone like me possibly do for someone like you? Dr. Pollari's humility almost feels real.

You could tell me something, says Adrian.

And what is that?

If I look different.

Different?

Adrian doesn't want to influence Dr. Pollari's answer. *Different from before,* he says. *When we met. In any way at all.*

Beneath his mask, Dr. Pollari is smiling just like he does on the social media accounts Adrian scrolled through last night. He does so easily and photogenically, although the doctor considers himself a serious man, an observer and philosopher of human behavior. (This, as he tried to explain in his emails, is what Adrian doesn't understand about the two of them: that they share a profound similarity rooted in their separateness from other people, from which an intimacy could spring, if only Adrian would permit it.) When Dr. Pollari speaks to another person—whether that person is his office manager, his wife, or the clerk who sells him wintergreen gum at the kiosk on the ground floor—his face is like it is on Instagram, a portrait of a happy man. The moment the other person looks away, it returns to a natural stillness whose only human witness, in all fifty-three years of Dr. Pollari's life, has been Adrian.

It's been a long time, Dr. Pollari concedes. The thumb and index finger of his right hand slide across each other too slowly to qualify as fidgeting.

You don't remember what I looked like before? Adrian counts his fingers without moving them, over and over.

Oh, I do.

When he laughs, Adrian startles, but then he laughs with him.

All right. The laughter suddenly ends. Dr. Pollari adopts a pose of sardonic scrutiny, his arms crossed over his white jacket. Lenses and watch flash. *Show me. I want to help.*

You do?

With a tip of his head, the irony bleeds away. His voice softens. *I really do, Adrian. Water under the bridge.*

Now? He's beginning to feel lightheaded. It has to happen before he loses his nerve.

Dr. Pollari settles into his chair. Rubs his hands across his khakis.

Redistributes his weight to the armrests, which creak as they bear up against his large, turgid body. *Show me*, he says.

Adrian stands up and reaches behind his ears. Until he was thirteen or so, Grandma made all of his Halloween costumes. At the end of each September, she would ask what he wanted to be this year. He would hold still for the casting of his plaster mask and submit to her painstaking tailoring, and one morning near the end of the month an ingenious new kit would be waiting for him, laid out on the dining table. Everything Grandma made was always a hundred times cleverer than Estela's Grapes. One year he was a ninja with throwing stars made from aluminum foil, the next a masked serial killer dripping with cornstarch blood, the next a jolly hunchback deformed by papier-mâché. When the holiday was over, Adrian liked to wear the plaster masks around the house, watching soccer with dad as a leering Richard Nixon or folding laundry with Auntie Rachel as a red-eyed ghost. He found it relaxing and sensed that his family did, too. He kept the masks, their edges crumbling, until they no longer fit his face.

When Adrian looks up, Dr. Pollari's mask is gone, too. His bare face matches the one in the photograph, though it's missing the smile, conveying emotions that Adrian can't identify. They size each other up, as if for combat. Neither Dr. Pollari nor Adrian had seen Mark's expression as he watched them shake hands the day they met.

Dr. Pollari's fingers move to his chin. His brow wrinkles. *You have changed*, he says, nodding. He seems much taller than Adrian, though he's still sitting down. The day enters from behind him, bathing him in the same light that dapples the park and scours the skyscrapers. The world's bigness draws the office walls away from Adrian. His heart drops through the floor, plummeting all thirty-two stories. The air-conditioning is cold on his chin and cheeks, cooling as it rises to rifle his hair. He's become a pinprick in a few seconds flat.

We've all gotten older. Except for you, it seems, says Dr. Pollari. He squints. *But you do look different. You really do.*

What was Adrian expecting to hear? He's still pink from his walk (he doesn't wear SPF, unless Mark forces it on him at Riis). His shirt is rumpled with drying sweat, his collar is stretched like a popped bicycle tire. He's not used to feeling shabby. *Well,* he says, *I guess that answers my question.*

It doesn't, of course. What was he expecting? Something definitive. Something specific. Even something bad. There's no chance of that now.

Dr. Pollari shifts his hips in his chair. *Did I help you, Adrian?*

The sun that shadows Dr. Pollari's face spotlights his own, generous as a Polaroid. The magic of long lashes is not their opulence but the illusion they foster: by drawing the viewer's eye into the sclera, iris, and pupil, soft tissues hardened by the light, they make the entire organ look both empty and full at the same time.

Yes, says Adrian. *I needed to know from someone who hasn't seen me in a long time. Who isn't in my life anymore.* This last sentence is delivered with an almost unnoticeable emphasis.

I'm glad, says Dr. Pollari. He smiles. *Can I ask you for a favor now?*

One of the reasons Adrian loves women as much as he does is that they expect so much less from him than men do. Both genders desire just as deeply, just as madly, in his experience, but he's found that men are less likely to question themselves long enough for doubt to take root. He can see why some people might be drawn to this quality—for its thrilling entitlement, its brutish force—but it doesn't excite him, any more than an avalanche would for its incidental power.

Okay, he says. *Sure.*

It's not until he's back on the sidewalk that his shoulders relax again. The security guard to his left looks studiously in the other direction. To his right, the lady selling Ziploc bags of tajín-dusted mango counts her change. The details of Dr. Pollari's request were not unspeakable, but neither were they remarkable. Adrian closes his eyes and slows his breathing until he can no longer hear his heart. He reminds himself that he will never come back here, and this slows it more.

He starts for the train station. Despite Dr. Pollari's willingness to cooperate, his question is still unanswered. What now? Well, he won't give up. He'll find someone else to ask. He thinks about the many *friends* he's had over the years, displeased with how difficult it is to summon one up in particular without first returning to a time or place. There are so many—how can he decide?

A rat streaks for the sewer grating, keeping pace with Adrian's stride. A crow flies overhead, a glittering vape cartridge in its beak. Dr. Pollari was right about one thing: what's happening to him has nothing to do with his appearance. Like *it*, this change can't be stopped by sunglasses, plastic surgery, a new diet, an infusion of cash. Rather than draw people in, like *it*, it's doing nothing at all. It's an absence, and it's growing.

Though he doesn't know where he's going, Adrian takes the stairs underground two at a time.

———————◇———————

On the VCR/TV, a woman draped like Salome dances in the foreground. Behind her, an alcazar stretches black against the dunes blurred by the setting sun. Her husband is dead and her lover's army is advancing. Adrian thinks Mark is finally asleep.

He had planned to stay the night, but he's feeling restless. He doesn't want to kill time in bed until Mark wakes up, sick again. He doesn't bother to pause the movie. It's pretty boring, not a lot of talking. Shot in black and white, too, which Adrian isn't a big fan of. He can't tell anyone apart, and he missed the title, *The Four Horsemen of Arabia*, which Mark will write on the side of the tape tomorrow. He glances up to see the camera pan to a dusty regiment of soldiers marching under a cluster of Joshua trees.

There are several apps he can choose from. As ever, he would prefer a woman, but at this hour a man is just easier. He turns off his notifications so he doesn't disturb Mark and responds to the first message he receives, pursuing it to its conclusion while ignoring the flood of dick pics that immediately come pouring in. The man has a wide face and a welcoming potbelly. His height is, theoretically, five foot eleven. He sends a photo of his cock, long, dark, and circumcised, squeezed into an erection by a slender band of silicone. Adrian doesn't have to send anything. They arrange to meet right away.

Adrian tiptoes down the hall and leaves his wallet on the side table by the front door—this way, it will be harder not to come back. He usually prefers to go home afterward, but he promised Mark he would be there in the morning.

The windows of the Dodge Ram are blacked out, the wheels slightly deflated. The man is older than he was in his photos but as tall as his profile claims, and he smells good, too: vetiver, tobacco, bergamot. They don't drive long before the man pulls over.

There's a long fence against the road. Behind it lies Green-Wood Cemetery, greener now that it's summer, even in the darkness. Adrian cracks the window and sniffs, the air hot and wet in his nose. There are lights on the road, but the cemetery isn't well lit; on this block, there aren't any storefronts that need protection from burglary. The moon will oversee him and his new *friend*.

As he unbuckles his seat belt, *it* stirs in his ribs. Adrian is excited. *I bet we can get inside*, he says. He's done things in cemeteries before, but not in New York. He looks at his date expectantly. Men will follow him anywhere.

But the man's seat belt is still fastened. He's peering through Adrian's window, making a face at the spears of fieldstone and polished slate. When he scratches his cheek, Adrian can hear his stubble.

I thought you said you wanted carplay, says the man.

Adrian is almost aghast. He can feel *it*, so why can't his *friend*? He fumbles for something to say. *Don't you think it would be fun?* He's not good at being convincing. He's never needed to be.

In there? He scoffs. *I think you need therapy, man.*

⬩

Adrian awakens to Mark's bathroom sounds. The windows have just begun to glow, which means he's been asleep for only a few hours. When the toilet lid slams shut, George's frilled ears twist to catch the sound.

Adrian opens his Contacts list and begins to scroll. A therapist, like the man said. He surely has dozens among his *friends*, but which one? And where? It's not as if he was ever in the habit of including anyone's advanced credentials after their name. They're all in here together, psychologists and psychiatrists (what's the difference again?), counselors, health coaches, spirit guides. The people who feed you peyote in the desert and solemnly observe as you trip balls. The people who boof you with ketamine and talk you through your dissociation. Evangelists of CBT, DBT, ABA, DMT, MDMA, etc. He scrolls slowly, bleary from sleep, waiting for a sign.

It comes to him like a feather landing in his hair: Lola. He hasn't seen her since before he met Mark. He scrolls to the name—she's one of four, in fact—the one she asked all her clients to refer to her by. He remembers thinking that this was unprofessional. *Lola* was too sexy for mental healthcare. Two of the other Lolas have a surname, but the one he's seeking does not. Lola suited her back then. Would it now? They will both be passing judgment, he knows, if she's willing to see him.

Adrian sends Lola a text and sets his phone on the nightstand. George stirs and stretches his body slender. His paw comes to rest on top of Adrian's wrist. The cat grins, begins to purr. His nails protract slightly, clinging to Adrian's skin. Adrian lies there, wanting to fall asleep again but unwilling to move the little paw.

In the bathroom, Mark is talking to himself.

Please. Lola gestures to the overstuffed chair across from her own. Adrian sits, keeping his posture straight. After what happened with Dr. Pollari, he wants things to be as formal as possible. When he called, he asked that she wear a mask, and she readily agreed.

The room is silent except for the pleasant murmurs of her desktop fountain. To his surprise, *it* has been activated—when exactly that occurred, Adrian isn't quite sure—and now it hovers between them at one of its lowest registers.

It's nice to see you, says Lola. Based on the contours of her face, her hidden smile appears to be genuine.

Thank you, says Adrian. Lola still smells like sandalwood, sage, and patchouli. Her office is Spartan yet disorganized: there is a store-brand box of tissues, framed flower prints, a few books on attachment theory, a half-melted candle, too many phone chargers. Having seen her rates online, Adrian had expected leather and jade and a fancy humidifier, perhaps an anteroom overseen by a fresh-faced girl with poorly spaced tattoos. But he's been to Lola's apartment. Why should her office come as a surprise?

Adrian and Lola met at a housewarming in Prospect-Lefferts. He and Mary had only just arrived when his friend seized his elbow, using her other hand to cover the right side of her face, as if half-blinkering a nervous horse.

Oh god, Mary hissed. *My therapist is here.*

Adrian followed her into the kitchen. *Now what?* He was desperate to peek around the corner. He had never been to therapy before.

Mary rifled through the bar cart. *We have to pretend like we don't know each other, I guess.*

It didn't seem like such a big deal to Adrian, but Mary's jawline had gone red, a rare sign of unease in a person as self-assured as she was dramatic. His heart melted for her. What shameful secrets had she confessed to this therapist? She yanked open the freezer and frantically scooped ice into a glass.

He wanted to touch her cheek, but instead he told her to wait. There weren't many people in the living room, so he zeroed in on the therapist's swarm of curls right away. As if on cue, she turned toward him. He cranked *it*. After a moment of stricken hesitation, she returned his smile, clutching her drink to her chest. Like everyone else at the housewarming, she had seen Adrian the moment he arrived. She was captured by his eyes, the heaviest features in his deer-fine face.

At Adrian's beckoning, Lola followed him down the hall, where they made their French exit on rushed feet, socks wrinkled in the sockets of their boots. He told her he liked her dress—cream with lilac roses, an old-fashioned pattern with a cutting-edge hem—although he didn't at all, actually. Going downstairs, he took her hand, gripping hard at her meek efforts to pull away. He was excited by their shared ambivalence: he was forcing himself on her, as heterosexual men were supposed to, as an act of loyalty to Mary. With his free hand, he texted his friend that he'd catch up with her later. She hearted the message.

A few blocks from the housewarming, Lola went into a liquor store for a pint of whiskey. Adrian took sips when she offered, but she kept most of it for herself. They walked for a long time, talking about her, or attempting to. Every time he asked a question, she would ruthlessly direct it back to him. It was clear she would have to be drawn out.

You're kind of private, aren't you? said Adrian. He was keeping an eye on the bottle.

I guess I have to be, said Lola. In her line of work, she explained, good boundaries were a matter of professionalism and of the well-being of her patients. The bottle was nearly empty, but she spoke as clearly as when she had introduced herself. *Lately*, she said, *I've started to wonder if I do what I do because I like that distance*. He could see her breath.

She lived on the edge of Fort Greene. As far as they had walked, Adrian didn't think she would ask him upstairs. But around the corner from her place, she bought a bouquet of pink Persian buttercups at the all-night deli and placed it in his arms so she could unlock the door.

The kitchen table was a mess: a coffee mug of clear liquid, two amber prescription medicine bottles, a ball of twine, black nail polish, a one-by-one-inch baggie of powder, a Bluetooth speaker with a loose screen, a book of postage stamps (two flavors: "Statue of Liberty" and "In Loving Memory of Great American Dancer and Performer Gregory Hines"), spare change in three different currencies. He set the flowers on the table, where a petal touched a peso. He leaned against the wall to remove his boots and pull up his socks—black, crew, limp from wear.

I only have water, said Lola, clearing yellow curls from her face. She opened the fridge to show him.

Though Adrian didn't like to lie, he didn't mind when others lied to him. They had their reasons, as he had his. *Water's good.*

Lola went to her neatly made bed in the corner, and Adrian followed her with their glasses of water, which he set on the floor. She picked a playlist on her phone. The first song was treacly pop, coming from the broken speaker with a layer of fuzz. The next one wasn't much better. By the third, it was too late to turn it off. Lola didn't pull down the comforter. After a while he was looking up at her, watching her move, holding her hips like he didn't care if they got away.

Lola's hair is different now. Her curls are longer and more relaxed. The yellow has become an expensive bronze.

God, Adrian, she says. Her hands still hardly move when she speaks. *It's been so—*

I have to ask you something.

After deliberating about the best way to explain the situation, Adrian has decided to be fast and blunt. He doesn't want to give this old *friend* too much time to think. That's where things went wrong with Dr. Pollari, he believes. It's for this reason that he didn't tell her anything over the phone, only that he needed to see her at her office as soon as possible. No apologies, no small talk, no hints. Certainly no explanation for why he'd suddenly shown up again, after all this time.

What is it? Lola asks. *Is everything all right?*

I'm worried that people can't see me anymore.

Lola raises an eyebrow. She changes gears surprisingly fast. *Well, I can see you*, she says. She speaks in the same tone of voice as she did in her bed: adroit yet comfortingly monotone.

That's not what I mean, says Adrian. *It* is still there, flickering like a broken TV, but stronger now, and getting stronger.

Lola tents her fingers. *Can you say more?*

Adrian thinks about Mark, who knows almost nothing about him that hasn't happened in his presence. There are the broadest of strokes about his family and their deaths, his move to New York, his life among his *friends* and friends, but little else. Telling Lola what's been happening to him since everyone stopped wearing their masks would require sharing information not even Mark is privy to. It doesn't feel right. He wonders if he can get what he wants without saying too much.

Since the pandemic, he says, *people have been looking at me differently. Like they don't see me the same way as before.* He makes himself laugh to show Lola that he recognizes how absurd he sounds. *I guess it kind of feels like I'm disappearing.*

Lola's fingers remain tented. Her sensible flats tap rhythmically against the hardwood. *It* throbs.

Nothing like this has ever happened to me before, Adrian goes on. *So I guess I need to find out what's going on. Because it's all in my head. Right?*

Lola nods, but not in agreement. *Can we try something?* she says.

Sure.

Lola goes to her desk and slides something out from the back of a drawer: a plastic hand mirror. There is a brief unpleasantness in Adrian's right eye as it catches the sunlight. Grandma had one just like that, he remembers.

This is an exercise I do with some of my clients, Lola says, motioning for him to stand up. Adrian doesn't flinch when she places her hand on his hip to get into position behind him; he's an inch or two taller. When she lifts the mirror, their eyes align in the glass, their curls distinguished only by their color. *Now, tell me what you see.*

Though Lola's bed had looked cheap, it was surprisingly comfortable. When she asked if he would see her again, Adrian rolled off the mattress, his feet kicking over the glasses on the floor. Neither broke, but water everywhere. *Do you have a towel?* he asked. When she emerged from the bathroom with one, he was dressed again, pulling on his boots.

Mary's apartment wasn't far, but his damp socks were catching up with him. By the time he got there, a blister had formed on his left heel. He hadn't texted or called, expecting her to be asleep, but there was a light in the second-floor window. A shadow lifted its hands like a supplicant. His friend answered the door in her bathrobe and led him to the kitchen, where her microwave curry was almost ready. Her face was shiny, as if she had just finished her nightly skincare routine. He checked the time. It was almost three.

So what happened? Mary's eyes were glued to the humming box above her head. Once, when they were both very drunk, she had told him that she'd never stopped believing in the faith her parents had raised her in. Theirs was a cruel and unforgiving god, which was why she didn't like to burden her friends with him. But she still couldn't shake it, no matter how much therapy she did. *Hell,* she had said, flushing from the throat, *isn't for being bad, but for not being good enough.*

I don't know, said Adrian. He had thought that Mary would be grateful that he had gotten Lola away from the housewarming. That she would find it all very funny.

Well. Kendra's was a bust, anyway. After you left, I came back here and fell asleep. Just woke up for some reason. Usually I sleep all night.

The microwave made a noise like a tropical bird. Mary pushed some buttons and it started humming again. In the hallway behind them, a stream of R&B flowed lazily from her bedroom. On the wall next to it was a long, streaky mirror. Adrian could see his hair, his face, his body, his arms and legs. All of himself, except for his stocking feet. When the microwave stopped again, Mary stood on her tiptoes. In the mirror, all he could see of her was the fuzzy back of her dad's old bathrobe, and, when she lifted it for balance, the grimy bottom of her naked foot.

Adrian peers into Lola's hand mirror. *I don't know what I see*, he says.

Do you see yourself? Lola gently shakes the hand mirror.

Of course, says Adrian, irritated. The morning after the housewarming, he had texted Lola back, but he stopped responding after a day or two. He suspected that she wasn't the type of *friend* to push it, and he was right. After that, he never heard from her again.

You're wearing a mask, Lola points out.

So are you.

Lola's eyebrow jumps again, as if she knows something he doesn't. *We could take them off.*

Okay.

The hand mirror dips downward as they bare their faces. Echoing each other's movements, as if removing clothes before getting in bed together. She still smells like patchouli, but now that his mask is off, there's sweet tuberose, too. She lifts the hand mirror again and they look together. He thinks of her in bed, her body above his, her hands tracing his chest.

The mirror flashes. Adrian sees a few crow's feet and a new stud through her right nostril. Otherwise, her face is the same as he remembers. The afternoon shines on her teeth, bright against her brown skin. Her lips are still red. He's so close he can see the blood vessels in her eyes, but he can't understand her expression.

Lola repeats herself. *Do you see your face?*

Do you?

Yes, Lola says. *But that's not the point of the exercise.*

Mark

As Adrian closes the bedroom door behind him, Mark awakens. He tries to call after him, but his voice catches in his throat. Now the room is dark and he is alone.

He needs to pee again. Where is Adrian going? Will he be back? He reaches for the pills. Still there. He reaches for his phone. 6:33 p.m. on July 11, 2021. He doesn't know when he fell asleep.

The honey never really goes away now. Being awake means feeling it worm its way to the limit of every last arteriole, lighting up even the dead tissues—the hair, the fingernails—that shouldn't feel anything at all. Today it was most manageable in the morning, when he felt strong enough to putter around the apartment. He swept the kitchen floor around Adrian, who was slicing cucumbers for gazpacho. He did some yin yoga poses in the living room. He read the Sunday edition of the *Times*. COVID, Trump, climate collapse, an unidentified body dredged from the lake in Prospect Park—the mayor was demanding a greater police presence to prevent such tragedies. He remembered going to Central Park to cruise when he was younger, afraid of cops, afraid of getting mugged, afraid of getting sick. But he had done it anyway, forcing his legs to carry him over the little footpaths deeper into the trees. Were the other men afraid? When they touched him, he forgot his fear. It didn't return until he was back on the street again, glancing over his shoulder before pulling his ID and cash from his right shoe and putting it back in his pocket.

After noon, Mark began to feel his energy flagging and returned to his room. He counted the tapes stacked against the wall. Twenty-one down. He knelt and steadied his low, neat columns, making sure the lip of each tape was flush against the others. As he zipped the bag closed over the thirty remaining (the thirty-first, *Hot World*, waited for him against the wall, a little separate from the others), the exhaustion hit him like a train. With it came wretched waves of stomach cramps, a loosening of his muscles. He needed to go to the bathroom, but when he tried to stand, vertigo bowled him over and he lost his breath. Would he faint? He cried out for Adrian, who came right away.

After he helped him use the bathroom, Adrian took him back to bed. Mark was tired to the bone and the cramps hadn't abated, but at least the dizziness was gone. What would he do the next time this happened and Adrian wasn't home, just him and George, helpless together? *I'm okay*, he said.

I know, said Adrian. He pointed at the VCR/TV. *Do you want me to put one on?*

Mark shook his head. He wanted to sleep, and if he fell asleep during one of the movies, he would have to start it again from the beginning. Even though he enjoys some of them, his distaste increases with each finished film. They weigh on him, draining what little energy he has left. He needs to watch them, though he doesn't know why.

Mark heaves himself upward and feels for the floor with his bare feet. Where is George? Not in the bedroom, which smells unpleasant, close and contaminated with his own breath and farts and sleep. He stands up and finds he can walk all right. No dizziness, just pain. He goes slowly down the hallway, past the bathroom, where he glimpses the framed photo of himself with Lucinda, still raven-haired like Lydia Lunch, at his first show.

Adrian is sitting studiously at the dining table, his hands poised over the laptop. *Hey, you're awake.*

Mark can't help but smile. *Hey.* Sometimes he wishes that his friend wore glasses—they would make him look so cute—but of course he has perfect vision.

Adrian smiles back. He smiles only when he means it, which Mark loves about him. The impulse to kiss him moves through his body so swiftly that for an instant he believes it's the honey. But no, not everything is pain, even now. The next impulse, to paint Adrian, should feel better than the first, but it doesn't. Anyway, it's too late for that. And with this composition? Not to mention the light isn't even there for it. The window shades are drawn and the bulbs are hostile. But a painting is not about conditions, Mark has always believed; was it Cézanne who said that light does not exist?

What time is it? he asks.

You were asleep for a long time, Adrian says, glancing down at the screen. *That's good.*

I'm sorry. Were you planning to go somewhere? Mark can feel the drugs in his eyes. His back is killing him.

It's fine, says Adrian. *Are you hungry? There's gazpacho.*

Mark is nauseous, but he wants to say yes to his friend. Though the hallway stretches for a mile, he trudges back to his bed, where George awaits him on his pillow. He gently pushes him off and props himself up against the headboard. Adrian brings in the new tray and sets it on his lap. The bowl of gazpacho is garnished with mint and cilantro. There's also a glass of water, a half-empty bottle of red Gatorade, and more pills.

Mark scoops out the herbs before he takes a spoonful. The vinegar makes his eyes water. He sets down the spoon. He remembers how one day, near the end, Mom wept as he fed her. The summer afternoon was mysteriously overcast and he had been angry with Ruth—why, he no longer remembers. When the first tear rolled down Mom's cheek, he pulled the spoon from her mouth as if it were a knife.

Does it taste okay? Adrian asks anxiously.

Mark doesn't want to hurt his feelings so he nods, clearing his throat. *Will you put one on for me?* he asks, pointing at the VCR/TV.

Romantic strings, crashing waves, geometric fountains. An American businessman traveling in Morocco hires a prostitute. They make love all night, then share a plate of apricots on the roof of his hotel as they watch the sun rise. The businessman has fallen in love. He begs her to stay: a young widower, he knows how precious love is, and how simple. He is determined to take her back to America. *Kiss*, the woman says, but this appears to be the only English word she knows. When he kisses her, she says another word that sounds like *soodin*. When he tries to pronounce it, she laughs, and he laughs with her. It becomes a joke between them.

I know what I know, the businessman tells the sinister young colleague who's traveling with him. After a series of obstacles, including an attempt at blackmail by the colleague, who is angling for a promotion the businessman is up for, and a harrowing chase through the back alleys of Casablanca, he and the woman have a hasty wedding and board the ship to America. As they watch Rabat recede from their cabin, the businessman presses her hand to his chest. *Will you miss it?* he asks her. But of course the woman does not understand him. All she can do is smile. *Soodin,* she says, and he laughs, pulling her close.

When the ship wrecks, the businessman is found floating in a life raft not far from the Canary Islands. A violin escorts the camera away and into the waves, which shudder like heartbreak. No credits. The VCR/TV falls silent.

What was that one called? asks Adrian, sleepy. He's lying next to Mark. The tray is at the foot of the bed, the gazpacho almost completely untouched.

Will You Miss Me? says Mark.

Adrian

Adrian doesn't expect to come across protests anymore, not like last summer. Most of the actions stopped during the first long COVID winter. He's a few bus stops down Washington, however, when a fleet of banner-bearing cyclists overtakes him, a block's worth blazing north to Barclays on a honking headwind of righteous indignation.

When the last Bianchi has passed, Adrian turns to cross the street, then turns again. Most of Underhill between Prospect Park and Atlantic was cordoned off for pedestrians last year, and now its sumptuous avenue-fatness has acquired the stateliness of an old botanical garden. The day's storm has already come and gone, lancing the afternoon's barometric bubble, leaving behind wet pavement and a lazy wind that stirs the sparkling trash.

Though he has an appointment to make, Adrian strolls at the ponderous pace of small-dog owners. He is thinking about women, but the only people on Underhill are otherwise. There is a streetweared pair of boys gazing into their phones, masks tenting on their wrists. There is a bearded man holding a child on his shoulders. *Teacher Barbara*, says the man, tipping up his head like a stargazer, *moved to*

Nashville during COVID. There is a person in overalls, and since Adrian can't tell what they are, he overlooks them as they do him, their shoulders passing within inches of each other.

Down on St. Marks, a woman meets a deliveryman on her stoop. She smiles at Adrian, but absently, before trudging back up the stairs. Through a window, he can see a gathering, a post-pandemic party of happy voices. There is a child's furious laughter and the sound of a metal spoon scraping a bowl. *Don't say it!* comes a voice, then the sound of shattered glass lost in hearty cheers. A plane's thunder cooks the air.

He checks the time. His appointment is in fifteen minutes.

Vonna saved my life, Cora told him. *My PTSD was so bad I was attacking my girlfriend in the middle of the night. Remember her? Victoria? She was going to break up with me. Vonna helped me with that. And then Victoria went and worked with her, on her vaginis-mus that she'd had since she was a teenager. It got completely bet-ter. Total size queen now. Vonna's the real deal.*

Adrian rings the buzzer for Healing Hands Brooklyn. He once read about a foreign country, he can't remember which, where residential buildings are doorless and it's customary to announce oneself by standing outside the entryway and making a noise. Something repetitive, like the first two bars of Betty Boop's calling card. When the buzzer goes off, he pushes inside.

The stairs are narrow and winding, like the helix of a medieval tower, lined with prints of abstracted nude women. The nudes embrace, dance in fields, eye each other across sunlit carpets fes-tooned with blocky flowers. Their bodies are sinuous, but their faces are sketched in short, brutal slashes, expressive but ugly. Adrian thinks of *The Gargoyles*.

On the second-floor landing, he opens the door and steps inside. Behind a desk, the receptionist, a middle-aged woman in butter-colored linen, is staring down at her phone.

Hi, says Adrian.

The receptionist doesn't look up.

He tries again, raising his voice. *Hey.*

The receptionist sniffs and rubs her upper lip, her mouth hanging open over the screen. She's not wearing earbuds. Adrian steps closer to the table and waves his hand through her line of sight. The receptionist, comfortably seated in an ergonomic chair, doesn't notice. Above her head is a placard that says *Please respect this quiet space*, with an illustration of an index finger held against purple lips.

There's a card holder next to her hand. Adrian tips it over, spilling the squares of plastic onto the glass desk. The receptionist jumps in her chair.

I'm sorry, Adrian says as she rushes to collect the cards.

Oh, god, what a mess, she says good-naturedly, as if she knocked them over herself. *You're our 3:30, right?* She leans back to look at her screen.

That's me.

And have you been to Healing Hands Brooklyn before?

No. Her eyes have transitioned from her phone to her computer. *It* is at a low ebb, but *it's* there. Through an open door behind her, he can see a small room with a massage table. Though he's uninterested in the receptionist, he decides to try. He raises his eyebrows, inclining his head suggestively.

The receptionist grins and leans toward him over her desk, as if joining him in an exciting secret. *You're so lucky to have gotten Vonna for your first time,* she whispers. *A lot of people have to wait, you know. Some of them never get to see her.* She can't feel *it,* he understands, any more than she could see him when he came into the office.

Adrian has already met Vonna, who had dropped into the adjoining seat at a matinee screening of *The Conformist* just as the lights went down. Cora had gotten their tickets, but at the last minute, something—Adrian can't remember what—had happened, and he had to watch this foreign film, with its shadows and stabbings, by himself. From the opening scene, he could feel the person beside him undulating with emotion, though he himself was mostly bored. The lights came on again to reveal a plain woman with fascinating clothes and a penetrating gaze. *I could feel you next to me the whole time,* she told him, recoiling a silk Hermès scarf around her throat.

At the bar, still almost empty, Vonna told Adrian that people often overlooked her until they were close enough to feel her energy. Then they understood her power. That was the word she used— *power.* Like *it,* Vonna's appeal was a gravitational field, drawing people in while holding them at bay. Adrian was unmoored. As a woman, Vonna compelled him; as an acupuncturist, she disturbed him. She was one of the few people that he had ever brought back to his apartment; he was afraid she would have needles at her place, waiting for him.

But it's a beautiful experience, Vonna exclaimed when he confessed his phobia. He was nursing a beer while she abstained from alcohol, preferring water with bitters, no ice (cold fluids disrupt the digestion, she said). *For both the acupuncturist and the patient. I mean it! Profoundly physical. When you push the needle in, it makes contact with the nerve. It hurts, just a little bit. Not enough for you to suffer, but enough to let your body know it's time to heal.*

Adrian didn't even want to hear about it. *I don't get it,* he said, shuddering.

Vonna grinned. *You don't need to for it to work.*

Vonna prefers what she calls an active consult, says the receptionist as she scans Mark's credit card. *She likes to feel people out.* She points to a door behind him. *Go in there, remove everything except your underwear, and get face down on the table. Please keep your mask on. She'll be in shortly.*

Adrian leaves the door ajar as he strips. He arranges his things in a neat pile before stowing his shoes under the table. The dim room is at a comfortable temperature, but sweat coats his skin. He lies down on his belly. The door is behind him, at his feet. He feels his sweat collecting on the paper stretched across the vinyl. Not so long ago, the receptionist would have come into the room and removed her A-line skirt without him even having to suggest it. His throat constricting, he gets up to peer through the crack in the door. Her face is hidden by her computer, her shoulders slumped in relaxation. He reminds himself of why he's here: in exchange for offering himself up as a new patient, he will learn if Vonna remembers him and, if he's lucky, what is happening to him.

Adrian lies back down again, closes his eyes, and attempts to relax. He puts away notions of leaving, of going back to Mark's to hide under the covers with George. He anticipates the sensation of a needle piercing his skin and forces himself to smile, as if teaching his body to be unafraid. If he imagines it happening without actually *seeing* the needles, it's not so terrible. See, nothing to be scared of.

As Adrian's pulse begins to recede, so does *it*. His shoulders sink lower onto the paper. He knows that this is important. He doesn't want to disappear. (What does that even mean? It's not dying, is it?) He wants to remain as he's always been: beautiful. He wants his life back. He will have it, he tells himself. He will have everything he wants.

The door opens. There is the momentary click of the receptionist's keyboard before it closes, latching. The soft scratch of sandals on the tile. A throat clearing.

Adrian resolves to be brave. He won't have to look at Vonna's needles, he tells himself, and by then he'll have gotten what he came for. When the first alcohol swab glides across his skin, he jumps, then steels himself again. With patient swipes of her fingers, his exposed skin is cleaned, from the base of his skull to his Achilles tendon.

This is your first time. Vonna's voice is loud and, as Adrian remembers, a little shrill.

It is. Will she recognize his voice, too?

We'll review your medical history later, says Vonna. *This is my way of getting to know you. If anything hurts or bothers you, just let me know.*

It suddenly revs like an engine. His heart racing, he listens hard as she steps away to tinker with a metal tray attached to a cart. What's happening?

Oh, says Vonna, so low he wonders if he imagined it.

He can feel her moving, hear her rattling the tray. Now *it* courses through every inch of Adrian's body. He's trembling, dripping with sweat, when two fleshy pincers seize the back of his right thigh.

I don't know what to make of this. Vonna sounds as if she's thinking aloud, like a character in a play soliloquizing for the audience. *They won't go in.*

Go in?

Your skin. Your body.

It flares like fireworks over brackish water. Terrified as Adrian is, he is still more terrified to be sent away. *What if you tried it on my face?* He can come up with no logical reason for why she should, so he doesn't try to justify his suggestion.

Vonna doesn't reply, but at her hands' pressure, he rolls over, lifting his head out of the hole in the table. Now on his back, his mask loosens. She's wearing one, too. Her hair is greyer than it was before, and she is thinner than he remembers, but she is undeniably herself: the waxy brow, the striking cheekbones, the thick, sturdy arms. The fingers of her right hand are squeezed together as if holding a needle, though the room is so dim and the needle so small that he cannot see it.

Watch, says Vonna, lowering her fingers to his thigh.

Adrian feels like an overturned turtle. *No!* His sweat rolls off the edges of the table. *It* is going crazy. *I can't watch!*

Grimacing, Vonna withdraws the needle. *Just look at this then.* She brings it a few inches away from his eyes. It's bent, as if she tried to push it into brick. She pulls the tray closer to the table and Adrian sees that there are three other needles, a trio of fishhooks without any bait.

My face? Adrian attempts again. *Would that work?* He's electric. Before she can deny him, he takes off his mask, freeing the diamond around his nose to fresh air.

Vonna removes hers, too. She leans in close, as if his face were as small as her needles. They smell each other's breath. His heart hammers, his blood races. At her neckline, the lower half of her pale throat is changing. Like gourd flowers, the skin sunsets, a speckling effusion. Something about this betrayal of emotion makes Adrian feel brave, though she does not seem to recognize his face. He readies himself for what comes next.

Just hold still, says Vonna.

The needle appears to be coming right for his eyes. Vonna's face is out of focus, tight and growing. Adrian wants desperately to kiss it. He imagines Mark's face. He thinks about what he will make him for dinner tonight. He thinks about Arturo and his cookbook. He thinks about the view from the kitchen window in his apartment. Of the roses below, red as Vonna's breast. When the needle pierces his skin, he doesn't feel a thing.

It's working, Vonna whispers.

Though her lips continue to move, these are the last words that Adrian hears. The rest is lost under his blood, which hammers like a brace of stallions drawing a chariot. When Vonna withdraws her hand, it is empty. She reaches for the cart and comes back to Adrian, again and again, points of pressure across his face, throat, and chest lighting up and disappearing each time her hand approaches him. Her lips move, her throat undulates. Her eyebrows are unchanging.

Adrian's head grows heavier, but he is not in pain. He can't feel his breath. When the blood begins to move down his body, he realizes that *it* has vanished, entirely, completely, and for the first time in his life.

The blood unleashes in him a certain euphoria. He stands so that it can move through his entire body, spill downward, drench him down to his feet. It's happening. It's happening. Vonna is in the corner of his eye, moving her body, moving her hands, her lips still silent for him. Adrian doesn't know. The crown of thorns lifts his curls. The blood softens his hair.

When Adrian awakens, there is no blood. He is lying in Mark's bed. He turns his head to look. George is there. Mark is, too. Mark isn't breathing. As Adrian reaches for him, Mark's cheek twitches, and with a snore, he gasps, his eyes roving below their lids. Now Adrian can breathe. He drops his hand onto George's body and strokes it until purrs vibrate the spun-glass ribcage.

Rubbing his eyes, Adrian reaches for his phone and opens his Contacts. He scrolls all the way to the bottom, lower lip twisted in thought. There's no one named Vonna in there, or anywhere.

Mark

White text over a white ass in a gold thong tells him the movie is called *Hearts In Space*. The camera pulls out and pans over an indoor film set. There's a grimy twin mattress, and off in the corner a shower without a curtain or a tub. Around the set, people are adjusting lights and smoking cigarettes. Everyone is skinny as hell. Mustaches, mirrored trays, diegetic music that's heavy on the bass.

Mark sighs. He doesn't tend to enjoy films about the porn industry. They're all so depressing. If he had a choice, he would turn this one off. But he keeps watching.

The synths blossom, the lens is creamed with Vaseline. The performers, two lesbians, one of them wearing the gold thong, are between takes. They aren't just colleagues, but lovers, kissing and playing with each other's hair as they wait. Finally the cameras roll again, but not for long. The director, a ginger with an unlit cigar in his mouth, is unhappy with their performance and keeps shouting, *Cut!* He yells at the performers and the crew. A woman's voice comes through above the audio. *We can't act. We can only make love*, she says. *That's our problem.*

After another bad take, the lesbians are fired. They scream at the director together. One of them upends a garbage can. *Fucking junkies*, sneers a crew member. Another blows them scornful kisses.

Dressing themselves in trash, the lesbians go to a strip club on Polk Street, where they gyrate and kiss each other's necks on a big black dance floor. They go to the corner to get high and watch leathermen massage their crotches. Bikers nod on barstools, fags grind by the jukebox. One of the lesbians argues with a bouncer. They get kicked out. They walk for a long time and fall asleep behind a dumpster in an alleyway. When they wake up, they walk some more. They have adventures in the Mission and SoMa, quarreling everywhere and fucking where they can. Night and day follow each other, become each other. They ride in cars. They snowangel on the grey beach. They have eyes only for each other, and the headlights. The movie ends when they OD together on a rooftop, under the stars and Coit Tower. No credits.

Hearts In Space reminds Mark of a lesbian he used to know. Leticia wore cat-eye glasses without a prescription, with pink rhinestones in the corners. They met when he was drinking and she was using. She got clean, and then she got sober, and then she got HIV from a blood transfusion. He went to visit her a few times before she died in '87 or '88. A few months later, her lover returned to her ex-husband, who took care of her and her two children on the condition that Leticia's name was never mentioned.

Mark rarely thinks of Leticia anymore, though he always tears up when he does. Her memory prompts another: George as a squealing, suckling kitten. Arturo bottle-fed him in their bed, holding him to his warm skin, speaking softly over George's head. Now George is getting old, but not fast enough. Mark's soon-to-be dowager.

George awakens, making the same squeaks he once did for his bottle. As Mark reaches for him, the idea of throwing him out the bedroom window shreds his mind. George has no idea. He approaches Mark as he always has, with a baby's certainty. He takes him in his arms. Now the tears come.

⎯⎯⎯⎯⎯◇⎯⎯⎯⎯⎯

When Mark checks his email, there's one from Derek at the top of the pile. *REMINDER* says the subject line. Mark has a remote interview with a young up-and-coming artist slash activist for *The New York Times Magazine* scheduled for this afternoon.

I'm sure it's on your calendar, wrote Derek, *but things have been so hectic lately, I wanted to make sure.*

From inside the brief window of contentment that often follows his morning purge, Mark is annoyed. Honey at a dull roar, his belly half full with a soft egg and sugar-sweetened coffee, he becomes almost feisty. Something about going through with this interview while knowing it could be his last, all while Derek hasn't the faintest idea, promises a kind of satisfaction that he can't quite put his finger on. Drafting a terse confirmation, he chews up one of his big gummies and presses Send with aplomb.

⎯⎯⎯⎯⎯◇⎯⎯⎯⎯⎯

At 2:55 p.m., Mark is sitting at his desk in a clean collared shirt. He turns on his camera and examines himself on the screen. It's even crueler than the bathroom mirror. He looks thinner and older than he ought to, especially to someone like Derek, who doesn't know the extent of his illness. Degendered by his weight loss, he looks more like his sister than he has since puberty. But he has his alibi: in the span of a few months, his mother and sister died. Who wouldn't look like shit? Even if there's cause for suspicion, Derek still won't guess what's in store for Mark. How could he?

At 3:00 p.m., Mark clicks the link. Derek and a young woman with pink hair, her roots a tender brown, are waiting for him in their boxes.

Welcome, welcome. Ha ha, says Derek. *Mark's been pretty busy lately, so in the interest of his time, we can just get going right away.*

I'm so nervous, says the artist slash activist. *I've been such a fan since I was in high school.* Though she's speaking about him, Mark feels that she's mostly talking to Derek.

You'll be great, Derek tells her. His glasses are pristine.

Mark smiles, but then he notices the VCR/TV in the camera behind him. His smile falters. He resists the urge to turn the camera off. Derek and the artist slash activist are still talking. He recalls the gummy. He does his best to keep his face steady. Smiling and open and still.

The artist slash activist seems to have taken Derek at his word, talking much more quickly than any normal person would. *So Mark, for over thirty years, your work has long been associated with . . .*

Straining to keep up, Mark places both his hands on the desk in front of him. He considers asking her to speak louder, but he adjusts the volume instead. She still sounds muted.

. . . the liminal space between one pandemic and another . . .

He leans forward, anxiously trying to anticipate her question in its entirety.

. . . the uncertainty of queer futures conceived of as part of their strength, lending to their resilience in the face of . . .

The gummy is in full effect, Mark realizes. He's not sure why he took so much today. More than he usually does, even, when he has no one to talk to except Adrian. Derek's face is taking up too much of the screen. There is a noise in the apartment—George, doing something. Somewhere, a car backfires.

. . . so as a queer artist, is that something that's been on your mind?

Mark wasn't expecting this to go well, but he hadn't intended to embarrass himself like this. He tries to remember what he's heard, seeking a concept, a phrase, to latch onto. There's nothing.

Um. You know, I don't really know how to answer that.

The artist slash activist is silent for a few beats, as if waiting for him to continue. But Mark just sits, looking at the VCR/TV behind him on the screen. There's a tape inside it. He can feel its pregnancy.

Mark, says Derek. He's smiling with all his teeth. *Ha ha.*

Poor Derek. At least he's being honest, and isn't that what they want from him? The damage control on this one is going to be a real pain in the ass.

Let me try reframing it, interrupts the artist slash activist. *As an artist who came of age at the height of the AIDS crisis* . . .

Mark hunkers in his seat and furrows his brow in concentration. He wishes he had a pen or a pencil to take notes, to show how committed he is to listening.

. . . *and institutional failure, not to mention the economic effects on working artists* . . .

Alas, this one is getting away from him, too. Mark wonders if he would be able to understand her under normal circumstances. If he wasn't high and dying. He glares into the camera, seizing each word as it comes, then losing it the moment the next one appears.

. . . *so since that was more of a comment than a question,* says the artist slash activist, tittering as she looks at Derek, *maybe you could just speak to that, you know?*

A softball. Okay, thinks Mark. He takes a breath to steady himself. *The world is small,* he says. *But art is big.* He nods.

The artist slash activist begins nodding, too. Derek has his elbow in his palm, his fingers squeezing the bridge of his nose. Both have screwed up their mouths like asterisks. It seems as if something more needs to be said, but Mark can't think of what that might be. To his relief, the artist slash activist starts talking again. Derek looks relieved, too.

With surreptitious movements, Mark clicks on the tab leading to the artist slash activist's website, which he was looking at earlier. There is a bio, as there is on his website. *She/They, Poet, Painter, Cultural Strategist, Fur Parent, #AmWriting . . . to show the importance of representation for marginalized people . . . has made a life out of speaking truth to power.* There is a list of publications for which she has written: the *Times, The Paris Review, The New Yorker*, a startup-run literary journal sponsored by a museum whose major endowment is from a dead oil magnate. Websites and universities, an honorary degree. His stomach hurts.

Mark? Derek's voice is tinny. Mark looks at the VCR/TV, his screen's second figure. *Mark, are you cutting out? Maybe you need to hear the question again?*

Oh, says Mark, *yes, please.*

The Gargoyles, prompts the artist slash activist.

The Gargoyles, says Mark. He knows he sounds stupid. It's what he wanted, or thought he wanted.

I'm sure people say this all the time, says the artist slash activist. *About the composition, the sensuality, the way it insists on itself, especially in contrast with your other work, which has always been so understated. It's ostentatious, isn't it? It's not living in this scarcity mentality, as we say. Beneath the mystery,* The Gargoyles *feels to me like it's very pro-pleasure. A part of me wonders if it's asking:* What else is there *but* pleasure?

Mystery? Mark's anger collides with the honey. Together they grow, a river of heat that moves without reason, surging through his spinal cord. Suddenly, he can focus. Mystery? *The Gargoyles* is not mysterious. Even Adrian could see that his first project after Arturo's death was about that loss. His gargoyles are carved from stone but, as paintings, lack substance. Protective symbols that ward off evil, their ugliness has a purpose real life rarely affords: they are in constant, excruciating exposure to the elements, in exchange for a sense of security. And yet, tragically, even this is ultimately artificial. Losing Arturo was an inversion of Mark's natural life. Now everything is outside, and nothing within. It's as clear to Mark now as it was when he was standing in his studio, watching them dry. How else can *The Gargoyles* be understood?

What else is there but pleasure? Mark demands. His voice has risen to a shout. He pounds his fist on the desk. *Many things! Many, many things!*

Adrian

Adrian gathers socks from Mark's bedroom floor. There are machines downstairs, but there's an out-of-order sign on the door, so he has to go to the laundromat on the corner. Thankfully, there isn't much to wash. Mark wears the same thing day after day. What little there is smells sour. He wonders if a wash is even enough to get it out.

Back soon, he yells, slamming the door behind him.

There are only two other people in the laundromat, both watching the silent TV with Spanish subtitles. Adrian sits in an empty chair and opens his book, which he took from Mark's shelf without glancing at the spine. It doesn't matter what it is—he knows he won't like it. Mark's books are all about theory or artists Adrian's never heard of, most of whom who aren't considered famous by normal people's standards. There's hardly any fiction, certainly not the kind that Adrian likes. But he needs to be distracted from his phone, which he's worried will tempt him to go somewhere, with someone. Mark didn't make it to the bathroom before he threw up this morning. Adrian cleaned him up and put him back in bed, then cleaned the carpet with George sniffing around his ankles. His arms beside Mark's, the latter's all veins. Claustrophobic as it makes him feel, he's beginning to wonder if he should leave the apartment at all.

Adrian opens the book at random, reading a page before skipping ahead to another. He gathers that it's about a gay painter who became famous for his ugly paintings of the pope before he died in the nineties. The jacket copy sketches a life that was long and strange and sad, but the pages fail to capture his attention.

After five minutes, Adrian gives up. He opens his phone and scrolls through his Contacts list, whipping his finger from bottom to top. Every time he looks through the thousands of names, he comes across one he doesn't remember. He's reading a note about Pao, a daycare worker he met in Jersey, trying to jog his memory—was her hair long or short? Didn't she have braces?—when he suddenly senses that he's being watched. Without moving, he flicks his eyes. The man is sitting in a chair across from him along the opposing wall. His attention shrinks the room.

Still deciding what to do, Adrian concentrates on the screen until a stray sound, the click of a washing machine unlocking, gives him an excuse to lift his face. A few feet to his right, a woman is taking her clothes out of the dryer. Now the man is watching her. The lower half of the woman's body sticks out from the giant porthole, moving as she reaches for her wet clothes.

He decides it's time for an experiment. When he drops the book on the floor, the man glances his way. Their eyes meet. Neither of them are wearing masks. Adrian opens his legs, the inseam of his shorts blue against tan skin. Golden hairs, periwinkle fibers. *It* rumbles. The man continues to watch. Adrian picks up the book, then sets it down, pointedly looking now. Something is going to happen. The woman has gone to the back of the laundromat, where Adrian can no longer see her. Now he and the man are alone.

Fag.

The man's voice is low. He gets to his feet, his brow furrowed and his hands fisted. He repeats himself. Adrian looks at the woman. Her earbuds are in as she steadily folds her laundry and stacks it in her basket.

What the fuck you looking at?

The man is taller and bigger than Adrian. His baseball cap is askew. His skinny jeans are shiny with stretch. His face is flat, his color dull.

Nothing, says Adrian, holding out his hands. *It* rides as high as the J train over the Williamsburg Bridge.

Fucking talk back to me. The man takes a step forward. Though his voice is loud, the woman doesn't seem to hear him.

Um, says Adrian, holding the book in front of him.

The man slaps it from his hands in one slow, swinging movement. The woman keeps folding, glancing at the TV.

Adrian runs, leaving the book on the floor and the laundry in the machine, knowing he won't be back. The front door is propped open, the entrance humming with flies. Behind him, the man yells.

Adrian chooses not to hear. Now *it* is nowhere to be found, but a burst of energy propels him over the pavement. The man will never catch him.

A few blocks away, he ducks into a deli. Hiding by the ATM, he texts Mark. There's no response, no bubbling ellipses. The man behind the counter keeps eyeing him, so he goes outside again. He waits in the shade of an awning for ten minutes, which he times down to the second. Still nothing from Mark.

An unexpected relief brings feeling back to Adrian's fingers. Mark must be asleep, or else he doesn't need Adrian. This is his excuse to go somewhere, anywhere. He opens an app and turns on the green light.

Mark

A man works in the city to afford a nice three-bedroom home in the suburbs. His wife stays at home with the kids, all clones of their hideous mother. The man slaves at the office all week long, even in the summer, when Manhattan becomes a slimy inferno overridden with rats and the chumps too poor to flee. There's a tight shot of him leaning over a drafting table, sweat spotting his forehead, tie loosened with exasperation.

One afternoon, when the man is riding the train home from work, he sees a sexy woman wearing red lipstick, a tight red dress, and red heels. The man is so bewitched by her that he follows her off at her stop, but she disappears in the busy station. Shaking his head, the man decides he might as well get something cold to drink before heading home.

The mercury above the register says 93 degrees. As he's pawing through the icebox near the back of the deli, the man notices a doorway covered with a beaded curtain. He looks at the man behind the register, who raises his eyebrows.

Five, says the man behind the register.

He forks over the money and walks through the beads. The camera shows his eyes, wide and catatonically still, as if he's in a trance, before moving behind him. It follows the man—balding, slung-shouldered, brown slacks—through the clattering drapery.

The peep show has three booths. The man peers into the first, where a nude woman dances sensually behind dirty glass. In the second, a nude man does the same. The man looks into the third, but the camera doesn't reveal what's inside. He enters.

Day after day, the man returns to the deli, paying to hide away in the third booth. He stays longer and longer, stopping in before work and leaving early to come again in the afternoon. The man behind the register demands more money for entry, and the man pays it. He loses his job, but he keeps coming back. His wife weeps, begging him on her knees. His best friend takes him out for a drink, gets angry, points directly at his chest. His wife leaves him. His friend and his parents can't call him because he's moved into a flea-bitten studio, not far from the deli, that doesn't have a phone.

Late one evening as he's leaving the deli, the man sees the sexy woman from the train walking down the street. Lipstick, dress, heels. The man follows determinedly, but just as he's about to call out to her, a truck drives between them, and she disappears again.

When the man returns to the deli the next day, the beaded curtain is gone. Now there is only a wall. There is a woman at the register the man has never seen before, and she doesn't know what he's talking about when he asks about the beaded curtain.

Mark pauses the movie. He had a sip of wine at the beginning of *The Booth*, but it made him feel queasy, and now he has to go to the bathroom. Somehow, he makes it without having to crawl.

To his disappointment, the nausea passes after a few minutes on his knees. Discomfort without relief? What a waste. He limps back to his bedroom, where the wineglass still sits, full and tepid. He wants to throw it out, but he doesn't want to get up again. His phone glows. He sits down on the bed. A text from Adrian. *Should I come over?*

Mark doesn't respond. He puts the phone down next to the wine. He lies on his back and stares at the ceiling. Then he remembers: he forgot to turn *The Booth* back on.

Mark is in bed, naked. He has an erection. Arturo is next to him, fully clothed. The wineglass is still full. The VCR/TV is still on. The screen is so bright that Mark must squint to see his lover.

It's been so long, says Arturo. He looks the same as he always has.

We have no privacy, says Mark. Despair floods him. *We can't touch each other again until we turn it off.*

When Mark awakens, the VCR/TV is still on, but he is alone. Not even George is here. He doesn't know what time it is. He steps into the tenebrous hallway on legs stiff as sticks. He totters. He barely reaches the toilet before he vomits the sour dregs of his last sip of wine.

Adrian

Raised in Alphabet City, Min had a map of Lower Manhattan in her head. She and Adrian spent an entire day together, riding the trains, looking at bridges, fording the crowds of tourists, eating mustardy hot dogs, bumming cigarettes. Late in the afternoon, she took him to her apartment. They said hello to her roommates, all squeezed in front of the TV, and went to her bedroom. Her kisses were salty.

That was back when Adrian was on his first smartphone, the dawn of his cloud and its thousands of contacts, of which Min was one of the first. When he goes looking for her card, the note says, *In hypnotist school. Funny.* He doesn't remember her being particularly funny, but he certainly laughed a lot when they were together.

Min answers after the first ring. Her voice sounds the same. She remembers Adrian right away. Adrian smiles, alone in his room. *It* wriggles.

Are you a hypnotist yet, Min? he asks.

Wow, you remember! says Min.

At Min's office, Adrian sees her long hair has become a bob. Her once-pale fingernails are shellacked in dark red. Her features, though still plain, are more animated than he remembers. When they met, she was dressed blandly, in rumpled linen and broken-in clogs. Now she's in a blazer and a short skirt, her heels just low enough to retain the designation of *business casual*. Smiling like a news broadcaster, she leads Adrian to a couch. The smile transforms into a grimace of solicitousness as she suggests he take off his mask.

It's totally all right with me, she says, *I've been vaccinated.*

I'm fine, says Adrian. It's not time yet.

So you're interested in getting hypnotized, huh? Her smile returns.

Sort of, says Adrian.

Is that why you called me? For a free session? She brushes her fingernails through her hair, five ermine peering from the darkness.

No, says Adrian. He laughs to match her laughter. *I have a question to ask you. But I think, if you hypnotize me first, that might help with the answer.*

Min frowns. *Why?*

Because of the mask, Adrian says. On Min's website are photos of clients wearing leather hoods over their faces. *Sensory deprivation will facilitate hypnosis through total dissociation*, the copy says. Perhaps, Adrian thinks, if his face is entirely masked before Min sees him fully, she will be able to see the difference—pinpoint

what has changed since she saw him last, almost a decade ago—
that he still can't.

I see, says Min. To his surprise, she doesn't ask him to explain
further.

When she hands Adrian the hood, it takes a minute to find the
hole for his head. It's large enough that he can pull it over his N95
without unsettling its loops from his ears. A zipper along the back
pulls it closed. Under both layers, it's a little harder to breathe.
He concentrates on his respiration. When *it* moves in response
to these changes, he allows himself to smile, knowing he's unseen.

We begin, says Min. *Now, repeat after me.* Sharp and crisp, she
sounds like an elocution teacher. When they met, she had mum-
bled, annoying the old man who sold them their hot dogs.

Adrian nods. The eye holes are small, so he can see only bits of
Min's face at a time. Breathing deeply, he sits as still as he can,
feeling the texture of the couch under his fingers.

I look out through black holes.

I look out through black holes, Adrian repeats. He angles his head
like a bird to see different fragments of Min. Her eyes are closed,
her hands crossed over her lap.

I am reassured by my own limits, she goes on.

I am reassured by my own limits.

I am bound by my impermanence.

I am bound by my impermanence.

Then nothing. Adrian waits, but the silence persists. *It* is withering. Panic like a road flare. He knows he hasn't been forgotten—
he's right in front of her, after all—but then again, what if he has
been?

Was that a prayer? he prompts her. It's the first thing that comes to
mind. He waits for signs of life from *it*.

Min, her eyes squeezed shut, grins like a jack-o'-lantern. Though
she is still young, as young as Adrian, anyway, she looks tired—
aged without added distinguishment. Adrian tries to remember
what drew him to her when they first met, when he had been
standing stock-still in the middle of the rush-hour scrum, searching for the 7. Min had tapped on his shoulder and asked where he
was headed. *I'll take you*, she said, proudly seizing his hand.

Prayer? I don't believe in that stuff, Min says. *It's all right if you do.
But that's not really related to what we're doing.*

Her voice is mocking. Wherever *it* emerges from is like a smoking
hole in the ground. If Adrian met Min a year ago, he wouldn't have
given her the time of day. Now he's desperate for her notice. He
wishes he could be somewhere else. He feels his phone buzz in
his pocket.

Now, says Min. *I want you to do something for me.*

Despite his feelings, Adrian nods obediently, tensing his body in
preparation.

I want you to wake up.

Min is on the couch beside him, close enough to touch his thigh. A pool of leather spreads across his lap. The N95 is on the arm of the couch. The leather smells good. Min smells like nothing.

So, does that answer your question?

Adrian feels lightheaded. *But I didn't ask it.*

You did, says Min. *You just don't remember right now.*

She walks Adrian back to the lobby. His head hurts. He's very thirsty. *That's normal*, she says. *Hydrate, maybe take a nap, and you'll be fine.*

Mark's apartment isn't far from Min's office, but Adrian can only think about his dark, cold bedroom in the center of Brooklyn's noisy, scorching heat. When Min leans forward, he allows her to wrap her arms around his body.

Rate me on Yelp, okay? she says, closing the door behind him.

Mark

Mark's feet are so swollen that none of his shoes fit, not that it matters. The farthest he's going today is the bathroom. He's not hungry anyway. He should drink water, but he's not thirsty, either. He hopes his first movie of the day will be a pleasant one. He's not in the mood for anything dark.

The movie opens on a girl standing in the window of an old house. She's an orphan who lives with her grandmother and aunt. A handsome youth moves into the boardinghouse next door; he attends the seminary in town. The orphan girl writes his name over and over in her notebook. When they encounter each other on the sidewalk, she always finds a reason to strike up a conversation.

So far so good, thinks Mark.

In the window of the boardinghouse, the orphan girl's grandmother and aunt sadly shake their heads. The orphan girl is ugly. A prettier girl may have been able to convince the youth to leave the seminary, but not she. They tell her to give up on the young man, but she doesn't listen. When the handsome youth takes advantage of her affection, spoiling her virtue the day before he's to be ordained, the brokenhearted orphan girl tells her grandmother and aunt that she wants to join the church herself.

On the eve of her vows, the orphan girl receives a letter from her rich old uncle inviting her to come live with him. He pledges to support her financially, he writes, if she will provide him with companionship for the rest of his fading life. In exchange, upon his death she will inherit his estate.

Uh-oh, thinks Mark.

The trouble begins the day the orphan girl moves into her uncle's mansion. He chases her around the breakfast table and paws at her body while she plays the piano. He does not mind her ugliness, perhaps because he is far uglier than she. He delights in her powerlessness. When she cries, he roars with laughter. He rips up the letters she writes to her grandmother and aunt and throws the pieces in the fireplace.

The orphan girl locks herself in her bedroom, refusing food and water. That night, she has a dream. Her dead aunt's wedding gown, standing as if filled with an unseen ghost, revolves before her, brilliantly white. The next morning, the orphan girl comes down from her room and pretends to have changed her mind. She tells her uncle she has fallen in love with him, but she won't give herself to him until they have married. It can't be done legally, but she insists on a sham ceremony. Her uncle is so pleased that he grants her everything she asks for: champagne, new shoes, and his wife's wedding gown. The ceremony is to be held that afternoon.

That evening, as her uncle is laying her down on the bridal bed, the orphan girl's smiling face suddenly twists into a rictus of fury.

From the lining of her dress she pulls a dagger, hidden there by her aunt's grandmother. The grandmother had worn the dress as she escaped the country during the war, when she didn't know if she would have to defend herself or even take her own life. While the orphan girl's uncle is bleeding to death, his flailing body knocks over a candlestick by the bed. The fire consumes the curtains and eats through the room. The house burns around her, trapping her and the corpse in the inferno. The final shot is of her face, peaceful as an angel, the flames reflected in her dark, beautiful eyes, overlaid with *The End* in Gothic script. No credits.

Jesus, Mark thinks. *Just ghastly.*

He wants to change the tape, but his ankles hurt too much to stand, even though his pills should have kicked in by now. He picks up his phone to text Adrian, then sets it back down again. He stays awake for hours, picking at his fingernails.

Hey, says Mark. He checks the time. It's almost 11:00 p.m.

Hi, says Adrian, shutting the door behind him. George is draped over one shoulder. His head lifts and their noses touch. His friend could just as easily be talking to the cat.

Sleepy? asks Mark. He's hopeful.

I guess so. When Adrian notices the wineglass on Mark's night-stand, he slips George from his shoulders and sets him on the floor. He takes the glass away and returns from the kitchen with a clean one filled with water. He leaves again and returns with two more, both full of water, to place beside it.

Will you put that in? Mark points at the tape on top of the VCR/TV. Adrian does, pushing the requisite buttons. A piano rumbles to life and a white statue of a beautiful woman rises from a lovely, summery city park. The words . . . *And In Health* bloom across the screen. The piano capers. Pigeons chortle in the dust.

Moving his eyes but not his head, which remains pointed at the VCR/TV, Mark watches Adrian undress on his side of the bed. He empties his pockets. He peels off his shirt, pausing to sniff the fuzz of his left armpit. He unbuttons his shorts and tugs them down over his thighs.

Mark's friend is thinner, he notices. His ribs are more prominent, and his briefs sit on his body, rather than cling to it. The lost weight seems to mostly have been subtracted from his lips and posture and forehead, making his eyes even bigger. *Everyone looks prettier when they cry,* Mom used to say.

When was the last time you went to the bathroom? asks Adrian.

He wants to know if he should help Mark go now, before they fall asleep. As if he were a child.

Mark can't think of a reply that doesn't confirm this treatment. *I don't remember,* he finally says. He knows this is unbelievable, but to say anything else would be to risk cruelty. He remembers Ruth.

Okay. Adrian smiles. Passive aggression has never worked on him. *You just let me know when you want to go.*

Now Mark feels chastened. Adrian gets under the blankets, his earbuds still in. Something seems to occur to him. He reaches for Mark's forearm. *When are you going to go to the doctor?*

If Mark's heart were a bird, it would go seeking twigs. *I will soon,* he lies. He thinks about pulling Adrian close. George makes biscuits on the comforter between them.

I think you need to. Adrian has a way of fixing his eyebrows during those rare instances that he exerts his will.

Don't worry about it.

Okay.

After playing with his phone for a few minutes, Adrian sets it down on the nightstand. He sinks into the pillow and closes his eyes. Mark wonders if he smells bad, if Adrian would say something if he did. The piano from the movie is gentle, consistent. Adrian begins to twitch. From the corner of his eyes, Mark watches him go.

Has his friend always been able to drop off so easily? Mark tries to think back to the first time they shared a bed together. (Is Adrian memorable?) Adrian soft and tight as neoprene, breathing without a sound. He'd had too much to drink at the hotel bar. Mark brought him back to the room and helped him undress. He held his hand while he sat on the toilet seat and concealed his pleasure upon hearing his friend's firm, clear stream of piss. He plied him with a cup of water. He tucked him into the queen and got into the one adjoining it. If Mark wanted, he could reach his hand and touch Adrian's hair. Dimples in his lower back, like thumbprints left by someone else. Why had they been at a hotel? Mark can't remember now. (Is Mark memorable?)

A muscle spasms in Adrian's cheek. Mark believes that he is one of the very few people on earth who is immune to him, but when his friend is asleep, even he is stricken by his beauty. Unconscious, the Adrian he knows becomes a man again. His strands of thick brown hair split with gold, his eyelids trembling with his heartbeat. Mark is not like Adrian's *friends*; he has known this since the day they met. But when he sees Adrian at rest, there's room to consider the possibilities. He's surprised to feel himself getting hard. When was the last time that happened?

Mark watches his friend instead of the movie. Adrian's eyebrows aren't thick, but they have body. His eyelashes are like fur. His lips *are* pink. When he dies, will Adrian be alone forever? Mark wishes to touch the tip of his nose. He puts his finger so close that there is almost no difference. Adrian's breath is low and slow, regular as a ceiling leak. George slips out from under Mark's arm, arches his back, and drops silently to the floor.

———◇———

. . . *And In Health* is a screwball comedy about Gerald and Rosie, an unhappily married couple of New York City swells. Gerald wears white bow ties and tails; Rosie wears fur capelets over gowns that reveal her skinny chest with elegant cutouts. They banter beautifully but feel trapped and bored by the endless parties and charity galas. In a simultaneous attempt to force the other to call it quits, both are trying to get caught attempting affairs that never seem to go off: Gerald woos a young heiress with rocks for brains; Rosie tempts a soybean scion who can't read between the lines. As the hijinks escalate, both arrange to meet their paramours at a beautiful white statue in Central Park, where they had their first kiss years before. They arrive one snowy night to find not their would-be lovers but their own spouses. The banter finally fails: in confessing their shared desire to end the marriage, they regain the spark they found here beneath the statue just as a blizzard blows into the city. They return home in each other's arms, but Rosie has fallen ill from the night air. Gerald stays by her side. After a sleepless week—with a few appearances from their dowdy housekeeper, a malapropist physician, and their adorable terrier to lighten the mood—her fever finally breaks. As Gerald kisses her, the chorus rises to a triumphant note and the statue appears in a shimmering overlay across the screen. No credits.

The VCR/TV falls dark and silent. A quick one, only eighty minutes. Adrian is still asleep. Now Mark is really alone.

Mark gets out of bed. When he stands, his head swims and his heart hammers. Feet burning, he limps to the VCR/TV and pulls the tape out of the slot. He clumsily stacks it on top of *The Damnation*, which he watched yesterday before *All The Women Typing*. He couldn't tiptoe if he tried, but even as he lurches back down onto the mattress, Adrian remains asleep.

The honey surges, turning his bed into a flat cage. Mark regrets having moved at all. But there's nothing to be done now. If Adrian weren't here with him, fast asleep, he would let himself moan. If Adrian weren't here with him, would anyone else be in his place? Will he die in this bed? He thinks of Mom's bed. He should have died there, like his mother and sister. His failure to do so is vaguely embarrassing, like a personal shortcoming. Instead he's three thousand miles away. It's as if he's gotten lost. No—as if he lost them.

Mark waits—what else is there to do? Forever transpires before there's a change in the air around his calf. An apparition crests the bed. He holds out his trembling arms to George, making a case for his own body. Suppressing a groan, he rolls over on his side and strokes his fur. He wishes he could hold him, folded together like Pompeii victims, but George does not tolerate such embraces for longer than a few seconds. After a series of desultory licks across Mark's skin, George settles, his whiskers tickling Adrian on the other side. Adrian still doesn't wake. The cat purrs. The honey dulls.

———————————◇———————————

In the morning, George is curled in the crook of Adrian's fetal arm, his friend's browned blond hairs encircling the cat's black and cream fur. Mark has a few minutes to watch before he needs to go to the bathroom again.

Adrian

When Adrian hits the pavement, his body reboots. Color to black-and-white, then back to color again. The driver blazes on to the next intersection, his elbow hanging out the window. He doesn't even tap the brakes.

He pulls himself to the curb, sucking in hot, bitter air. The familiar physiology of the near-death experience drenches him with sweat. Nausea lengthens the distance between his throat and his belly. Spots dance in his eyes, speckling the pockmarked sidewalk, the desiccated brick, the trash-strewn planters, the garbage bags wet with dog piss.

How had the driver not seen him? People on the sidewalk move around and away from him, but none look at him or change their stride, much less place their hands over their hearts, feign swoons, ask him what he's doing for the rest of his life.

———————————◆———————————

As the front door closes behind him, Marks calls to Adrian from his bedroom. He wants to take a shower.

Adrian helps him out of bed. He guides him to the bathroom and steadies him while he undresses. Mark sits on the toilet while Adrian tests the water's temperature with the back of his hand. When he reaches for the detachable shower head, his shoulder and hip hurt.

What happened? Mark points at the rising red mass on Adrian's thigh.

Adrian pokes the aching place, turning it white. *Fell,* he says. The skin on his arm is already scabbing. Mark is looking at the pictures on the wall behind him.

After his shower, Mark slowly leads Adrian back to the bedroom and waits on the bed while his friend gets him clean underwear, clean shorts, and a clean T-shirt. Adrian pulls the underwear and shorts up to Mark's knees so he can reach them. When Mark is dressed, Adrian sits on the bed next to him. He puts his bruised arm around his friend's shoulders. Though he's several inches shorter than Mark, he feels bigger than him. If they both got on the scale, he probably would be.

<hr />

Adrian opens his eyes. He's lying on Mark's side of the bed, fully clothed. In his dream, someone was trying to start a car, but it kept stalling, belching black fumes into the air. He realizes the sounds are coming from the bathroom.

He's about to go check on Mark when the toilet flushes. He relaxes. While he waits for Mark to come back to bed, he pulls his phone out of his pocket and opens his Contacts list.

Adrian scrolls at random, in search of an idea. But the movement hurts the pad of his thumb, a strip of pain reaching from above his wrist to under his ulna. It's the hand that hit the pavement when he fell. There should be an ice pack in the freezer. He wonders again how that driver didn't see him. Broad daylight and everything.

On his way to the kitchen, a memory occurs, like a bad idea: the hot-pink Honda, the lime-green paint. His lunch box on the front seat. *Sweetheart. Very safe. Very very safe with me. Sweetheart.* The woman looked like Mom if she dressed like a teenager. The sides of her mouth were wet. When she started the car, it made a horrible grinding noise and Adrian thought that maybe it wouldn't go. But it did, and she raced out of the school parking lot. Adrian put on his seat belt without needing to be asked.

They were almost to the city limits when the woman pulled into a gas station and parked at pump 4. She got out of the car, where the wind stole the ends of her hair and reshaped her XL T-shirt. The Honda was still running, her wallet in the cupholder. She walked away. He missed her before he even lost sight of her in the trees.

Mark

He and Ruth are drinking wine together, like they haven't in so many years. (*I'm not compulsive about anything.* Ruth always said that.) Mark spills his wine on the table and uses his finger to write foreign words in the liquid. Ruth seems to understand them. *Where's Mom?* asks Mark. Mom isn't with them, but she is the undercurrent of the dream. *That is what it means to be siblings,* Ruth says.

When Mark awakens, Adrian is asleep beside him. George is somewhere. Careful not to disturb his friend, Mark's hand roams over his own body. His chest, where the hair grows. His belly, which is bloated. The rest of his body is sapped of its fat: his arms, his thighs. His fingers can feel his pulse under his skin. When he holds his breath, his heart remains, slow but accounted for.

He realizes the pain is gone. Nothing hurts, aches, throbs, or burns. Being alive is all that Mark can feel.

So it's finally happening. How much time is left? A month seems unreasonably long, but tomorrow is surely too soon. He wants to wake Adrian, but what is there to say that wouldn't force an explanation—of what the painlessness means, and why he knows? A single secret is a lying life. He sits up to scan the comforter for George, but it's too dark. He could open the drapes above his head, but he doesn't want to see the moon.

Not far from the foot of the bed, the VCR/TV is still, empty as shadow and taller than it should be.

⸻◇⸻

Mark answers without opening his eyes.

Got a minute?

Hey. Derek. Why didn't he check the screen? Because he assumed the call would be from Adrian, even though Adrian never calls.

So that opening is this weekend. I wanted to tell you that you shouldn't feel any pressure to come. Ha ha. You know, it might be a good idea to just stay in . . .

Mark doesn't know what Derek is talking about.

. . . and I know that interview was a little rocky. But their team was really gracious about it. They aren't even going to . . .

Mark sits up and puts both feet on the ground. They're still swollen, though less than they were last night. Now that the gouty pain is gone, the swelling seems like a ring of protection, a life vest of fluid and air. He stands without a hitch, and while his first step doesn't hurt, it doesn't hold solid beneath him. He twists his ankle, nearly falling to the floor.

What was—

Sorry, says Mark, steadying himself on the nightstand. His ankle should hurt, bad, but it feels asleep. Pins and needles. *Tripped on George.*

Oh, yeah. Good old George, says Derek. He has never been to Mark's apartment, but naturally he's seen the paintings of a black-and-white cat. *Anyway, I got a call from Jen—Jen Preston?—this morning. She's the one who . . .*

Mark minces to the wall and takes one of the last movies from the bag. He minces back and slides it into the VCR/TV one-handed. He presses the button. He checks his feet. They look like condoms filled with water. His toenails are too dark. With each step, he tries to favor the left foot, the one he didn't twist. He wonders if the right will swell even more.

. . . I just don't want you to feel like I'm asking you to hide or anything, you know? But given everything that's going on, and that interview, and—you know. It's so hard for everyone right now. It's not just the pandemic, everything is crazy. You of all people deserve a little time. A little space. Ha ha. Don't answer any emails. Just zone out and watch some TV.

Whatever you say. His own voice sounds strange to him. Does it sound strange to Derek? He imagines his agent on a Zoom call, holding a brass urn dusted in black powder with Mark's name on it. *Yeah, maybe I'll stay in tonight.* He's not even sure he can leave the apartment by himself.

Adrian

The men converge on her again. Now all Adrian can see is the part in her hair, like the white shaft of an arrow. He presses through the crowded bar toward the back wall. On the dance floor are a few dozen beautiful men and a fistful of beautiful women. To his right, a trio of go-go dancers arch on pedestals. He stands under an unironed pride flag, craning his neck for a glimpse of her face.

Finally, the men she's with—all friends, obviously—part enough that he can see her again. When one of the men begins telling a story, she listens attentively, cool without a trace of coldness. When the punch line arrives, the men throw back their heads and clap their hands. She slides a hand through her hair and behind her ear, gravity pulling her bracelets down her forearms.

Adrian is lowering his beer bottle from his mouth when she finally notices him. As their eyes meet, his skin tightens, warm and prickling. She smiles for him. He smiles back. They have each other's attention.

The first of her friends to notice him is wearing cutoffs. He's about her height, with a mustache and silver earrings. Adrian watches him nudge another man—this one tall, in white mesh—and their eyes find him together. A triangulation occurs. Her friends examine him with interest and something like indignation before the man in cutoffs puts an arm around her waist and leans his ear to her mouth. The light from the disco ball lands on her forehead, eyelids, nose, and teeth. Platinum overflows the ladle of her collarbones. Her squared chin frames generous lips. They nod to each other. She hands her drink to the man in white mesh and disappears into the crowd.

Adrian is about to wonder where she's gone when he feels a hand on his shoulder. She's behind him, so close that their hair writhes in a shared electrical charge. Her fingers trace his shirt, stop briefly on the gold chain, then move down to his wrists. She has large, angular breasts and long, slender feet. High cheeks, suggesting secrecy. Adrian nods himself even closer. He wishes their hair were the same color. Her voice is only just audible in the loud bar, but he understands her: here is the variation on his life's theme, one he hasn't heard from a woman in an eternity.

Now she's raised her eyebrows and closed her lips. She has asked him a question. Adrian smiles and nods, not caring what it was. She takes his hand and guides him from the dance floor. Behind them, the laughter of her friends has already blended into the hum of the crowd.

From the sidewalk, to the train, to her apartment in Gowanus, neither of them say a word. She leads and he follows, trailing by their linked fingers. She's wearing a silver halter top and Chelsea boots. He feels like he's on his very first date.

When they're finished, she kneels on the mattress to push open the window. The AC unit ululates. *You can smoke if you want,* she says. When he tells her he doesn't have any cigarettes, she produces a box, handing him one and keeping another for herself. She lies back down and scoops her breasts with her forearm, squinting at the skyline. Morning will eventually come from that direction, he thinks. While she watches her wedge of Brooklyn, the smoke-stacks and the freeways, he admires her.

Adrian wants to say, *I'm so glad we met.* Instead he points at the script tattooed between her elbow and wrist. *What's that mean?* he asks.

She laughs a little cloud. *That's what's going on my tombstone,* she says. For Pleasure. *Pretty corny, huh? It's old.* She blows a real smoke ring.

Adrian has never thought about his tombstone before. He realizes that for the past five years, he's taken for granted that Mark will manage everything after he dies. (What he had assumed before that, he doesn't know.) Even though Mark is thirty years older, something about him outliving Adrian has always felt right.

Adrian realizes that his night is over. He must return to Mark's apartment, hours later than he said he would, and face his friend there. He had told himself he would find something quick at the gay bar, then hurry home to help Mark get ready for bed. Something in the bathroom or a nearby car would be enough. Instead, he came here with her, and lost all this time.

Are you from out of town? she asks. *I've never seen you at Alberta's before.* The velvety texture of her halter top, wadded up near his hand, looks satisfying to stroke.

I live here, Adrian says, with finality. It doesn't occur to him to explain that he'd never been to a gay bar before last night. That he'd never wanted to, had certainly never needed to! To explain that going to one had always seemed, to put it indelicately, like shooting fish in a barrel. To tell her that, before everything—his vaccination, and the masks, and COVID—when he wanted to meet anyone, but especially men, he could do it everywhere, anywhere, all the time.

She shrugs and stubs her smoke. Adrian starts getting dressed. At any other time in his life, any other woman in her position would have been asking where he lived, if she could come visit him, whether he was single, did he know how beautiful he was? Now it's 2021 and she's looking at her phone, absentmindedly scratching the arch of her foot with a rigid toe. She is the first woman to see him in so long, to see him and also want him, and it's still not what it was before.

Adrian doesn't want to go back to Mark's, but he has no urge to linger, or to find someone else. Although he likes the idea of returning to Alberta's, he doesn't feel the need to do so now. Maybe some other time. Maybe with Cora. She could join him, like this woman on the bed had joined her friends. He thought of how her friends had looked at him. Their interest wasn't anything new, but his response to it was. He feels a curiosity that reminds him of his childhood. Remembering the man with one arm, the one at Miss Linda's salon, he carefully ties his shoes, as if securing the sails of a ship.

Although Adrian would like to see her again, he doesn't get her name or phone number before he leaves. At the bottom of the stairwell, where the warm, stale air is thick as sour cream, he checks the time: 4:54 a.m. He realizes that he hasn't felt *it* for hours.

<hr />

He finds George hunched outside the bathroom, hackles up, ears in reverse. The door is ajar. Adrian pushes it open with V-for-victory fingers.

The door's path mirrors the archway of sanguine vomit across the tile. Mark is on the floor, his right arm disappearing behind the toilet, his body an eroteme without the dot. His eyes, inky and unfocused, go to Adrian. His chest begins moving as quickly as George's, as if both breathe for the same small heart.

Neither man speaks while Adrian squats to put his arm around Mark's shoulders and lift him to his feet. It isn't so difficult. His friend has lost almost fifty pounds in the past year. Vomit, dried into a crumbling patch on his T-shirt, is ground into the fibers of Adrian's. They slowly stagger back to the bedroom. George trots after, tail close to the ground.

Adrian leaves Mark panting on the bed. When he returns with wet wipes and a damp washcloth, Mark has removed his shirt but not his sweatpants. Adrian pulls them off. He cleans Mark's face with the wet wipes and the rest of his body with the washcloth. He goes back to the kitchen for a glass of water.

When Adrian returns, his friend is stretched on the bed like a strange collage. Mark's head, mouth agape, face unshaven, looks like the portrait of a man hanging in his living room (the first time

Adrian visited his apartment, Mark had laughed when he asked if this Peter Hujar was a friend of his). Mark's pale torso, twisted and spent, is like Christ's in an old painting they saw at a museum in Madrid. And Mark's feet look like Leo's in one of the Fire Island photos, although they are not sandy and tanned but clean and ugly.

Here, says Adrian, holding out the glass to his friend.

Mark can hold it by himself. While Adrian was in the kitchen, he had counted out a handful of pills. He takes them one by one, spilling water on his bare chest. *Thank you.*

Adrian does his best to sound firm. *You need to go to the doctor.*

What I need, says Mark, *is a bedpan. A bucket. For when you're not here.*

I'm going to be here more, says Adrian. *I didn't mean to be gone so long tonight.*

Mark laughs.

How long were you in there?

Mark averts his eyes. Adrian doesn't want to know anyway. *I'm sorry*, he says. *I thought I'd be back.*

Well.

I still think you need to go to the doctor.

I don't care what you think, says Mark. His laughter ends on a high, cracking note. *I just need you here sometimes.*

I was going to come back.

You didn't tell me that. George, who had crept to Mark's side, winces and bounds away. *You don't tell me anything.*

I didn't know, says Adrian.

Well, me, neither, says Mark. *I'm not a fucking mind reader.*

Mark

Adrian slept on the couch last night. Since his alarm went off, Mark hasn't heard a thing. It's barely 7:30, an hour at which Adrian's rarely awake, unless he hasn't been to bed yet.

Mark listens keenly from his bedroom, where he's been since a forty-five-minute session of writhing and shitting water that began around 5:00 a.m. No more vomit, at least. Adrian's silence betrays his presence but nothing else.

At around 8:00, he hears the front door slam shut. He wonders if Adrian will come back today.

———————◇———————

Mark has always been irritated by the idea of an essential wound, the holy accident that artists' lives are boiled down to, typically found on a museum placard, term paper, or documentary. His preferred metaphor is planets without atmospheres: over the course of their existence, people are worn away by meteorological attrition until there's nothing left. Anti-*Argos*. And long before then, they're more crater than substance. When does destruction really happen? That's what Mark wonders. (After Arturo died, he had felt too alive. Painting *The Gargoyles* made him feel more dead, a relief.) At the end of his life, he's a vehicle for pain, memory, and lack. A true crescent moon, no trick of the light.

Mark sees this attachment to the essential wound everywhere, especially among artists. With them, he often comes across the need to be understood more than the wish to understand. *Life is a wound*, Mark thinks. He doesn't understand anything.

To kill time, he counts his pills. In the nightstand is a notepad he brought back from Almendra. While Ruth watched a movie, he spent an hour in Mom's bathroom taking inventory of all the bottles in her medicine cabinet and a drawer under the sink. Some of the bottles had Mom's name, some Ruth's. He wrote down each medication, the dose, and how many pills or spoonfuls were left.

When he finished, Mark checked on his sister. She was watching James Caan drill into a bank vault. Wearing Mom's nightie, lying on Mom's side of the bed. It was in that spot, after a week of almost constant sleep, that Mom's eyes had suddenly opened. She looked around the room like a baby. When Mark spoke to her, she answered apprehensively. She didn't appear to believe what she was saying, although she spoke lucidly until, a few hours later, she died.

He stayed in the doorway, watching. Ruth seemed strong. Her hair was loose; she always declined when he asked if he could put it up for her, to keep the heat off her neck. Over the sound of the movie, he could hear flies near, coyotes far.

It's not what I expected, said Ruth.

What isn't? Did she mean the movie? Neon lights turned a used-car lot Picasso blue.

Kind of thought there'd be more people here with me, she said. She kept watching the movie.

Well, you know. It's just not safe. All the hospice nurses wore masks, as did Mark, both when he was around them and away from the house. Ruth's body couldn't handle COVID. Neither could his, most likely.

His sister frowned. She knew it was a lie. His joints were hurting badly, so Mark sat down on the bed next to her. The honey was alive, just like him. If he touched her, could he share his life with hers? Even if it was painful? He leaned toward her, but she flinched, and after a few seconds she pulled away.

Is there anyone you want me to call? Mark asked. He searched his memory for incidental people, acquaintances whose relationship to Ruth he could pretend not to know the extent of, so as not to embarrass her with the truth: that there was no one to call. *Julianne?* She and Ruth used to work volunteer shifts together at the natural-food co-op. *Kate?* He wasn't even sure if there had been anyone by that name. *Ken?*

Ruth's body stiffened. *Off,* she said, throwing her fingers at the TV. Mark couldn't find the remote. He got up and turned it off manually.

What's wrong? It was too early for this. It was not yet time for this conversation.

Will you do something for me, Mark?

What? Mark felt imperiled, suddenly certain that she was going to ask him to help her commit suicide.

There are these tapes in my closet. In a bag. I need you to get them to Ken. He thinks he has all of them, but he doesn't. Are you listening?

You have them? Why? He leaned again, though not close enough to risk touching her.

Why? There were tears in her eyes. *I don't know why! I took them. I wanted to see them first, before everything was cataloged. Maybe there would be some insights I could share. Or I could be the one to see it, for the first time, the one that becomes really important. A lost treasure, or like a new classic.* She laughed shrilly. *Or maybe I'd just end up keeping them all for my own private collection. Then there would be something left of me when I died. Something of value.*

Of course, Mark said. He thought of the wealthy man who had originally owned the movies, a person with an estate, and descendants, and mourners. The pressure to reassure her, even if it meant lying, trembled on his forehead like a bead of water, but he resisted. *Of course I'll give them back to Ken.*

But wait until after, okay?

Of course.

I just need it to be after.

Mark was too selfish to ask her why, but he had to say something. *Are you sure you don't want me to call him now?*

I'm sure. Now Ruth was laughing. It quickly became a cough that tore through her chest until she gasped for air.

Adrian

There's only her first name. Nothing in the notes. It's rare that Adrian doesn't write a note for one of his *friends*.

The phone rings for a long time. He worries that Moira's dead, or worse, that she's living but doesn't have a phone, which seems like something that would be true about her. Just as he's beginning to panic, she picks up.

———————◇———————

He's not due at Moira's for several hours, but Adrian is afraid that if he doesn't leave Mark's apartment early, he never will. When his alarm goes off, he leaps to his feet and gets dressed where he stands. Before he leaves, he tiptoes down the hall to confirm that his friend is still asleep.

He goes to Verses for coffee, then heads for Prospect Park with his warm paper cup. The espresso works fast, affecting him so strongly he thinks he hears lyrics in the church bells.

It's going to be 97 degrees today. It's still in the low eighties, but he keeps to the shade when he can. He sees joggers, walkers, little children chaperoned by nannies. A man emerges from a faint trail to wordlessly proposition him, but Adrian pretends not to notice. *It* is awake. *It* feels good, like swimming in cold water. But if he gets started now, he's afraid he won't stop. He can be distracted, but not by that. He finds a shady place and lies down in the grass. He wishes he could go back to sleep. For a long time, he watches the branches touch each other. When the sun spills over his calf, he gets to his feet again.

His walk ends when he emerges from the park by the movie theater. He checks his phone. There's a movie in twenty minutes and it's sure to be freezing inside. Perfect.

He has to clear his throat at the ticket booth, then tap loudly on the glass, before someone notices him. His stomach hurts. When was the last time he ate? He gets in line for popcorn. He's thirsty, too. A Coke, why not? More caffeine. Two teenagers and a tired old man in rumpled polo shirts work behind the counter. He says *Excuse me* louder and louder, raising the volume of his voice until one of the teenagers sourly takes her place behind the register.

The teenager checking QR codes doesn't bother with his. All the seats, the big ones with the thick headrests, are empty. Adrian picks one that's dead center, wishing that this could feel indulgent. The popcorn tastes like paper and the Coke isn't sweet. He lets them cool and flatten, respectively, and falls asleep before the previews are over.

⸻◇⸻

There is a long time between the doorbell and the doorway, Moira's face widening in between.

Hello, she says. *Hello, Adrian.*

I need help.

I know.

Her wrinkles are so tight that her skin almost looks young again. Her white hair is pulled back in a low bun. She beckons and he follows her down a wood-paneled hallway that leads to a cramped but clean sitting room. There is a round table, not too large, in the center, with two chairs. He has never been in her home before, which is also her place of business.

Have a seat, says Moira.

On the table before each chair is a steaming cup of tea on a saucer. Adrian looks around for a crystal ball, a rosary, things like that, but doesn't find them. He looks into his tea, expecting leaves, but there's only a bag of Lipton.

Cream or sugar? asks Moira.

Do I look different? asks Adrian. He's not wearing a mask.

Yes. She answers without hesitation.

How?

You're more beautiful than ever. I wish I could describe it. But that's never been my strong suit. Was always better at math than languages.

People can't see me, says Adrian.

Sometimes when things happen on the outside, it's because things are happening on the inside.

I think it was the masks.

Moira fishes the tea bag out of the water and deposits it on her saucer. *You do look different. Do you feel different?*

I think I'm depressed or something, says Adrian. When he knew Moira before, nothing made him sad. *I can't feel anything.* This is untrue, or not all the way true. He remembers his espresso from this morning. He remembers his dream about Vonna.

Well, says Moira. *Let's see what I can do. Cream or sugar?*

When they've finished their tea, Moira gets to her feet with gracefully labored movements, like an elephant rising from its knees. *This way,* she says, flapping her fingers. Adrian follows her down the hallway. She opens a door and ushers him into a closet. *Face the wall,* she says. *I'm going to take a picture of your aura.*

For the brief duration of the darkness, Adrian thinks about Alberta's. When the door opens again, Moira motions for him to come out. *We have to wait for it to dry,* she explains.

She pours him more tea. There is now a plate of shortbread cookies on the table. They both take one and eat in silence. When she's finished with her cookie, she says, *Just a moment.* She goes to the eastern wall of the room, where she counts a series of light blue tiles with her index finger, twice, thrice over. Then she returns to her seat at the table.

Did you see the shoes in the closet? Moira says. *The red ones?*

No. The cookie has cleansed Adrian's mouth of the burned popcorn. He feels a little better. *It was too dark to see.*

They were my mother's. When I was a girl, she only wore them once a year. They fit her perfectly, but she said wearing them felt like walking on knives. She would walk around the house all day. Cried the whole time. Sometimes she screamed. But she had to wear the shoes because they awakened her third eye. She tapped her forehead.

Wow, says Adrian.

Yes. Moira pours herself more tea. *My mother never got sick. Ever. And she always told the truth. Except when it was tax season.* She smiles.

There is a deck of cards on the table. Somewhere, far off, a rooster crows. Adrian thinks about Mark on the bathroom floor.

You know, says Moira, *I think the picture is ready.*

She returns to the table, holding the paper so he can't see the front. He's not sure if he wants her to turn it around. As she examines it, her brow darkens and her lips move silently, as if she's reading words on a page.

Something bad has happened, Moira finally says. *But not to you, Adrian.*

She turns the paper around, but he turns away. He refuses to turn back until she assures him that it's face down on the table.

Mark

The pills work fast. As Mark falls away, he looks at the two remaining tapes on his nightstand, next to his phone and his water. His body drifts for a long time. All that's left is the soft and passive reception of light and some sound.

He comes back. For a while he waits, building up his strength to put in the penultimate tape. After a while, he sits up to count the pills. Between his stash and Ruth's leftovers, there are forty-nine left. Enough. He breathes deeply, willing himself to get to his feet.

Ruth's death was quicker than Mom's but much worse. Mark and Ruth joined Mom on the bed together, but it was Mark that Mom turned to when she said, *It's my time.* When it was Ruth's turn, Mark sat in the same place on Mom's old bed, wishing that his sister would have chosen to die in her own room. Ruth cried and cried. *I have nothing*, she said, wrapped in Grammy's quilt. *I have nothing left.*

Mark thought of calling a chaplain or minister—maybe someone through Calvary? But when he asked Ruth if that was what she wanted, she said no. He thought of calling Adrian on FaceTime, so she would have someone else to talk to, but when he texted to ask, Adrian didn't respond. Mark was glad he hadn't suggested it first.

It's not okay, said Ruth. *It's not okay.*

Mark was afraid. For the past year, all he had done was repeat the lies and platitudes they reserve for dying people, words that didn't mean anything to anyone and yet still needed to be said. *I'm here with you*, Mark told her. They were brother and sister, but there was nothing he could do for her. But he was there.

I have nothing and you have everything. Ruth's voice was too high. Her tears found no purchase, moving in desperate sheets down her tiny face. *You have it all.*

Mark felt sent away. This was not how he wanted it to be.

⸻⸺◈⸺⸻

When Mark got back from the mortuary, he found that he'd forgotten to lock the front door. Mom had never locked it, or the door to the truck. That kind of theft didn't happen out here in Almendra. But the oversight made him feel shaky, as if he'd done the same thing at home in New York.

He went through the living room. To his right, down the little hall, Mom's bedroom door was closed; behind it, the TV was still on, screening nothing. He kept going into the kitchen. To his right, Ruth's room. He went in and retrieved the duffel bag from her closet, closing the bedroom door behind him. He went down the back hall to his own room, where the door was still open. He packed another bag, including a few things from the bathroom, and found a personal lock for the zipper of Ruth's duffel, though he had no intention of checking it.

When he was ready, Mark sat down at the kitchen table and called everyone he needed to call. There would be a funeral, but he wouldn't be attending. He didn't know who would. He made all the other arrangements, for Ruth and for himself, using the list he had made when Mom died. Rarely was Adrian far from his mind, but for a stifling afternoon hour his friend did not once occur to him.

There was food in the fridge, wine in the pantry, plants in the living room, and the utilities to pay, but with the body gone, Mark didn't see the point in staying a moment longer. Though he hadn't yet booked a flight, he waited in the driveway for the car that would take him over the Golden Gate, into the City, past the multicolored slopes of ticky-tacky spilling inward from the San Bruno Mountains, to the clerestories of San Francisco International Airport. He'd figure it out when he got there.

Adrian

As Adrian runs, *it* froths to life, burning like hot oil in his belly. He hurtles through the gates of Prospect Park at a dead sprint, merging onto the asphalt that rings its fields and forests like a moat.

Mark

George remains at the foot of the bed. He won't let Mark touch him, but there is something about his reticence that is respectful. He purrs from afar, for Mark.

Come here, whispers Mark. *My baby.*

George won't. Mark cries.

Adrian

Everyone is in Prospect Park tonight. Adrian has to slow down to wend through them. A few times he shoves someone aside, shooting away at a sprint before they can take offense.

The park falls to his wayside, peripheral colors that blur like light speed. Green lawns and ticking thickets pool around the lake and its dead tributaries, down where the temperature, which dropped slightly with the sunset, is a little more bearable. Flashing with blunts, roman candles, and sunglasses, the pastures and fens are a hall of mirrors, the road a parade. The people of Brooklyn have brought their lives with them: children, animals, cell phones, blankets, whole watermelons, sandwiches, plastic half-pints of deli salad, two-liters of generic soda brands, soccer balls, beach chairs, dirt bikes, and Bluetooth speakers to pick up signals and share secrets.

As he was leaving her apartment, Moira had reached for him. *It felt very far away.*

My mother used to say that an accused man is desirable, she said. *You might want to think about that.*

After

A young woman, her criminal boyfriend, and her mother are living in a convent. Straightforward enough, and yet Mark can't follow the plot. When *Sister Sarah* ends, there are no credits, just like every other tape. Mark didn't like it. He wonders if he would have enjoyed it at another time in his life.

George, purring, watches him stagger to the wall, where he retrieves the last movie from inside the duffel. Hot World, Mark says, holding the tape to George's little nose. *You remember, don't you?*

The cat gives it a sniff and returns to purring. His chest swells and shrinks slowly and evenly.

Mark puts it in the VCR/TV and presses Play. The first heavy rhythms of the score rise from the darkness. He gets back into bed and starts taking pills, a few at a time so he doesn't choke. He loses track of how many times he swallows. Already he can feel them down in his belly. It occurs to him that he could vomit. Well, too late to worry about that now.

The VCR/TV screen looks bigger than it is. Black backdrop, red script—Mark remembers. A dusky sun dawns on a postapocalyptic landscape, the kind you can still shoot out West, in the titian brainpan of Arizona or New Mexico. The score is more rhythm than harmony. He attempts to make himself comfortable.

Mark smells him first: the sweat and the fear. Adrian appears like a dark trophy in the doorway. There is nothing inside the silhouette. Featureless in shadow, his friend appears to be turned away from him, as if he came backward down the hall.

Mark saw Adrian's hair and shoulders first, the first time. He hadn't been out much since Arturo. His friend Jonathan had assigned a man named Matt as his date, though he reassured Mark that there were no expectations. He was to think of Matt as nothing more than a new friend (with potential!). Mark met Matt at the corner, noting, with irritation, that Matt was handsome. Mark extended his hand to shake, which he immediately regretted—what a weird thing to do. Finally, they went inside.

After five minutes of conversation, it was clear that Matt was too happy. Mark already regretted coming. Surprising himself, he had stayed sober when Arturo died, but in that moment he wanted a drink so badly he'd have fought for it. Pointing a finger at Matt— *Just a minute*—he slid into the crowd, nervously scanning for a waiter. He needed something sugary, like a Coke. When he saw the white shirt and black pants, the youthful build and brown curls, he hurried to tap his shoulder.

Adrian turned. Mark blinked. Perhaps not a waiter. He was too beautiful not to be an actor or a model or a boyfriend. But then again, some of those were also waiters. But this young man was holding a half-finished drink in his hand and his shirt was unbuttoned below the solar plexus. Definitely not a waiter. Not at this party, anyway.

Adrian smiled. Mark wished to see him in the rain. With a terse apology, he wheeled around and walked away.

You all right? said Matt. He picked up where he left off, making what should have been an interesting job—casting director—sound dull. And yet he smiled with every other word, leaning comfortably into Mark's airspace. *It's easy when you're happy,* thought Mark, resigned.

But Matt could carry on the conversation more or less by himself, which permitted Mark to keep an eye on the beautiful young man. He was also with a date, an amber-coiffed Anna Wintour type who kept two of her fingers on his left elbow, like she was searching for a pulse there. Like Matt, the beautiful young man smiled often, but he spoke very little. Mark thought about painting him.

Adrian knew the man was watching him. He had rarely felt *it* respond more strongly. He kept Mark within eyesight while his date—who had the same given name as Mom, but went by Bo—talked with the woman beside her. The man watching him was older, with brown hair and an earring. Clean-shaven. *It* kept building steam, and as it did, people began drifting toward Adrian and Bo, gradually bringing the majority of the attendees to their side of the long studio. A few tried to take pictures of Adrian when they thought he wasn't looking, or perhaps they didn't care if he was. A woman, fingers in her mouth, stood a few feet behind him and giggled. His head cocked toward Bo, Adrian didn't appear to notice anyone until they needed to be shooed away.

Mark studied the beautiful young man's disinterest in those around him. His date was obviously enjoying the attention he drew, though she kept up the patter around her. When the woman went to the bathroom, the beautiful young man approached him, surrounded by whispers and glances, the room edging toward frenzy.

They talked. When they discovered that they were both from Northern California, from the same area code, even, born a hundred miles away from each other as the crow flew, Mark was giddy. *My mom and sister are still there*, he told Adrian. He pulled out his phone to show him pictures he had taken on his last visit. Poppy-pocked fescue tumbled from misty barbed wire, tender foxtails, grazing cattle. *That's Arturo*, he said, pointing to the pale hand palming the sycamore. The fog, obscuring the bay in one direction and the Central Valley in the other, made the hills into mountains and the pastures seem endless. *See how beautiful*, Mark said. Adrian smiled. They both knew the verdance would scorch and yellow by June.

Adrian gave Mark his number, then went home with Bo. Mark searched for Matt to tell him he was leaving, too, but his date was already gone. He took the train, his phone locked in his lap; he didn't want to reply to Jonathan's messages, and he wanted to wait as long as possible before he texted his new friend. At home, he fed George too much wet food and forgot to wash his face. He fell asleep to Adrian. All night, he held the brush in his right hand and watched the concentric perfection of his oils shudder with his footsteps.

Adrian left Bo's place the moment she passed out. When he got home, he went right to bed, but he couldn't sleep. Even then, hours later and all alone, he still felt *it* very strongly. At this intensity, *it* was like having a pair of vast and muscled wings beating powerfully overhead, their feathers anchored to his flesh by exquisitely sharp nails. At Bo's apartment, her heart had raced. She made declarations. She fantasized about tasting his blood and bearing his children, the latter of which she was too old to do by a decade at least. Tomorrow, when she awakened alone, she would feel like she was hungover, though she'd had only a glass of champagne. *It* was nothing to Mark. And yet Adrian knew he was thinking about him.

Adrian passes the VCR/TV on his way to the bed. *Are you okay?* He's still catching his breath.

Are you? Mark's voice is weak.

I don't know. Sweat soaks Adrian's collar and lower back. He goes to his side of the bed, taking things out of his pockets.

There are still some pills left on his nightstand. Thinking quickly, Mark begins to cough. *Will you get me some more water?* He reaches for the half-full glass on the nightstand. *Another one, just in case.*

Sure. Before he turns to go, Adrian clicks on the lamp on his nightstand, but it's out.

Mark coughs again. *And I guess a lightbulb, too.*

What?

Mark points at the lamp. *New bulb.*

It's working. Adrian tugs the chain twice to demonstrate. *It's on.*

Mark strains his eyes, blinks and blinks. Then he understands. The shadow that's overcome his room is inside him. He looks hard. George is barely there, at the end of the bed. The doorway is barely there. The duffel bag, the VCR/TV. *Hot World* plays on. It's double nighttime, there in the postapocalyptic landscape. The screen is so dark he can hardly see the players outlined against the sand.

What's wrong? says Adrian. He crawls to him over the comforter, clarifying as he nears. The tan skin, wet and unflushed, except for his lips. All these years, Mark thinks, and he has never painted Adrian. Why not? Adrian would have done it for him. He would do it right now, if Mark asked.

Something's wrong with my eyes.

Adrian's face blurs as he pulls his head away. *I'll be right back*, he says. The lamp throws a halo on the wall, above his curls and his curving shoulders, a close-knit shadow that Mark can no longer clearly perceive.

When Adrian returns with the water, Mark has finished the remaining pills. As he approaches the nightstand, he notices the bottles. Mark waits. George mips.

Adrian hesitates. *Here*, he says. *It's heavy.* He lifts the glass with one hand and guides Mark's jaw with the other. The water is cool and delicious. He drinks all of it. He imagines it spilling down his throat to his belly, onto the pile of pills and over the glacier of honey frozen inside him.

Adrian gets into bed and lifts himself up against the headboard. He pulls Mark's head against his chest. Mark lets him move his body without resistance. He can feel Adrian's wetness and warmth and heartbeat.

As if Adrian knows how rapidly Mark is losing his sight, he begins to describe what is happening in *Hot World*. On the screen, blurred figures disappear into rockfaces, or into other figures gathered in the foreground. Bodies seem to collide, only to pass through each other, a crowd of negligibly differing shades of coal and slate and oyster. Skylines and sunsets, skylines and sunsets. Mark doesn't know where these figures are, or why they're there, or what they're doing. Only the music knows. He lets it all wash over him.

Although the movie continues on, Adrian goes quiet after a while. He is stroking Mark's hair, smoothing it with his fingers. It feels like a long time before he speaks again. *Mark,* he says. The score is nearing some kind of crisis. Synths. Kettledrums. Resounding metal.

Mm. Mark coughs. He realizes he was dozing.

Do I look the same to you?

Mark feels his friend turning his head. He squints upward toward the shape. *I can't see, you know.*

Not at all?

A little. He smiles.

Adrian smiles. *And?*

His beautiful friend. *You know what I think*, says Mark. He is firm, but then his smile falters. *I'm sorry I didn't paint you*. He can still feel them in his belly. He is stricken by what he almost did.

It's okay. And it is, Mark realizes. His friend smiles gently. *Why didn't you?*

Is George still there? Mark can hardly see the screen. The desert looks like an ocean.

Yes, Adrian says, his fingers in Mark's hair. *We're all here.*

Good. There is still no pain, only a deepening feeling of relaxation.

Why didn't you? Adrian repeats himself.

Mark knows that beyond the heaven of the perfect translation is the heaven of a single language, but, as has been the case for his entire life, he can't find the words. For the last time, the title flashes across the screen. *Hot World*. No credits.

Acknowledgments

If I confess that *Casanova 20: Or, Hot World* was difficult to write, I run the terrifying risk of someone replying, *Oh, I could tell*. This book demanded more vulnerability than I was prepared to give, and I couldn't have written it without the help, encouragement, and examples of many brilliant and generous people.

Thank you to my agent, Julia Kardon, and to Megan Fishmann, Andrea Córdova, Rachel Fershleiser, Ashley Kiedrowski, Lily Philpott, tracy danes, Mikayla Butchart, and everyone else at Catapult who helped make *Casanova 20* real. Thank you to Barrett Briske for understanding me in a way I didn't realize I needed.

Thank you to Jack Thompson and Ellis of Cipher Press for your kindness, vision, and willingness to fuss over me.

Thank you to Huw Lemmey for being a guide.

Thank you to Cristine Drach, Frankie Faul, Torrey Peters, Elizabeth Harvey, and the great Bambi Katsura for your friendship. To each of you: I think about what you said all the time.

Thank you to Sophia Hoffman for wanting to read everything. Your honesty gives me courage.

Working with my editor, Alicia Kroell, for the second time has forced me to completely reevaluate the art and craft of editing. What have you done here, Alicia—run a race? Assembled a puzzle? Extinguished a house fire? While I'm still not sure, I'm shockingly pleased with *Casanova 20*, and for this no one can take more credit than you. It is an honor and a delight to benefit from your delicacy, insight, and wisdom. I hope I will again.

For the record, *Casanova 20* is indebted to E. M. Forster, James Purdy, Jean Genet, John Rechy, Manuel Puig, Samuel Delany, Red Jordan Arobateau, Gary Indiana, David Wojnarowicz, Guillaume Dustan, Andrew Holleran, Rabih Alameddine, Robert Glück, Alan Hollinghurst, Sarah Schulman, and Alexander Chee.

Jade, your patience continues to save me. Thank you for allowing yourself to be a creative effigy and for your beautiful, unwavering certainty, which I rely on more than you know. Anesu, I thrive in your patronage, about which there is nothing cold or distant. Thank you for always being the man I need. Like this book, love isn't easy for me to write, but I feel it with both of you every day.

And finally, my muse, Marcus. Thank you for being my little friend.

DAVEY DAVIS is the author of *the earthquake room* and X. They live in Brooklyn.